I0630099

BROKEN ARROW

APOCALYPSE CHRONICLES
BOOK 3

DARREL SPARKMAN

ROUGH
EDGES
PRESS

Rough Edges Press
An Imprint of Wolfpack Publishing
9850 S. Maryland Parkway, Suite A-5 #323
Las Vegas, Nevada 89183

roughedgespress.com

Paperback ISBN 978-1-68549-294-6
eBook ISBN 978-1-68549-293-9
LCCN 2023936146

Broken Arrow (*plural* Broken Arrows)

noun

1. (*US, euphemistic, military*) An accidental event that involves nuclear weapons or nuclear components but does not create the risk of nuclear war
2. (*US, military*) A code phrase indicating that a ground unit is facing imminent destruction from enemy attack and all available air forces within range are to provide air support immediately

BROKEN ARROW

ONE

NEITHER REASON nor anticipation can fathom the effect of the last drop falling into a bowl causing it to overflow. Jim Lane had metaphorically spilled blood into that bowl for half his life, some of it his own. Given enough time, the results are obvious and flowing down the side. Nothing shows up like blood.

The blood of enemies. The blood of loved ones. The blood of countrymen. All spilled in fervent cause, believing right is on your side. Or not. Sometimes it's just being at the end of your rope and saying to hell with it.

He'd often wondered how the end would come. Not for him personally, although the possibilities were varied depending on who he'd pissed off on any particular day. He could envision anything from gunshots, heart attacks that leave you with that big, surprised look on your face to being gored to death with tiny cuts by those exuberant Pygmy goats with devil's eyes, prancing on your body. The little bastards.

The end of the world as we know it can happen in so many ways. Or forget the world. How does a country die? A slow rot from within, chipping away morals and liberty for the good of the masses? Or perhaps an EMP, or electromagnetic pulse, brought about by some malicious country or ideology—or a CME, a mass coronal ejection, like the ones of 1860 and the near miss of 2012. Either would fry all the electronics and move everyone back a hundred years. Just imagine people punching on the screen of thousand-dollar cell phones that don't work.

In the modern world, enemies from within, or without, need only push a button to make that happen.

Maybe the big rigs would stop running for a few weeks. The reasons could vary—dial in gas prices going through the roof, gas shortages, pandemics—manufactured or not, protests, or myriad other reasons. Products that America is dependent on could be delayed in container ships off the coasts, unable to offload and be delivered across the country. Just in time inventories would be depleted. Perishable goods become scarce and then nonexistent. Hungry people are unpredictable. Chaos would reign.

Any good guerrilla fighter knows that when you are being invaded—cut off the aggressor's supply chain.

Or, his personal favorite, maybe the country descends into chaos if it runs out of coffee. It was as good a reason as any.

Reality leans toward the biblical verse that portends that the end would come *as a thief in the night*—when we are asleep as a nation and unprepared, all brought on by a creeping apathy that engulfs any free society. People give up freedom for convenience. While the masses convince themselves that it made a difference who they voted for in the grand republic, the government kept getting bigger and exerting more control—cradle to grave, we'll take care of you. Right.

Then comes a pandemic, along with all the requisite finger-pointing. But the cure was more about who makes the most money from a vaccine than doing things that work. Disasters were made political. Nationality was made political. Through the CDC, medicine was made political. Skin color was made political. Public narrative was pushed for the most advantage in a thirty-second sound bite.

The country, as a free society, has enemies and they foretold decades before how it would happen. First, we'll take your schools, your children's minds...like cancer, from the inside. Make them hate. Make them ridicule. Make them dependent. Make them love the state.

We against they. Us against them. And the 24-hour news cycle pushed and fed the monster. To be a good citizen, you must be mad about something all the time. The injustice of free thought and expression became an affront to the masses.

And he was as lazy as the rest of the populace. It was easy to give over control for comfort, to have some agencies take care of problems, to take responsibility. Many people just said I don't care, let them do what they want, it doesn't affect me. When that happens, the oppressor ticks a checkmark in the win column.

Distractions were all around, from sports to social media. The clarion call of clashing cymbals seducing attention to watch me, watch me—don't look over there. All you have to do is put your head down and work two jobs to make ends meet and pay taxes on everything. An easy existence. Sheeple.

Jim glanced at his laptop. The screen was alive with

the bouncing bubbles of a screen saver, taking away any semblance of writing a story. He sighed, his pencil tapping a discordant beat on the table, gaze fixed on nothing. The biggest fear he had was that he had succumbed. Nothing left to fight for, nothing to stand up for, ready to join hands while singing campfire songs. He supposed there was a place for that. Somewhere. Imagine.

It wasn't that he lacked experience. Ten years in the service doing dog work for the Army Military Police. Then, another ten years working for a shadowy organization called the Shepherds, specializing in high-risk rescue. After the previous year of being caught up in the so-called Russian invasion of Limestone County and then more recently with the Good Old Boys drug cartel, his friends in law enforcement told him he'd done enough— too much, actually. Stand down. His skill set was not needed. After all, who needs a killer.

So he stepped back. Content to prepare for the day that the house of cards came tumbling down. Not that he wanted it to happen. He just couldn't see things playing out in any other way. And as he flipped through the electronic pages of the book he was writing to save the world? The plot changed every time he watched the news. His characters scampered away like squirrels wearing clown costumes.

Jim Lane slammed the lid on his laptop in frustration. The crazy was coming, slipping through everyone's fingers like a noxious gas leak.

And he wasn't ready.

TWO

JIM LANE WAS WIDE-EYED, enduring another sleepless night, when the screen of his cell phone lit up the ceiling. Yearning for any distraction, he leaned over to look at the nightstand.

The cryptic message popped with black letters on bright white.

Jailbreak. 10-15 Godspeed.

His first reaction and only logical and informed response, bypassing the hollow feeling in his stomach, was a softly mumbled, "Well, shit."

The return phone number of the sender was a string of zeros, but he knew who sent it. Sally One-Eye was his handler with the Shepherds and was constrained by her own set of government overseers likely watching her every move. But those young and all-knowing cubicle denizens and desk jockeys in government buildings would not recognize the old-style police ten code. She'd abbreviated it even more. This wasn't an official message. It was personal. *Jailbreak* was their code, taken from her love of football, where the defensive line goes through the offensive line like water through a sieve, making the quarterback run for his life or get sacked. The ten code, *10-15*, which differed over many organizations, meant civil disturbance—major disaster. *Godspeed* was...well, self-explanatory. Start praying.

It was a simple message telling what was happening and why. The not-so-simple meaning of the message, discussed a lifetime ago over a few beers, was that the populace was mad and out of control—society break-down was imminent. The more complex message was that people had reached the tipping point driven by political and social anarchy. The peasants were fed up and rushing the castle with scythes and pitchforks. The Huns were at the gate. Checks and balances were gone. With anger overriding reason, confusion overriding logic, blood would flow. People were mad...most didn't know why. And the main message, the one you didn't have to overthink to receive?

You're going to be on your own, brother. Soon.

There was one unquestioned rule governing everyone trying to prepare for disaster—the preppers, doomsday-ers, and smart folk with an eye toward the future? Every contingency, every corollary to Murphy's Law would prevail. You're never ready. Never. Ever. Ready.

Even a casual observer would know that the country was on a collision course with itself. It wouldn't take a shaman waving an eagle feather through the smoke of burning peyote to predict the results. And the government would implode trying to gain control by force.

Though he'd tried to pull away from the organization,

the Shepherds were his overwatch. An entity dwelling in the shadows, using agents to rescue high-risk assets, or lately to take out domestic terrorist wannabes. And now, they'd reached out to him again. Not orders to saddle up and go, but a simple warning. Duck and cover. Incoming.

Later, after his nerves stopped jangling and misfiring, he leaned his forehead against the cool windowpane, staring into the darkness. Light winked over a mile away, seeming to move in the vertigo-inducing blackness of the moonless night. The valley below was dark as a well ten feet down, the surrounding trees silhouetted by a lighter sky awash with cold starlight. Some of the brightest lights above the tree line were mere remnants of long-dead suns. The lesson in that eluded him, but he knew it was there. Somewhere.

The cool night was a paradox to the heat of the passing day and welcome relief as he stood naked in front of the window in the bedroom. Sweat coursed down his body after the same old dream. Lately, any loud noise could set it off. But most of the time the noise was in the dream itself, muffled and indistinct, leaving him shaken and bewildered.

Every culture has the tale of two wolves perched on your shoulders—one represents goodness, the other evil. The lesson is that your path in life depends on which wolf you feed the most. His fear was that the winning wolf, declaring its goodness, might be the shapeshifter written about in old legends.

Of course, most reasonably intelligent people would know anyone standing between two hungry wolves was an idiot destined for a confused and violent end—wolves are not forgiving. Life was a crap shoot, either way.

He took a deep, ragged breath and glanced at a stirring in the darkness behind him. The muted red numerals of the bedside clock on the end table read four a.m. The mocking projection seemed feral in intent. Is loss of sleep time lost, or gained? If the head doctors were to be believed, loss of sleep could lead to madness. Another conundrum inside the riddle called life.

HER BREATH WAS a warm caress as strong arms from his warrior princess snaked around his chest—her scent...her taste, a recent memory. Alina pulled herself tight against him, face nuzzling his shoulder with a kiss, then two. He felt her breast on his left side, the right having too much scar tissue to register the delicate touch being offered.

"You're soaked. The dreams again?" Her voice was soft, giving the question a certainty of knowledge from other sleepless nights.

Following her tone, he spoke in a whisper. "Sorry I woke you."

He'd flinched from her contact at first, ashamed that the violence of his past would trigger an escape reflex even after all this time. Trying to slow his heartbeat and ignore the instant infusion of adrenalin was a useless gesture.

"Don't worry about it," she said. "You talk in your sleep sometimes, especially when you're tired. Too many bodies? Too much blood? Those memories are things that you have to let go."

"Maybe. Though, neither of us are strangers to that. You seem to cope better." Altercations with a small mafia army and later a cluster of drug pushers in the last two years were a testament to his understatement. The Chinese had seemed to put the curse on them of living in interesting times.

"Maybe I'm better at dealing with it, but it doesn't make either of us immune," she replied, squeezing him tighter.

"No. It does not." He paused a moment, relishing the closeness. "You should get some sleep."

She yawned into his back. "Too late."

His skin cooled as she pulled away. "It's a strange thing. When you don't sleep, I don't either. What's the saying? Equally yoked? We need help, Jim. This can't go on. I actually *like* to sleep. It's rejuvenating. Mother Nature says so."

He grinned in the darkness. "Not invigorating?"

It was hidden in the dim lighting, but he knew he was receiving the stink-eye. "Yeah, I know," he continued. "Maybe it's time."

He'd been fighting it for years. Too many killings, too much blood spilled. Some justified, some...well, maybe they were. In hindsight. That was his reputation. Quick on the trigger, no quarter given—none asked. Subtlety was never his forte.

Needing help? Of course, he did. But the idea was easier said, harder to act upon.

It was curious that the woman he'd once hated with a passion might be the one to make it happen. Those he'd loved...did not. They treated him like a domesticated bear—useful if kept under control, but never, ever turn your back on it.

He trapped her arms to pull her close. The old saying was correct about there being a fine line between love and hate, and that line, at least for them, was passion.

Her entry into his life was full of it. Her earlier betrayal, by any definition, was the same. And now her total commitment to him, what she described as finding her true purpose in life was jaw-dropping. She claimed to want children. His children. She claimed her biological clock was ticking. While she was thinking babies, his thoughts were more of IEDs. There was more than one kind of improvised explosive device in this world. Her biological clock was one of them. There was a word he was using a lot, lately. Off. It just sounded off.

Both had checkered pasts and unquiet souls. How much difference existed between killing for purpose, enshrouded in the white-hat persona of sanctions and orders—and being an enforcer for one's family...an assassin? Even if that family was elbow deep in lawless practice?

His service to country was aptly compared to the bull in a china shop syndrome. Her service to family, a reckoning arriving silent as a wraith. A night panther with no remorse. Theirs were divergent roads traveled with similar results.

"I have a suggestion." Her tone was a question and delivered like she feared he'd shut her down before she got it all out. "Jacy Mane is still doing online classes. Maybe she knows someone associated through her physician's assistant program. We'll do the research and find someone to help. But it may take some time because that person will need security clearance. And you'll need more protection than just a doctor-patient privilege—things in your past would scare the bejesus out of some doctors. Hell, in both our pasts. So, I'll need assurances from them."

"*You* will need assurances?" His glance was curious. Her, not him?

"Yes, me. I have interests to protect. You're one of them."

She paused a moment before continuing. "It presents a problem. On the one hand, I will not lose you and subjecting you to a shrink may change you into something neither of us can live with. That scares me. On the other hand, I don't want you to become one of those statistics shown on television. I'll risk anything to avoid that. How's that for my own psychotic view? Maybe I should find two doctors."

"You're a demanding little wench." Turning in her arms, he held her close, kissing the top of her head as she snuggled in. "You've thought about this, and I appreciate your concern, and you're right. Do what you can. I'll leave that part of it in your capable hands. I'm aware I need help and haven't been easy to live with. And for the record, I would never do...that. If I were disposed to eat a bullet when things are bad, I'd have done it a long time ago. Besides, the way things are going in the world, someone else is likely to do that for me. There's a bad feel to the night."

"Did I hear your cell phone vibrate earlier? Who'd be messaging at this time of the morning?" She paused a moment. "Wait...Sally?"

"Who else? It was anonymous, but I'm sure it was Sally sending a message. It was a warning that a large amount of excrement is about to hit the oscillating fan blades. The end of the world as we know it...just that kind of stuff. Nothing new. It's predicted every week. If they keep spinning the wheel, someday it will hit. It's only a matter of time."

She huffed and shook her head. "You and your damned Internet. Stop reading the headlines. The fourth estate was corrupted by the socialists a long time ago when they got into the teacher's unions and colleges. Most of the journalists they turn out are biased—actually, all of them are one way or another. They are taught to stir up the commoners. Then, if it bleeds, it leads."

"Things are falling apart," she continued. "And it's what they want. We know it's happening, so you don't have to read about it every day. The violence in the cities is orchestrated for the most part and doesn't have to affect us. If it does leak out into the country, we're ready for it. You've prepared well."

"Well, aren't you the smart one? You know I'm an Internet junkie. Reading and watching is like keeping score at a game, ticking off little check boxes. Between the pandemic and social unrest, our country seems to be in a death spiral."

He yawned a moment, surprised because he didn't feel sleepy. "Both sides are being called extremists, but the attacks from the communists are non-stop. After that fiasco in DC, they're labeling about eighty million people terrorists. Sooner or later, someone is going to start shooting back—which is what their leaders want. The tip of the spear on both sides are just cannon fodder for their leaders, playing bad situations like a giant chess game. You should worry, too."

Her voice was resigned. "I do. But it doesn't consume my day. I worry for you the most...for us. You need to see the light, not the darkness. We'll just play it out as it comes. Besides, they're not communists."

He shrugged. "They are socialists. A very famous man once said the only reason for socialism is communism. It's the endgame and the final boot on your neck."

"Look," he continued. "It sounds like you want to sit around singing campfire songs. If there's one thing I've learned from life, it's that thinking good thoughts doesn't bring about good endings."

The silence stretched into minutes before she replied in a whisper. "Will we be okay?"

"Truth?" He didn't know if the question was related to the world situation, or to their personal situation. Either way, the answer was the same.

She poked him in the ribs. "No. Lie to me."

"I don't know." He knew she was glaring at him.

"Thanks for that. At least you're honest."

Changing the subject, she leaned away from him, wrinkling her nose. "You're getting ripe. Trying to exhaust you into sleep last night has a price, even if it didn't work."

"Hey. My manly bloom comes from honest labor. Although I did think you were making me train for some kind of marathon." Thankful for the change of subject, he made a grab for her...pulled her close. "And I do sleep better tired."

"Stop." She tried to put anger into her tone but failed when it turned into a soft giggle. "We need a shower."

"Yes, we do." His low, disappointed sigh filled the room. "Then bed?"

She shook her head. "We'd have to change the sheets, they're soaked. I need to put them in the washer, and I'm too tired. That's a daytime job."

The jumbled bedclothes weren't all a result of his night sweats and bad dreams. She tried to pull away again, but it was a passive effort. Glancing at the bed, he conceded. "Couch then. We'll wrap ourselves in a blanket and watch the sun come up—assuming the world doesn't end before dawn."

Her forehead rested on his chest in surrender, damp hair nudging under his chin, before she turned away. Her soft laugh gave him hope for life beyond the darkness.

"Yeah. There is that."

THREE

CHARLES FREDRICKSON and Martha Reinhold leaned against their motorcycles, parked next to a KFC on the west side of Springfield, Missouri. Since COVID protocols were enacted, the drive-thru was the only part of the fast-food restaurant that was open, so they parked under a shade tree, holding their boxes.

"I can't believe you picked the name Red Dog Charles. And what's with that ridiculous tattoo on your head? Surely that's not permanent."

"C'mon, Boots." He rubbed sweat off his head with a brown paper napkin. "It's good for our disguise and mission. I don't think any recognition software could pick us out, and nobody in this part of the country knows us. Besides, you know the money is good, so we make sacrifices."

He looked at his reflection in the mirror mounted on the handlebar. "They told me it would stay on for a month. That's all I need. By then, we'll have done our job here in town with the local clubs and started building a stronghold by Lake Stockton. If things go as planned, we'll be in good shape to control a lot of country. If things escalate like they're supposed to, law enforcement will have a lot bigger problems than chasing us."

"I still don't see why we left St. Louis. We had a good thing going there. It's easy to be invisible in a big city. We kind of stick out here."

"St. Louis is going to burn. All the cities are going to burn. When there's a huge number of people in a small area, the chances are greater that we get caught up in something we can't control. We have some tough people, but thousands of scared citizens would roll right over us."

"You trust this Gomez guy? He's unknown to us and working with some very bad people. I don't like working with people we don't know."

"Like we just got out of Sunday school? You're starting to sound whiny. Are you going soft on me?"

"Just asking, Dog. This plan of yours better work, or you'll be in deep shit."

It didn't help that she was starting to ask questions. With what he knew of her history she was a wild card, but even wild cards have their uses. He finished his chicken and threw the box into the ditch next to them. "Actually, I don't trust Gomez one bit. But he has skills we need. He's ex-military and supposedly has all the supplies we want, particularly guns and things that go boom—and money. Lots and lots of foreign money."

"Yeah, sandbox money."

His answer was sharp. "You getting choosy?"

"Nope." She gathered her trash, stowing it neatly in the box and putting it in a nearby container. "So, after we take his money, we get rid of him and take over. Right?"

"No, Boots." He shook his head with a grin. "When

it's time, you will take care of Gomez, and I will take over. Don't forget the pecking order here."

She drew a blade from her boot and ran the edge across her leather jeans while looking around the parking lot. Looking at him, she knew he could see her agitation.

"Dammit, woman. You're not a damned vampire. You can go a few days without killing someone."

"I could." Her stare was intense, never blinking. "But if we don't take care of this soon, I may have to start looking closer to home."

His gaze met hers until she looked away. "This is a bad world we live in, Boots. It's stressful, and it's gonna get worse. When the day comes that you want to give it all up, when you're just so bone tired of it all that you can't go on, then you go ahead and pull that knife on me. That's your day for Valhalla—or the gates of hell. I'm not sure there's a difference."

After standing in an uncomfortable silence a moment, he continued. "Alright, we'll cut someone out of the herd around here before we leave. These days, we'll be long gone before anyone notices. Maybe that girl at the drive-thru...she was just too damned chipper for this time of day. Or some homeless guy. There are some tents in the woods right across the highway. You might get two or three for the price of one."

"No way. They're too dirty and would probably welcome death. I'm thinking a soccer mom or someone in the mall parking lot—someone who just can't believe such a bad thing is happening to them."

Dog sighed, shaking his head as he straddled his bike. "Okay, but it's got to be quick. We have things to do. There's a Walmart right around the corner."

"It doesn't take long. I just like to look in their eyes

when the lights go out." She returned the knife to her boot. "So, what's the plan when we get to the lake area? Just hang out with this Gomez character? Come back and burn down Springfield? What?"

"Stockton Lake is surrounded by forest, especially on the south side. Folks live in those hills thinking they're self-sufficient, away from everyone—most places you can't see from the road. You know, the prepper types. Funny thing is they don't have any kind of security. That makes it easy. We start knocking them off, one by one, and put some people in their places. That gives us control of a wide area. By the time anyone notices what is going on, we'll be set. No one will be able to move us out."

"Where are we going next, after we visit a Wally World shopper?"

"We'll pick up the club members first. They're hanging out at the Powder Puff Junction on I-44, and then we'll go visit a guy."

"Jim Lane? I've heard he's hell on wheels."

"Yeah, I've heard that, too. From the local intel we have, he's the only one I'm worried about. He's one of those guys that acts all tame and friendly, but you don't want to cross him. People have wound up dead doing that."

Boots smiled. "Sounds yummy. Can I have him, too?"

"You'll overeat someday." Dog stared at her a moment. "You know that, don't you?"

"Gotta big appetite." She grinned and dropped her brain-bucket over her head. "And you like to watch."

He reached out and pulled her close, running his hands up her torso—naked under the leather vest.

"What are you going to do when it turns cold?"

"You need to make sure we're through with these

Halloween costumes before then. My bullet-points might break off."

———

LATER, they sat in a Walmart parking lot near the perimeter. They didn't have to wait long. A nearly new SUV with a sticker on the back showing dad, mom, children and two dogs made the choice easy. It was the middle of the day so the kids would be at school and dad at work. Mom was shopping. They could see her walking toward the vehicle pushing a cart piled high with groceries and clothes, a broom handle sticking up along with a mop. She was dressed in a crop top and yoga pants, pulled tight enough to show cracks on both sides. Small, blond, and feisty. Just like Boots liked them.

Most people have zero situational awareness, something you really should have when parking so far from the store—probably parked this way because she needed to get her steps in for her fitness calculator. She'd already pressed the unlock button on the key fob, the tabs making a clunking sound as they popped up. Stopping abruptly as she came around the rear of the SUV toward the side door, her mouth and eyes went round like a cartoon character.

Boots pulled the grocery cart hard toward her. "Let me help you with that."

Still clinging to the handle, maybe thinking Boots was trying to steal her groceries, Soccer Mom took a deep breath to scream, but Dog came in from behind and forced her forward and slamming her belly into the back of the shopping cart, reducing the scream to a small squeak. Boots didn't want her groceries.

Opening the side door, they pushed the dazed woman into the vehicle. Boots followed her in and Dog shut the door behind them, leaning on it. With the heavily tinted windows, no one could see inside. The car bounced a few times on its springs and then stopped. He moved the cart around to the front, where it wouldn't roll away.

If there were any chance of discovery, Dog would have tapped on the window. Since he didn't, Boots took a few extra moments. Finally, climbing out of the back door, she returned her blood-stained blade to her right boot, straightened her vest and walked over to her bike, straddled it and raised the kickstand. She stared at Dog without expression, ready to leave.

Looking around one last time, and knowing the security cameras weren't pointing their way, and the security truck with its blue strobes was a half-parking lot away. He went to his ride. He'd learned long ago not to look inside after Boots was through.

They left the Walmart parking lot on slow idle, hardly raising a ripple in the sea of humanity rushing to and fro, heads down and intent on their little corners of life.

FOUR

THE MONTHLY MEETING of the Lake Stockton
Redneck Cage Fighters was in full session—open invita-
tions, place your bets and the winner takes all. Minus the
cage. Betting on the fights was encouraged, being a
welcher was not tolerated.

Jim Lane was resting on an upended section of a cut-
down log, glad it was fresh cut and not full of ants.
Several impromptu seats and benches littered the area in
not-so-pristine condition. One grizzled man in overalls,
no shirt, and untied lumberjack boots pulled his
chainsaw from the bed of his pickup and made his own
seat from a cut-down log lying nearby—no limp wrists or
B-type personalities in the bunch. He'd started the
chainsaw by holding it over his head and pulling once on
the starter rope.

Jim Lane had trouble focusing on the contests, which
was bad because if he didn't concentrate, he'd get his ass
handed to him. The text message of the night before left
him unsettled. And the conversation with Alina left him
moody. The situation defined the euphemism of waiting

for the next shoe to drop, generating thoughts of what to do and how to do it. And the biggie? How soon? If it was very soon, life as usual would not go on. It was like saying that the world will end tomorrow...or maybe not.

Any kind of message or statement like he'd received instantly generated the fight or flight response. And then, when your mind stops running in circles, you realize you can't do anything about it. You've done what you can. The pieces are in place. Let it play out. Don't be *Chicken Little* proclaiming the sky is falling. A good analogy came to mind. Whether you agree with the circumstance or not makes no difference to the circumstance.

People had been predicting TEOTWAWKI, or the end of the world as we know it, for a long time. The only question about it? Would it come fast or simply appear as a slow-moving cancer, ever increasing and spreading incrementally like falling dominoes? He doubted there would be any point that someone could point to and say, "There—that did it."

Looking around, he knew his heart wasn't in this form of exercise anymore. Or more to the point, of being the entertainment. Many came to see if he would lose. Strangely, there was no animosity about it—just curiosity, like watching a horse race.

The clearing he faced was on a bluff above Stockton Lake. The grass and leaves covering the ground were worn through to the hard-packed rocks and dirt below. A semi-circle of pickup trucks and beater cars were backed up on the periphery, tailgates down, trunks open, kegs and coolers of ice in abundance. Brats and meat patties were on the grill—burgers and bangers.

His was the final bout of the afternoon and he was distracted as his stomach grumbled, either from protesting the smell of mystery-meat burgers or the lucky kick one of the fighters from the last bout had delivered. He'd gone through the sequences of one-on-one and two-on-one. Now there were three men facing him across the way. He sighed and stood, rubbing away blood from a cut over his eye, watching the men glancing at him and whispering together about a strategy to win. Or maybe sports. Maybe admiring someone's sister.

The huge man running the show walked to the center of the clearing, holding a wad of cash. Commensurate with his size, a large-framed and low-slung .44 mag revolver with a walnut grip was strapped to his hip. Even money would be that "We The People" was inscribed on the butt plate.

"Aw'right. Aw'right. Aw'right." The man's unusually high voice cut through the music and laughter. "Bets are closed. Time for the last fight of the day. And remember? No weapons." He put one hand on the butt of his pistol, while staring around the circle. Seeing no dissent, he raised his arms and then brought them sharply down.

"Gentlemen? Begin."

Jim faced a pugilist, already in his classic stance and shuffling forward, making little puffballs of dust with his feet. Wearing tight-fitting leather gloves, he held his fists up and ready. Clearly an amateur move to wear the gloves, which would be loose when wet and make them a hindrance. There were already wet spots on the leather. He had no intention of giving the pugilist time to break a sweat and prove the point. The man clearly wanted to protect his hands, but Jim knew hitting someone in the head or face was the last thing you should do. You'd bruise or break bones in your hand and then be ineffective.

The second man was trying to be a kung-fu specialist weaving crazy signs in the air while making squeaky sounds that surely attracted birds from a great distance, maybe a moose or two. He was sure the man had stood in front of too many mirrors. The fact that the man was in ripped and faded jeans, a checkered shirt, and cowboy boots of unknown lineage made him chuckle. It was clear that agility was not his forte.

The third man just smiled at him, waiting. Curtis was going to be a problem.

It looked like they were following some kind of chivalry and would not gang up on him. At least, not yet.

As Jim moved toward the center of the clearing, the pugilist came in hard, throwing a left at Jim's head that met open air while following up with an uppercut with his right...same results. A classic move on the punching bag hanging from a tree in your backyard. Those were power moves and would hurt. No point in standing still for that. Jim slipped the first punch, stepped back slightly to make the second miss, and then planted a short, solid left in the short ribs exposed with the man's uppercut. Ribs cracked as the pugilist winced and then dropped his elbow to protect himself from another blow, leaving him open for a quick jab to the throat. The one thing the organizer never mentioned was rules. Scratch the pugilist.

Kung-fu bounced around, waiting for his chance. When Jim backed away from the first opponent, the second ran at him while leaping in the air, trying to deliver a kick to the face that would separate Jim's head from his shoulders—at least in his opponent's mind and especially with boots. The promo posters always look spectacular with this move, and the man's reflection in his image-enhancing mirror probably did the same.

Jim didn't do the expected, which in all the movies required him to be immobilized by the piercing scream, stand in awe at the attacker's prowess and take the hit, then do a back flip ending in a tuck and roll. Being tired and not in the mood, he simply waited until the man was airborne, stepped forward, grabbed the man's leg, and pushed up. The move dumped the man flat on his back, leaving him open to a stomp to the balls. Kung-fu man curled into a fetal position and vomited, mewling like a hungry kitten. Scratch Kung-fu man.

Backing away, he located the third contestant standing with his arms crossed, smiling at him. The drunken spectators were yelling and screaming at them. More than one scuffle erupted around the half circle, not surprising given the amount of beer flowing, and comical as they expressed their own ability in brawling by keeping from overturning the charcoal grills and avoided spilling their drinks. That was an underrated skill.

The man's voice was barely heard over the crowd. "I think this is my day, Lane. I'm feeling it. I'm going to mess you up."

"Why didn't you jump in before?" Jim's breath was coming in a deep, easy cadence. He knew the man, they'd sparred before. What Curtis didn't bring in expertise was made up with toughness and a go-to-hell wildness in his eyes.

Curtis shrugged. "Waiting for you to tire a bit, although those two weren't much of a challenge. Never liked crowds anyway."

Jim had gone through five men to get this far, and his last opponent of the day was right. While Curtis was fresh and eager, Jim was tired, no longer feeling the angst that motivated his participation in the contests. He dropped his hands to his side. "Tell you what, Curtis. You win. You can have the prize money."

"No. No," the man chided. "Trying to back out? Well, that's right insulting."

Curtis glided across the clearing, moving with an ease that concealed speed. His first strike was to the groin, old school.

Jim pivoted, taking the kick on his hip while executing a knife-edge strike with his hand to the side of the man's neck. He partially missed but followed up with a fist under the xiphoid process of the breastbone. Curtis was having trouble breathing as he backed away.

"I can see you're a reactionary." Curtis finally stood straight, stretching his stomach muscles and rolling his neck around. "I'll bet you don't know how to attack me."

Grinning, Jim nodded. "You're right. If this were a real-life situation, I'd have shot your ass by now."

Most fights don't last long. Arms get tired, knees get weak, chests start heaving for air, vision gets blurred, or someone makes a mistake. Curtis was small and wiry, lightning-quick with his hands. Jim was hampered because he didn't really want to hurt the man. They traded blows for almost two minutes before Curtis closed with Jim looking for a headlock, a classic wrestler's move to get in a clinch and seek a little rest.

Slipping his right arm up past his opponent's neck, Jim stepped behind the man's anchor leg and flipped him over his hip. The man being flipped has a choice. Tuck your legs and land on your knees, maybe blowing out your kneecaps or stretching out to try and absorb the impact with the ground. Landing hard on his belly, Curtis was stunned a moment. Coming down hard, Jim planted an elbow in the man's spine, right about number fifteen that controls chest muscles. Curtis gave a hoarse scream, back bowed, hands convulsing in the dirt as he found it difficult to breathe for a moment.

Jim stood, wiping blood from his face. Scratch Curtis.

The clearing erupted in a screaming melee of bodies as part of the crowd rushed the last pair of combatants. In a gleeful profusion of kicks, punches, and elbows, the crowd's momentum pummeled Jim to the ground, landing next to Curtis. Fighting back to his feet, he stood over the man, trying to keep him from being stomped. Most of the men, and surprisingly a couple of women, were fighting their own friends in a frenzied release of pent-up adrenalin. It was a typical bar fight under the trees, country style.

The slapping sound of gunshots echoed through the clearing. One shot wouldn't faze the crowd—three froze them in their tracks, faces looking wide-eyed for the source, hands grappling frantically for pistols they'd forgotten to bring or that had fallen on the ground.

Sheriff Josh Barnes stood at the edge of the clearing, a mustard-dripping burger in one hand and his pistol in the other. This wasn't a crowd that he had to worry about his back.

"Alright. Break it up, folks. This is over. Now, if I remember right, I'm thinking this old Glock has at least a dozen more rounds in it before I have to throw it at some-body. Y'all best eat some burgers and brats to neutralize all the alcohol in your brains with grease before you pack up and head on home. You hearing me?"

It was a reluctant crowd responding to the sheriff's order, giving each other embarrassed looks, knowing full well the officer could have arrested them or simply started firing into the crowd on an assumption that bodily harm was being done to someone and lives were in danger. They started gathering their gear and brushing off leaves and dirt as Barnes finished off his burger in three bites and then snagged a beer out of a cooler.

Barnes held up the beer, looking at the owner, eyebrows raised in question. The reply came with a laugh and dismissive wave. "On the house, Sheriff."

Jim helped Curtis to his feet, then stood brushing dirt off his own clothes and gazing at the receding crowd. What the hell had just happened? Shaking his head and walking back toward Barnes, he was confronted by the huge man who'd held the bets.

"Here are your winnings, Lane. It was a profitable day. Most everyone bet against you, thanks to your stellar personality, but you earned it."

He didn't like the man's expression—decided he didn't care. "You got your cut out of this?"

The promoter nodded, regarding him with a hard eye. "I always get my cut."

"Figured." He held the wad of cash a moment and then handed it back. "Use it to fix those boys up. Curtis may need a chiropractor."

The promoter shook his head. "They knew the risks when they signed up. I don't like to see losers win."

Jim held the man's gaze a moment. "I'd be real disappointed to find out that money didn't get divvied up between the fighters."

Their conversation wasn't private. Most of the spectators that hadn't left were listening to the byplay, and the promoter knew it. "Alright. I'll split it up, but that's kinda breaking the rules. I don't like to do that, so I'd be obliged if you don't show up again."

"Be sure you do it. Don't forget to carry the one. Long division doesn't seem like your strong suit."

"Funny. I'll use the calculator on my phone if you don't mind." The man stomped off.

Barnes stepped up and took his friend by the arm, and called after the promoter. "These dummy promises to never grace any of your"—he looked at the forest and people around them—"whatever the hell this is…again. I think he's done."

The big man nodded, suddenly in a better mood. "Good. The boys don't show up to fight unless they think they can win. This guy could go pro."

Curtis moved up to them, nudged Jim's shoulder with his own, and then put his hand out. "Maybe I'll get you next time."

Shaking the man's hand, Jim shrugged. "Doubt it. I think I just got retired. Sorry for the elbow shot. I get a little crazy sometimes in a fight. Adrenalin and fear are a bad mix."

Curtis laughed. "A little crazy? When you were standing over me fighting off that crowd of drunks, you were grinning. You enjoyed that shit. Thanks for that, by the way. I guess I owe you one."

"You're welcome, and you don't owe me anything." Jim smiled at him. "You didn't deserve to be stepped on while you were resting."

"Resting? Shit, I was paralyzed. I'm gonna remember that move." With a finger wave, Curtis walked gingerly away.

"Curtis, you seem smarter than this. Why take part in this?"

The man laughed. "Hey. I got kids in college. My chickens aren't laying, and two of my milk cows went dry. We don't have much for spending money until I sell some beef this winter, so I try to earn a little extra."

Jim reached into his gym bag for his checkbook. "What'll it take to tide you over?"

"No, no." Curtis held up a hand. "I can always find something to do, and we don't take charity. We'll get by."

He knew the worst thing he could do is step on the man's pride. "It's not charity. Just consider it a loan."

"Besides," he joked. "I've got a rich girlfriend."

"Really?" Curtis shook his head. "What, are you a kept man? Are you doing stud service?"

He held a small grin until Curtis spoke again. "Aw, man. Does she have a sister? If the money is right, my wife might be okay with it."

Jim wrote out a check for a thousand. "Right. Your wife would nut you like a pig."

Giving him a serious look and after hesitating, Curtis took the check. "I owe you."

"Yes, you do. You can show me your secret catfish hole. I know it's up Turnback, but I haven't found it yet."

It was Curtis's turn to grin. "Not happening. I drug a sixty-pound Flathead out of there last week. Been eating on it ever since." The man tipped his hat to both. "Y'all have a good day."

Watching the man leave, they drifted over to Jim's old Dodge pickup. He always won the prize for heaviest tailgate.

"Speaking of cuts. You're leaking all over yourself." Barnes pulled Jim around by his arm and handed him a handkerchief to stop the bleeding on his forehead. "I'll turn your own question back to you. Why are you doing this, Jim? It doesn't make any kind of sense, even less than why Curtis shows up. What's going on?"

Forgoing the cloth, he shrugged, giving his friend a long pause and bloody smile before answering. "I got issues, Barnes. You know that. But out there?" He gestured behind them. "In that clearing? Things are not complicated. Kinda simple, actually."

"Issues, huh?" Barnes gave him a sad look. "Well? Do you have those issues all cleared up now? Because Lord knows, I'm sure the boys in the club want you to get all your problems solved before someone gets seriously hurt."

Pulling a weathered hand over his face, Barnes sighed in frustration before continuing. "Jesus, Jim. You have got to be pulling every punch you throw out there. One of these times you'll forget, and neither of us will like the results. You'll kill or cripple someone or give them a serious hospital stay. You could have broken Curtis's back, and you know it. I wouldn't want to arrest a friend, but push comes to shove, I can manage it. So go home. Don't do this anymore. If you need exercise, do naked yoga with Alina."

Watching some of the participant's vehicles pull out, enjoying the friendly banter about who had the most functional tailgate that didn't require turning in their man card, he finally responded. "Yeah, like that wouldn't be distracting. Look, I'm good. Okay? It's under control. More or less."

Barnes shook his head, staring at Jim. "That's what I'm afraid of. Which is it? More or less? Brother, what am I going to do with you? You're like a runaway steam engine with no relief valve, and you keep pouring in the coal. You're gonna blow a gasket someday, and I don't want to see that."

AFTER HE PARTED WITH BARNES, it took Jim a half-hour of cautious driving before he parked by his front step. The sleepless night, adrenalin surge from fighting, and then the subsequent drop had nearly frozen his muscles. Not taking time to cool down was catching up with him.

Alina's face was insentient as she came toward him— he could almost wish for anger or disgust. After staring at each other a moment, she came down the steps and put Jim's arm over her shoulder, helping him into the house to sit on a kitchen chair. For having such a slight and wiry frame, she was incredibly strong.

"Well, you'll be happy to know this." Her voice was soft as she gathered supplies from a cabinet drawer. "I've thought about it long and hard, and came to a decision. Jim, you're a damned fool. You look like a human punching bag. That cut is going to require stitches."

"Just use a butterfly for now." He watched her, wondering how much trouble he was in, and gave her a crooked smile. It seemed a strange circumstance that she cared, given their prior history.

"I won."

She glanced at his bloody face. "No. No, you didn't. And don't even try to make up any stories. Barnes called before you got here and sounded a little impressed, awed even. He said it was quite a little fracas. What's a fracas?"

He gave her a wry smile. "It's kind of a melee."

"A melee?" Her right eyebrow rose to an impossible height.

"You're mocking me...I can tell." He gave her a wary glance. Humor was not Alina's superpower.

She leaned hard into her Russian accent. "English is not my native language. You know that."

Jim leaned with his left arm on the kitchen table, legs spread and facing Alina. She stood between his knees and cleaned his face with a hydrogen peroxide-soaked cloth. So far, their road through life was bumpy and unsettled. Both were flawed and knew it. It was hard to believe she'd stayed with him—actually, sought him out the second time. An even greater mystery was that he'd let her. Actually, it wasn't that much of a mystery. In his forty-two years on the earth, he'd had two serious relationships. He was oh-and-two. Even the minor leagues would cut him.

While his life seemed to be a proverbial doomsday clock waiting for that last tick of the second hand, she seemed to improve every day. He marveled at that. They didn't speak of love—neither were big conversationalists. If he needed a word to describe her now, it would be settled. She'd lost that hard edge and seemed to have what she wanted, working to make it better both with herself and their little farmstead.

Picking up the conversation again, he said. "Barnes is a little old lady. Nobody likes a tattletale."

Rolling her eyes, she gave a very unladylike snort. "Not to change the subject from your adolescent views, but did you hear about the shutdown orders from the governor? They want everyone to stay home because of the virus. Only essential workers are allowed out, but everyone can go out if you need to go to the grocery or pharmacy...or anything else essential. It's contradictory and makes no sense."

"You just defined government." He nodded. "So basically, around here anyway, business as usual. You're talking about the virus with a death rate of less than three percent—some thinking it's closer to one?"

"Yeah. That one." She paused a moment giving him a stern look. "And it is serious. Maybe not for people our age who are in good shape, but older? Grandparents? Right now, it's a disease of 'overs.' If you're over sixty, overweight, or overly unhealthy from other issues, it's closer to ten percent. It's the real deal. Anyway, I-44 is a parking lot because the State Patrol is stopping people and issuing tickets, even for just going out of town and shopping for food. The big rigs are being stopped and turned around to their homes or nearest home base. It's wild and wacky out there."

"Wacky? Is that a Russian euphemism?"

"It's a word. Look it up." She pointed at her forehead. "See these wrinkles? They're worry wrinkles and should not be there. I don't need wrinkles. People are rioting in the streets about this. Kinda violates the social distancing thing. We both know what will happen if the trucks stop delivering supplies or if we even have a two-week pause in deliveries. Businesses will close, and some won't recover. What are people supposed to live on?"

At his startled look, she continued. "Oh, please. Gimme a break. I can read, and it's not like you don't have a whole library on the subject."

Nodding, he replied. "You're right. We geared up for this once. It didn't happen right away, and we got complacent. We need to reach out to Pablo and family. And maybe Jacy, although I'm sure she's aware. I'm surprised she hasn't called us."

He sighed, watching the front of her blouse wiggle as she worked on his forehead. Living in an out-of-the-way and secluded valley through a hot summer had made her a clothing minimalist. Finally raising his gaze, he smiled as she smirked at him.

"You are such a boy."

He needed to look up the definition of niggle. She seemed to be the real deal this time. His need for her was certainly real. Regardless of her past, the simple polishing of a worn, dusty gem had produced a stunning diamond. But there was that niggle, the proverbial itch you can't scratch, floating around in his often-confused brain.

He smiled past the pain in his forehead. "Of course I am, and you love it. Otherwise, fitting tab A into slot B wouldn't be as much fun."

The slap on the top of his head wasn't gentle. "Stop it."

She paused, putting a final pat and Band-Aid on his forehead. "So, what's this redneck cage fighting thing all about? You just meet and beat each other's brains out? Barnes is worried. Now that I know about it, so am I. Seems a stupid risk to me, especially since people aren't supposed to be congregating at all."

"When did you become such a rule follower? Look, it's just a way to blow off steam. Like exercise. And the beer and brats were good...at least until John Law came and busted things up."

She shrugged. "Not the version I'm hearing."

"Someone talks too much. Why do I feel like a kid missing curfew because I was out too late, and momma's mad at me?"

"You feel that way because momma *is* mad at you and so is your friend." She was trying to be stern, but his roving hands kept producing a small smile.

"Yeah. Sorry about that. I'm not used to having

friends. I'll have to read up on that. Maybe there's a phone app for it."

She reached out and caressed his cheek with fingers made rough by gardening and working outside. "Not used to having a momma...or a friend?"

"Well, the friend. You're not a momma yet, and you're certainly not mine."

Taking a long, slow breath, she backed away. "So, is this gearing up and preparing for the apocalypse a today serious project, or is it tomorrow serious?"

He gave her a slow smile. How bad could the world get in a day? His feeling was that TEOTWAWKI would come like a biblical fog stealing through all the nooks and crannies of life taking the firstborn and any other unwary soul...not like a runaway train.

"I'm thinking tomorrow is good."

She grabbed his hand and pulled him to his feet. "C'mon. We need to work on making me a momma."

"You sure about this momma thing?"

At his hesitation, she grinned and pulled him harder. "It'll only take a couple of minutes."

"Ouch." He pantomimed pulling an arrow from his chest. "That hurts my feelings."

Letting go of his hand, she walked away. "Really? Then get your butthurt feelings in here and prove me wrong."

FIVE

JIM LANE WAS ENJOYING the shade under his wrap-around front porch and the cool breeze, along with the requisite big container of iced green tea—the insulated mug kept it from sweating puddles on the table and ruining his notes. Fingers tapping idly on the side of his laptop computer, story ideas completely forgotten, he stared into the distance, pondering Sally's middle-of-the-night cryptic text from the previous night. It was hard to bring up any level of concern as he gazed over his peaceful valley. A published author had told him once that for any successful novel to grab the reader's attention, a body had to fall through the ceiling in the first chapter—preferably the first paragraph. So far, nothing had cracked the ceiling of his world.

He glanced at his computer. Was it time to change the focus of the story? He could use the headline from any news outlet on any given day to outline an apocalyptic ending. For now, the projected mid-point of his novel had been reached. Maybe. It was much the same with his life, and being a dismal failure at outlining and plotting, the story's characters hadn't told him where to go next. Mostly they were laughing at him, having already left the virtual building with no notice of intent. Maybe the bastards were better off gone.

It was hard to concentrate. Everything felt...unsettled. It was day two after the *jailbreak* message with nothing accomplished but contemplating the state of the world and wondering how to react. But the weather was nice, and his little kingdom seemed to be faring just fine. His gaze took in the sea of grass surrounding his cabin and the hardwood forests beyond.

September weather was bipolar at best, giving those who prayed for relief from summer's heat a small amount of hope. The small sea of grass in the parched valley of the Lazy J was grateful for a morning shower that passed through. His motley herd of multi-colored cattle grazed contentedly on the wet grass, tails swatting at flies with synchronized flair. Some were being raised for beef, a few others were milkers, which Pablo's wife and kids managed daily.

Most of the fescue was still green, the rest cured on the stem. He'd have to buy hay early this year. Or so his foreman told him. At best, all he knew about cows was feed went in one end and came out the other in slightly less pristine condition.

His foreman's children raised a herd of miniature goats, cute and fun to watch—except for the funny eyes. Those freaked him out. Their numbers were unknown. Apparently there wasn't any sure-fire method of counting goats that multiplied like rabbits. His guess was that they snuck into the trees and mated with magical forest goats to make a new highly prolific breed.

He was reasonably sure that only visions of children

wailing and crying kept Alina from thinning the herd. She couldn't figure out why the little rascals spent more time in her raised bed gardens than at home, if free-range goats have a home. If they knew how well she could shoot...and both Jim and Alina had vowed not to tattle about the magnificent eagle who'd swooped in and taken one of the smaller kids—goats, not human children.

———

THE HEAVY RUMBLE of motorcycle engines defying noise abatement sensibilities drew his attention as they slowed and stopped along the highway fronting his property. He couldn't see them, the road was hidden by a thick stand of trees and brush, but the half-mile distance did little to mute the distraction. Two riders guided their bikes off the blacktop and appeared in his driveway, bumping across the cattle guard and under the Lazy J emblem, slowly approaching the house. Both showed commendable expertise avoiding the potholes and washboards of the gravel drive with controlled ease. The machines had white T-shirts tied to their handlebars.

Gangs often used certain colors to show affiliation, but white? He sorted through as many options as his mind could process on a full stomach and lazy day. A white flag, then. Parley? Were they pirates? Or maybe they'd just taken a dip in the lake and were drying out shirts.

Keeping his gaze on their approach, he called inside. "Alina? Did you leave the gate open again?"

He often marveled at Alina Ivanov's white-blond Scandinavian looks, a contrast to her Russian heritage. She looked nothing like her father. Maybe there was a

Swede in her genetic woodshed. Her low voice drifted through the screen door. The main reinforced door was open to give the air conditioner a break, take advantage of the cool day, and save battery life from the solar array behind the house.

"Probably. Maybe," she finally replied. "That remote only works half the time. And before you ask, yes, it has fresh batteries in it, and yes, there is power to the gate. We need to fix that or open the gate the old-fashioned way. Maybe it was Pablo or some of his tribe. Oh, and Jacy came through earlier but left through the maze."

Pablo Estevez was his foreman who lived with his family at the bottom of the hill. His house was hidden in the trees and backed up against a bluff of fractured limestone and cold springs. The white and brown bark of huge Sycamores gave his place a Norman Rockwell setting. His wife Juanita and three little girls were generally all over the valley at any given time, riding their favorite electric golf cart with over-sized battery and near-silent approach. They loved trying to sneak up on small animals and grown-up humans going about their daily chores.

Jacy Mane was their neighbor and a registered nurse who raised horses for barrel racing—at least until that market dried up. She'd been training to be a physician's assistant until the world took a turn for the worse with COVID. So far, that career move was on hold. You'd think a pandemic would be the time to train *more* doctors and nurses.

If Jacy came through the gate and left their valley through the maze, she must have been looking for stray horses. The maze was a jumble of rocks and brush that bordered between their properties, much of it impassable. It made sense to come around and push any strays back toward her place. Although 'it was a natural barrier between their places, a curious horse could always find a way through.

Watching the biker's approach, Jim wasn't too concerned but didn't recognize the riders. Given the climate of the world and country in general, he decided to raise his threat level a notch.

"Can you come out here?"

"I'm in the middle of something." Alina's voice was unhurried, showing no interest in what he wanted.

"Well, get yourself loose." The comment came out sharp, more than intended, so he toned it down. "Sorry. We have visitors and I don't think they're selling tickets for the next barn dance."

"I can hear them."

Alina had moved in with a prior claim when his relationship with Sheriff Rita Morris died an agonizing, and according to his friends, predictable death. His resident Russian had an occasional idiosyncrasy, like hating clothes, and he wondered how that would play out in the coming winter. That she was the daughter of an ex-Mafia boss and was known for eliminating problems for her father by dropping a .22 caliber lead pellet into the opposition's brain pan was both a complication and help. She'd been an assassin, pure and simple. But his unquiet past was just as storied in a world devoid of pristine heroes. All the angels he knew were unable to fly with their singed wings, so no stones were thrown.

Although he didn't turn his attention from the approaching pair, he heard bare feet slapping on the hardwood floor.

"Shit. Who the hell...?" As she walked away, he could

hear her fading voice talking on her cell. With no pockets, he idly wondered who she was calling and where she carried that thing.

The bikes stopped in front of the porch and shut down with all the finesse of water gurgling down a clogged drain, the resulting silence only broken by the ticking of their engines as they cooled. The momentary quiet was broken by a meadowlark calling and receiving no answer except for a crow in the distance and fading.

SIX

THE WOMAN on the smaller motorcycle stopped a few feet behind the other. Backup? At first glance, he had a fleeting thought that maybe their situation was similar to his own, and the one in the back was the more dangerous of the two. She had an unsettling look to her, a face you couldn't focus on without wanting to look away.

The lead rider was a big man, clearly needing the extra size of the Harley Fat Boy. When he took off his brain bucket, it was obvious the woman would have all the hair. The only adornment on his head was an iron cross tattoo with a bright red outline. The butt end of the cross came to the crown of his nose. With his over-hanging forehead, he would have passed for a Neanderthal, except he didn't have eyebrows to grow together or any facial hair. His deep-set eyes would always be shaded from the sun. The man wore leathers and long sleeves that would be hot as hell, even on a delightfully cool day.

The woman took off her helmet, setting it on the handlebar of her Harley Sportster, and donned a pair of reflector aviator sunglasses. She wore a battered leather vest over—he raised up a bit to look—nothing except for an upper body covered in tats, including full sleeves down to her knuckles. A triplet of white-dimpled scars ran like a bear scratch across her chest. Like a model in body paint, it was hard to tell what was real.

He waited patiently as the biker cleaned bug juice off his sunglasses and face. The man gazed around the place, using the flag of truce as a rag, finally settling his gaze on Jim.

"My name's Red Dog Charles." His voice was mild, just passing the time. He continued in a matter-of-fact tone, clearly enunciating each word. "You've likely heard of me."

"Jim Lane." Jim nodded, stifling a smile. "Sorry, never had the pleasure. I doubt we have the same social calendar."

He bypassed the normal "nice to meet you" or "have a seat on the porch, would you like a beer?" He'd woke in a peckish mood, chasing virtual characters that wouldn't hold still and allow themselves to be written, and couldn't shake it. Maybe it was a premonition. The last two months were near idyllic, and most of the physical work around the ranch was done. Alina was close to manic in her quest for domestication, apparently determined to make a go of it this time. He'd be the first to admit that he was the main benefactor of her efforts— she spoiled him rotten.

The building project housing Pablo and family was finished. The two temporary travel trailers, owned by Barnes and Alina, were moved to different parts of the valley for privacy, should anyone need them. A future inhabitant was likely to be Jacy, who was still waiting for her husband Donny—don't call me Don—to come home from wherever he'd run off to.

Josh Barnes had settled in as the interim Sheriff of Limestone County while Sheriff Rita Morris was convalescing from a gunshot wound at an unknown location under Sally One-Eye's care. And Sally hadn't called with any more projects. After the puzzling text from two nights ago, she probably wouldn't. So things were good for the moment—waiting for the proverbial shoe to drop into a nest of yellow jackets.

At Barnes's insistence, Jim was now a retired gentleman rancher watching the world implode via the Internet, waiting for it to hit rural America. There was rioting in the cities and fighting in the streets by both sides of the political spectrum, while good folks in the middle were being hurt as they watched, not knowing what to do. All he knew was that nothing good was on the horizon. But isolation, like ignorance, is sometimes bliss.

And now this crap. Realizing he needed to fill the silence, he spoke to the biker. "I'm sure you're aware that Charles could be your first name or last? We don't have the familiarity for me to call you Red Dog, which I'll admit to being confused about. Wild Dog, Crazy Dog, Mean Dog—I'll admit to running out of euphemisms, any of those would make more sense. I don't see anything red about you, except for that iron cross stamped on your head. So I'll just say howdy."

The man refused to have his feathers ruffled, his expression neutral and unconcerned. "You can call me Dog."

He started to get off his bike when Jim held his hand up to stop him. "Whoa, now."

Keeping the man straddling his six-hundred-pound hog would put the biker at a distinct disadvantage should things go sideways.

"Hold on a minute, Charles. You ain't been invited to 'light and set' as we say out here in the sticks, so you'd best stay on the bike and speak your piece."

The man gave what may have passed for a smile in his mind but appeared to the world as a snarl. "You disrespecting me? I won't tolerate that. Not from anybody. We're not getting off to a good start."

"No disrespect intended, and I wasn't aware we were starting anything at all, good or bad. What can I do for you folks?" Jim's voice sharpened. "And tell your friend if she touches that pistol again, I'm going to light up her world. Although I do admire her choice of weaponry. That's one ugly gun."

Dog turned his head. "Boots, cut it out."

She snorted and tried to intimidate Jim with a baleful stare. He now knew a better definition of malevolent than the dictionary offered. He was staring right at it. She folded her hands in her lap. It wasn't lost on anyone that her hands were still within inches of her pistol. It was set for a cross draw in a slanted holster—something he favored himself.

"So," Dog continued. "Let's get down to business. I've heard you're the man that runs things around here. I figured we should talk."

"You heard right." Jim nodded, waving his hand at the valley stretched out below them. "I own every rock and blade of grass on the Lazy J."

Dog interrupted with a confused look. "You talking about your brand on the gate? I thought it was a fishhook."

Jim stared at the man a moment and then continued. "A fishhook would have a little circle on top...you know, for tying a line? A 'J' has a little cap on top...and...never mind."

He studied the biker a moment. "More to the point. This little grass kingdom is about all I can take care of on a good day. And we've not had many good days lately, so truth to tell, I'm about worn out."

The man stared a moment, anger hot flashing through his expression before he put it away. "You're lying, but that's okay. We both know what I'm talking about. We're men of the world, so let's cut to the chase. I already checked you out. You're ex-military. Then you disappeared for ten years, who the hell knows what that was about. To your credit, you put the mafia pussies down a couple of years ago. Then you got tangled up with some local redneck dopers and meth heads. They bit off more than they could chew. Mostly they just disappeared...that was impressive. Gotta hand it to you on that one."

Jim shrugged, watching Boots's hand creep toward her pistol like a baby needing the reassurance of a pacifier. "All that sounds like a revisionist history you won't find in the county historical society archives. All those things you've mentioned are water under the bridge and mean nothing. Sounds like you've done your homework, though. Very commendable."

He stopped and glanced at the door, wondering where Alina was before continuing. "But there's just the one thing you may not know that your spy should have told you. It's hard to tell what really happens in Limestone County. We don't have a reporter on every street corner. We have to pay a coroner extra to come in from a neighboring county and we rarely have the money for that. The family of the deceased usually pays for it if they're curious about why a loved one died. The local mortuary is close to bankruptcy from lack of business. Disputes hereabouts are often ended by calling a friend with a backhoe and a discrete parson for reading a verse or three over the unfortunate remains. Is there a point to your visit today?"

Dog nodded and shrugged, glancing at his lady. "Yeah, there is. Soon as I figure out everything you just said. I like that bit with the backhoe though. I may steal that."

"Plagiarism is a crime." He gave the biker a calm smile—calmer than he felt. For a polite conversation, this was ringing every alarm bell he had.

Dog paused, looking exasperated at being interrupted, making a show of looking around again with a big sigh. "Anyway, if I can get a word in? Some friends and I got together and left the city. We represent the cream of the crop from several different associations—"

"Why don't you just go ahead and say gangs? It's more accurate."

"—between the Rona virus and rival *associations*, it just wasn't fun anymore. We could manage it, don't ever doubt that, but relocating was a lot easier. I'm just here as a courtesy to let you know we'll be around the area starting some new business enterprises. If you keep your head down and out of our way, we'll stay out of yours. There's no need to get crosswise here."

Dog gave a perplexed look around the fields. "Whatever your business is. The main point being, we're not looking to butt heads with you. But if we do...?" He shrugged, eyes drifting toward the door as Alina stepped out. "It could get bad for you and the missus."

Boots hooted from the back. "Look at that pale little thing. Ain't she pretty, Dog? I bet you'd like some of that. I could get her for you if you like?"

Alina was silent, and that was a bad thing. Jim gave her a slight head shake. He gazed around the long veranda that fronted his cabin and into the fields beyond. Most days you could hear the wind sighing through the tall grass and trees, if the meadowlarks and Carolina wrens weren't too loud. It was a tranquil scene broken only by the two bikers watching him, and the war cry of an eagle in the distance.

Under advice from his friends, Jim had tried to disconnect from violence. Maybe he should try harder. But a famous man once said—if peace was equated as the absence of war, then it became abject pacifism turning the world over to the most ruthless among men. Wise words unless the boot was already on your neck. Once the boot is there, it's a little late for soliloquies.

His attention returned to a patiently waiting Red Dog Charles. "Just so you understand, I've been trying to turn over a new leaf...been trying for quite some time. It's hard, like breaking an old and well-used addiction. But make no mistake about it. We are not garnering a working relationship here. Since we're being civilized about this, I'll return your courtesy and give you some advice. Please don't discount the sincerity of the message."

Jim gave the man a level look. "Go back to the big arch in the sky. Maybe spend some money at the casinos. Enjoy the good things in life while you can. Take your lady out dancing and live for the day. Smell the roses. Eat the cake. You never know what tomorrow will bring."

"I don't know what in the hell you're talking about. I'm thinking you've talked all your enemies to death. This isn't a negotiation." Dog shifted on his padded seat and tried to see over the porch railing. "And I've got a problem with that advice. With the virus and all, those places are shut down, along with nightclubs and bars. We got no place to hang out."

Dog offered an expressive shrug. "Anyway, we kinda burned some bridges back home. Returning is not an option, and this lake area is nice."

His tone gave up all pretense of friendliness, rapping out in anger. "Pick a different lake. There are lots around, most with more tourists to shake down than this one."

Dog's fake smile was beginning to resemble a snarl again. "Maybe I need to reconsider my stance here. You're sounding kinda scared. I didn't expect to see you backwater like this."

Shrugging off the insult, Jim smiled at the man. "It's a one-time offer. You need to vacate. I'm asking polite. One professional to another."

Dog forced a laugh. "Nah, man. Lotta opportunities around here. Look at it from our point of view. It's damned near perfect. Your sheriff is all shot up and missing in action. The man in charge is on medical retirement from the State Bulls. I haven't met him, but he can't be worth much. And what's he got, two rookie deputies to work the county?"

Now where did he find that out? This guy had way too much specific information. Jim shrugged. "It's a small county."

"Maybe. But I'm thinking you need someone strong

enough to help keep the peace around here. It won't be long before undesirables start trying to move in from the big cities."

Jim nodded, wondering if Dog missed the irony of that statement and thinking that the exodus had already started. Where did Dog get all his information? It was specific, which meant they'd been around a while. Or at least a scout. His mind was full of old sayings and curious banalities.

The only easy day was yesterday won the contest. He sighed and shook his head. Movement on the ridge drew his attention, and he knew it was time to put an end to politeness.

"You know, you might say that has already happened. For your protection racket to work, you'd have to evict yourselves since you're the undesirables. Anyway, forgive the change of subject, but do you know what a yellow jacket is?"

The biker turned to his woman, and they shared a laugh. "You mean like a bee? Is that what you think you are? You gonna float like a butterfly and sting like a bee? They don't hurt much."

"A yellow jacket isn't a bee. It's a wasp, actually." He smiled at the man. "But we got something a little different around here. It's called a red dot. Hurts like a bitch. It's often fatal."

"What's that...?"

"Easy now. I wouldn't make any sudden moves. You've got one on your shirt right now." Out of sight behind the porch rail, he pulled his Glock, just in case things got stupid.

Dog glanced down and saw a red dot steady on his chest. As he watched, the dot moved slowly up his torso until he couldn't see it. He turned and glanced at Boots, watching a dot on her throat.

"That's not very friendly." Dog's voice was rough, and sweat speckled his iron cross before he ran his hand across the top of his head.

"Right now you are alive at my discretion." Jim stood, staying by his table so he wouldn't be in anyone's line of fire. "I assume you came to talk and look us over, maybe impress us with your wit? That's all good, and I appreciate the gesture, but you need to leave now. Don't take our civility as an invitation to come back."

Boots spoke up, sounding like four packs a day with a whiskey chaser. "You're not going to threaten us? Tell us how big and strong you are? What you're going to do to us if we don't leave?"

"Threats are pointless. You know that." He kept his attention on Dog, knowing Alina would take care of Boots.

Seemingly unable to stop herself, Boots continued. "Is that a pistol your little sweetie is holding? Maybe I should come up there and take it."

Alina was smiling, and he wished she wouldn't. He knew that smile, and it scared the daylights out of him. He didn't see it but heard her send a kiss Boots's way. Breaking trigger discipline, his finger rested on the first stage of the Glock's trigger, taking up a little slack.

His voice barely above a whisper, and with the first hint of concern in his expression, Dog didn't stop staring at Jim when he spoke in words well-spaced and soft. "Boots. Shut your trap."

Dog nodded, waiting to make sure she was through talking. "Let's not let the ladies get us into a shooting war. At least, not yet. I think we have the answer we came for.

But Lane? There are over forty of us, and not many of you. I gotta admit, sometimes my own men scare me—they ain't nice. You'll have to come out into the world sometime. Just so you understand. There's no need for things to get bloody. This is a one-time offer back to you since you gave me one. You mind your business. We'll mind ours."

Limestone County had been through some problems, but nothing like these people could dish out. His friend Josh Barnes was a retired Missouri Highway Patrol veteran and the infamous, at least in his own mind, Red Dog Charles was wrong about him. He wouldn't stand for their kind of trouble. Rita Morris was recovering but out of the fight for now. Her deputies would do their part but would need supervision. Even faced with those limitations, the biker gang could not be allowed to get a foothold in the county. What Dog didn't seem to understand was that the only person in the county that wasn't armed was the preacher, and he wasn't real sure about that.

"That's mighty nice of you, offering us a pass like that. I appreciate the courtesy." Jim sighed and shook his head, giving the man a hard stare. "Sorry, Dog. You're in the jungle now, and you already hit a tripwire. From this point forward, your only choice is going to be limited to either a Claymore or a Bouncing Betty."

Declining to answer, and after a baleful glare while donning his helmet, Dog started his engine and backed the machine away from the porch. Before leaving, he grabbed the white tee shirt and threw it toward the ground.

Maybe it was supposed to be a symbolic gesture. Maybe he thought it was like burying a spear in the dirt between adversaries, a challenge from ancient times. Maybe. But Jim had given up trying to discern the thoughts and inclinations of man a long time ago.

What Dog got with his gesture was a gusting wind that planted his false flag of peace into a raised bed full of tomato plants with mint and oregano trailing over the sides—bolting a startled rabbit from beneath the leaves. An equally startled calico cat gave chase before stopping to give an embarrassed look over its shoulder. It walked away, casually ignoring the situation and showing the kind of cool only a cat can muster.

Barely above an idle, Dog guided his rumbling Harley away, followed by Boots. The tattooed woman held her white flag high in the air before releasing it. Maybe her social finger pointing back at them was an accident, but he didn't think so.

Their departure was an education. Watching Red Dog Charles's slow retreat filled him with dread. A hothead would have left with spinning tires throwing gravel and insults. Jim would have preferred that ending. A good rule in most fights, if you want to defeat someone, is to first make them mad. Angry people lose their cool and make mistakes. This man seemed too controlled, like he'd just completed step one and was progressing to step two. If that assumption were true, it left an impression of a methodical approach to a problem. That suggested a level of planning and control that spelled trouble for all of them.

This visit was step one. It occurred to him that, no matter what happened with this encounter, step two was already in the works and going to happen. Step two worried him. And if this were a three-act play, the first act surely got off to a bad start. He shook his head, thinking he should have killed the man and buried him with his bike. And that omission was going to cost lives.

Pablo walked in from the rise on the south, holding his Ruger Mini-14 at down-ready and watching the duo ride away. More than a foreman, he was a friend.

Alina came to stand beside Jim, still holding her pistol. "Looks like our peaceful days are over. Again. I'll start back on birth control pills." She patted his arm and returned to the house, leaving her shirt draped over his shoulder.

He gave her retreating form a sharp look. "Wait. What?"

Before he could follow her into the house, Pablo stomped up the porch steps and divided his time between gazing at the closing screen door and the receding bikers. "Boss, we can't be doing this here. This is our safe haven. It could get nasty if they bring war to our doorstep. We got women and children to think about." He paused a moment. "Oh, and Juanita says you should buy your woman some clothes."

Jim snorted. "Doesn't surprise me, your wife being a staunch Catholic. Where do you stand on that?"

"Me?" Pablo grinned and shook his head. "I say yes ma'am and no ma'am in all the proper places and try to avoid trouble. Works for wives and significant others."

"Yeah, there is that. You're a good man, Pablo." He gave his friend a blank stare before looking back at a door that seemed to be mocking him. "You're right on all counts. If I run away from home, do you think I'd get far?"

"Don't pull me into your troubles, boss. I got problems of my own." Pablo's grin was getting wider.

Jim commented. "Speaking of problems, and given

what those bikers just brought to our door, you might reach out to your friend Gomez—kind of sound him out, see where his head is. I think trouble is coming to Limestone."

"I'll try." Pablo stared into the distance. "He doesn't come around much, and calling him a friend is a stretch. He's always been more of an acquaintance. Juana doesn't want him around the kids."

"Children or goats?"

"Either one." He gave Jim a serious look. "She wouldn't trust him with a pet rock."

"That's...enlightening. Second thought, don't bother reaching out. I'll do it myself, maybe get a read on the man."

SEVEN

PABLO WAS LEAVING on the near-silent electric golf car, and Alina had returned to whatever project was holding her interest. Still in a pensive mood, he returned to his chair.

He came from a family of idiots. It was the only sane answer. Sure, all he could remember as a child was foster care, but DNA doesn't lie. Idiots were back there somewhere.

Otherwise, he wouldn't have gotten involved again.

All he had to do was agree with Red Dog Charles that he'd mind his own business, be a good citizen and give the sheriff's department a heads-up.

All he had to do was comply with his friend Barnes's request, and earlier Sheriff Rita's request, to stay out of law enforcement business. *Mind your own damned business.*

But here he was again, tilting at the elusive windmill called doing the right thing.

He should just live his life. He'd earned it. He

deserved it. Right? He and his spooky goats and a fat calico cat.

And Alina.

Something was not right. Oh, they were pushing all the right buttons with each other. She treated him like a god. The sex was great. She was over the top in trying to be Suzy Homemaker. Hadn't he learned his lesson the first time? In a way, he was rolling with the punches too much. Something he just let happen. Go along to get along.

She was gone at odd times, usually during the day. How much shopping can one person do with nothing to show for it. And no friends.

Idiot. It must be in the blood. He'd never learn.

EIGHT

A FEW MONTHS PRIOR, Jim had changed a couple of ringtones on his cell phone. Alina got a regular, old-fashioned ring like everyone else. Sally One-Eye got the Darth Vader nine-note dirge.

It was nearing dusk after a light supper of stir-fry from the garden. They watched the calico cat and two miniature goats bed down for the evening in a raised bed of tomato plants and miscellaneous herbs, oblivious to the low growl from Alina. The cat would be up later to trip all the motion-sensor lights it could find—at least, that seemed to be its current mission in life.

Darth called, startling them out of melancholy.

Acknowledging a surprised look from his resident assassin, he lay his phone on the table and pressed the green button. "I'm surprised you called, Sally. Unfortunately, you never call with good news. Your text the other morning cost me some good sleep."

Alina kicked him under the table.

"You're on speaker with Alina and me," he continued. "I'm assuming you have encryption back. What's up?"

"Yeah, I finally got things going through private channels. Don't know how long it will last. It won't matter much in a few weeks. I'm just checking on your situation."

"Well, there's nothing going on around here like we hear from the cities. At least, not yet. One question—why the Jailbreak message? What's the big picture?"

"Sorry about that. I was sleep and caffeine deprived. A few things happened that blew my whistle." They heard papers rustling. "I'd think you would already know this, as much of a news junkie that you are. In old news, the left went all in for a soft coup and they pulled it off. People haven't realized it yet and it won't matter when they do. It was set up with a straw man candidate with no statistical chance of winning. They made sure enough votes showed up in the middle of the night and pulled it off without a shot being fired. We now have a one-party system ruling with executive orders, with no consequences in the foreseeable future. Remember the old saying. It isn't who or what you vote for...it's who counts the votes."

"I thought they couldn't prove the voting machines were bad."

Sally laughed. "Never had a chance. All the judges, even the Supremes, threw the cases out on technicalities. From SCOTUS on down, they never got their day in court. Personally, I think the courts were afraid of the results, afraid of a civil war. So in the name of prudence, they may have helped cause one anyway. Mistakes were made, thinking that after a delay for dramatic effect, there would be a chance to prove tampering, but everything was stacked against them. At that point, they couldn't go to the media because they are all in the bag for the communists."

"Communists?"

"A rule I've heard you state yourself," Sally said. "Watch what they do, not what they say."

Jim was shaking his head, although he knew Sally couldn't see it. "We've had the president and both houses of Congress represented by one party before. Both sides have, for that matter. Never made much difference."

"You don't understand," Sally continued. "The country is split down the middle, and it seems everyone is mad about something. One side has their hand out, mostly the people in population centers, for the government tit. The other side, what they call flyover country, wants the government out of their lives. The two will never come together."

"Look what's going on," she continued. "One political ideology controls the government from the top down including the military. They also control the media. Now they are on a witch hunt to try and shame and control everyone who voted for the other party...all those conservatives who disagree with them and don't want socialism. They now have a way to control them. For years they've controlled the curricula kids are taught in school, and parents let that happen. They control what people hear when they turn on the news—the dog and pony show called Congress is exactly that, all for show."

Alina broke into Sally's speech. "So, did you just call to rant at 'the man?'"

"Funny." Sally sighed. "Did you notice a word I keep using? Control? People are busy trying to make a living while businesses are being shut down, social distancing is mandatory, masks must be worn whether they do any good or not. Groceries are getting hard to find. And since the communists are scared to death of rural America, the price of bullets is like buying a car. Even a brick of .22 cal has gone through the roof. Doesn't matter how many guns are bought if the users wind up throwing them because they can't buy ammo."

"Kids haven't been taught much of anything in the last thirty years, that's why we rank below twenty compared to other industrialized nations. They certainly weren't taught love of country or the constitution. Now those kids are teachers, politicians, and military who can't decide which bathroom to use. Their allegiance is only to those who give them what they want."

Sally continued her rant. "Man, they screwed the pooch with that show of support for the outgoing president. The communists orchestrated the break-in with the demonstration at the capitol. Peaceful protesters had no idea they were being manipulated. It was bad because they scared the crap out of the legislators. Now they're acting out with no one to stop them and no media reporting to hold them accountable. If you tell a lie often enough, it becomes truth."

"All the left-wing mobs rioting around the country are ignored. Police departments are being stripped or disbanded. Patriotic gatherings are treated as insurrection...you think this isn't a jailbreak?"

"I'm kinda sorry I asked." Jim winked at Alina and then reached for her hand.

"Well, buckle up, cupcake," Sally responded. "Now we have the mock second impeachment that's illegal since the president is gone, but the main idea is to shame voters and the lame-duck political party. That will be covered by the newsies twenty-four-seven."

"All the news organizations are purging conservatives. Military and National Guard units are purging those who profess belief in the constitution and allegiance to the flag of the United States. Allegiance must only be to those in power."

"The current regime was voted in as having a plan to save us from the pandemic and then became a complete failure. No one can figure out the truth because they manipulate the numbers. The CDC has changed their story so many times they look like a politician following money—which they are. The COVID shots are going to politicians first, then selected military, and then people last, if ever. It should be the other way around to beat this thing...if it is a thing."

"Then comes the coup de grace. They feign ineptness and start to enforce a two-week quarantine. People in flyover country aren't buying it, but the population centers do. Now? It's a typical doomsday scene. For millions of people, there are no food deliveries. No jobs. No vaccines. People are dying. COVID is a sneaky bastard. All this is done on purpose. After it's all done, and after maybe six months of apocalypse, they'll suddenly try to throw out the constitution and seize control. A new government will rise from the ashes."

"I don't believe that will happen. What they don't see is there won't be enough left to govern. Jim, you're in a good spot, close to water and food sources all around. Pockets of people will survive. Pockets of the best prepared and meanest SOBs around."

He heard her sigh into the phone. "I'm counting on

you, Jim. You and your friends. I'll help as long as possible...which won't be long."

"If all this is true, then come to us, Sally."

"Can't. Still got agents in the wind. I can't abandon them, and you know why. Gotta get them home or die trying. Just like you rescued me years ago. After my job is done? Maybe. If I can. Godspeed, Jim."

He disconnected the call while Alina stood and leaned against a porch post, gazing into the long shadows of twilight.

"She didn't wish me Godspeed." Her voice was quietly bitter.

"Don't take it personal." He knew Sally disliked Alina, and didn't trust her at all, but he wasn't about to tell her that. She knew it anyway.

"If the world is winding up like she is talking about, why don't we see it here?" Her voice was soft, barely heard over the wind through the fescue.

He stood by her and pulled her close. "I'd say we're in a bubble right now. Big cities will have problems first. They always do with a tightly packed populace. Then it spreads from there into the hinterlands. It would be nice if we can get all our ducks in a row before that happens."

"Will we? Can we?" she replied in a pensive voice.

"Short answer? No. Not completely. We're better off than most, if that helps any."

"Why aren't we ready? Or I should say you, since you've done most of the work."

Thinking of all the things that could go wrong, he felt they were reasonably prepared for most of it. It was the outliers, things they hadn't thought of, that worried him most.

Jim shook his head. "Murphy won't let us."

Her gaze snapped to his, a warrior ready to defend the realm. "Who is this Murphy?"

"Murphy? He's the god of bad luck and pessimism. His law states that what can go wrong will go wrong."

She punched his shoulder again. "Idiot."

NINE

RED DOG CHARLES led a forty-strong contingent of bikers along the mile-long dirt road that led to Trader Jack's. The front parking lot, a pressed surface of creek gravel and crushed limestone, was shaded by towering oak and sycamore. As soon as he stopped, he could feel the cool breeze coming off the cold spring-fed creek that meandered away through the trees. It was a relief from the late-fall heat of the day. He glanced around, pulling off his helmet and watching the people behind him dismounting and standing by their bikes, stretching and grousing about aches and pains.

In the distance, he could hear another group coming toward them in ATVs. In the time they'd been in the county, they'd acquired several of the all-terrain vehicles. They were handy in a myriad of ways. He waited wordlessly with Boots, gazing at the building. Gomez came out of the building, flanked by two bodyguards dressed in full battle-rattle—bump helmets, ballistic vests, duty belts, and M4s attached to a one-point sling held at the down-ready position.

It was nearing evening and both guards had flip-down night vision attached to their helmets. He wondered how many more men like this were scattered around. It might make a difference...later.

Dog put on his best smile. "How the hell are you, Gomez? Expecting trouble?"

The Mexican shrugged. "Goes with the territory, don't you think?"

"So, do you have a place for us to stay—other than bivvy tents and hammocks? My people are tired." He spent a few moments gazing around the compound. "This is a sweet setup, by the way."

"Glad you like it," Gomez replied. "You'll find accommodation in back. I didn't expect you to bring an army to my door, but there should be room for everyone. A few may have to double up."

"What about inside the post? I've heard it's cozy in there." Dog caught the man in a steady gaze.

"Nope. That's just for a few trusted friends and me. There's not that much room in there for extra guests."

They were interrupted by a man driving an ATV, skidding in the gravel before coming to a full stop next to them. Dog gave him a quick glance, waving the dust cloud away from his face.

"We're kinda busy here, Tuck."

The man named Tucker turned and started to leave but stopped when Dog called to him. "Hey, wait a minute. Weren't you on detail this evening? How many split-tails did you pick up?"

The man sighed, looking fearful. "We tried the local hamburger joint and then the convenience store across the street. We even tried a couple of beer joints. We couldn't get anyone interested except one couple."

"I wasn't aware we ever asked anyone. We take who we want. And I sure as hell didn't put in an order for men. You know better than that." He gave an exasperated glance toward his host, shrugging with a "what can you do" expression. "So what happened?"

"Couldn't help it. The guy was into it. Anyway, she got naked for us in the football field parking lot. Then things went south."

"You were sampling the goods?"

"Tried. We knew not to damage her. Then the guy got cold feet, said we were too rough, then pulled a little shooter on me. Hell, she wasn't complaining."

Boots came up, moved the vest away from the man's shoulder for a visual and snorted before backing away.

The man shrugged. "It was only a .22. Not much to see." He rolled his shoulder. "Hurts though."

Gomez spoke up. "According to the FBI stats, more people are killed with .22s than any other caliber."

That got him a couple of blank stares. "Just trying to add to the conversation."

"So, what happened?" Dog was shaking his head, staring at the man.

Tuck grinned at him. "Then I got smart. One of our guys knows the area. We took them up in the woods above that ranch we went to, left the bodies there. We kinda posed them. I figured when they're found, that guy will get blamed."

Dog gave a disgusted sigh, glancing at Gomez before pinning Tucker with his gaze again. "You figured that, did you?"

Gomez stood with arms crossed. "I don't suppose you know that Lane and the sheriff are tight? He'd never get blamed for something like that."

Tucker stepped back. "No. I didn't know that."

Dog pulled his pistol and pointed it at Tucker. "So, no girls for the men to play with, and then you pull a bone-headed move that could get the sheriff looking at us, instead of just disappearing the bodies. That about right?"

"Boss, I..."

When he raised his gun, Boots grabbed his arm. "Let me. I need it."

Dog nodded to a couple of men, and they grabbed Tucker by the arms and pulled him off the ATV. "Alright. He's all yours."

As they dragged him away with Boots following, Tucker screamed. "No...no."

Fading into the twilight and following the men dragging Tucker, Boots pulled her knife.

———

DOG FOLLOWED Gomez inside and leaned against the counter.

"Drink?" Gomez asked. "That woman of yours seems a little...off."

"You don't know the half of it." He shrugged. "I'll take coffee, at least until I know how things are shaking out here. You sent for me. What's the plan?"

Gomez filled their cups. "I need you to sew up this lake area. It's a good spot, off the beaten track. It's been tried before with bad results, so if you don't think it can be handled, let me know."

"By handled, you mean Jim Lane and the sheriff's department?"

"I do. Right now, it should be easy. He's back on his

heels, out of the game. By the time he gets his game face on, it will be too late."

"Since you know this man, and I'm sure you can get close to him, why don't you take care of it?"

Gomez shrugged. "I have certain...benefactors. They require some things done in the cities, so I'll be busy, along with my men. I need our home base to be secure. I'm contracting that out to you."

"I already stopped by to see Lane." Dog leaned his arms on the counter, hands still close to his pistols, waiting for a reaction.

"What?"

"Seemed prudent. And as the saying goes, news of his demise may be premature. He didn't strike me as a pushover, and he sounded ready to rock-n-roll."

"I didn't say he was easy. But it's doable. You just need to catch him out on the road and make it happen."

"I was going to do it when we met, but he was cagey—wouldn't let me off my bike. I should have thought of that. He's not out of the game, as you put it. But the best way to make that happen is to break him. I got an idea on that. After he's broken, it's simple."

"It's your funeral. What about the sheriff's department?"

"We've dealt with every alphabet agency there is and haven't lost yet. I have a lot of men. Some hit-and-run ambushes should do it. Put in a 9-1-1 call and wait for them to show up. Just blow them away and go on about our business."

"Probably work," Gomez said. "How you going to break Lane?"

"Oh, that's easy. He's got a real domestic scene going

out there. I'm going to kill his woman." Dog grinned at the man.

Gomez looked away after giving Dog an uneasy glance. "We've had eyes on them, but I don't know her. Just some skinny blond chick who doesn't like clothes. She works in the garden a lot."

"I saw her when we visited Lane. She didn't look like much."

They turned as Boots walked in the door, specks of blood on her face and vest. Gliding up to the men, her voice was hoarse. "I need a place to clean up and rest."

Dog turned and grinned at Gomez. "I'll give her to Boots."

After learning of their housing, they turned to leave. Gomez stopped them.

"I almost forgot. There's one more thing. I'm long on food and supplies but a little short on firearms. My other project is using them up faster than expected. There's a little town a few miles south of here with a hardware store and gun shop. A little birdie told me he might have some auto pistols on the sly. They have a ton of stuff. Might check that out."

"Defenses?"

"Not much. It's just a mom-and-pop store, but like most folks, they carry. It should be easy pickings. The county deputies are miles away."

"I'll put some men on it, we can use the ammo."

Walking out of the store and toward several buildings that looked like old-fashioned bunkhouses, Boots spoke softly. "You trust that man?"

"Not much." Dog gazed around the compound. "For now we have to. We have similar interests."

"And then, after that interest is over?"

"This looks like a nice place to put down some roots."

Her hand caressed the handle of her knife. "And Gomez?"

"He's all yours."

"You take care of me so well." She leaned against him as they walked, the acrid smell of blood a sharp and pungent miasma around them. "We're a good team."

TEN

ARRIVING at the sheriff's building, Jim moved through the front doorway, past the receptionist, and plopped into a rolling chair left in the middle of Barnes's office. Thanks to the fake hardwood floor he was able to ride the beast until he impacted gently with the desk.

"Don't bother knocking. Just roll on in." Barnes shook his head after tracking him across the floor. "How'd you get past the gatekeeper?"

Leaning precariously in the squeaky-backed chair, he put his feet up on a two-drawer metal file cabinet. "Didn't see any receptionist. All I saw was Aunt Bea glaring at me, so I didn't speak."

"Aunt Bea?"

"You remember Beatrice, don't you? Your wife? Alina and I have a collection of old *Andy Griffith* shows. We've been binge-watching. Anyone ever call you Barney?"

Digging a noisy furrow through a drawer filled with knick-knackery of office supplies, Barnes smirked. "Stop it. I have a hard time taking anyone serious with a Scooby-Doo Band-Aid on his forehead."

"Besides," Barnes continued. "I've got more bullets than you can count. Due to budget cuts...well, actually not much budget at all, Wifey is our new unpaid receptionist."

On cue, her voice came echoing down the hall. "You need to sign the log as a visitor."

He grinned at Barnes and yelled back to her. "Can't. I'm not here." Leaning forward, he continued in a mock whisper. "She doesn't have a gun, does she?"

"I heard that. If I did, I'd shoot your ass." She appeared holding a heavy, official-looking book. "I used to have a wheel gun, but hubby took it away—something about my anger issues and his guilty conscience. Now, sign this book so I can go back to playing solitaire on my computer and pretend you're not here to get my acting sheriff husband in trouble."

He gave her an innocent look. "How would I get him in trouble?"

"Because you're a damned trouble magnet. Keeping you around here is like feeding a saltwater crocodile hoping it will eat you last."

"That's real cold, Aunt Bea. Josh is my BFF."

She snorted. "Yeah, your best friend forever is probably your only friend." Her stare turned soft a moment. "Why do think that is, cupcake?"

"Alina's my friend."

Her expression went through shades of red, pink, and then settled on pale. "Yeah, you just keep telling yourself that."

"Knock it off, you two," Barnes grumbled.

The heavy book dropped in Jim's lap. Stifling a grunt and snatching a pen from a cluster parked in an old coffee mug sitting on the desk, he checked the page marked with a paper clip. "Some of these dates of entry are older than me."

She shrugged. "I'm trying to put some order into the chaos around here. You can sign your name right under George Washington. We're holding his wooden teeth in the evidence locker in case he comes back."

Snorting, he signed near the bottom before snapping it shut and handing it back to her. He glanced at Barnes. "Acting sheriff?"

"Yeah." Barnes exchanged glances with his wife. "We finally heard from Rita that she'll be back in a few days. She seems to be well enough to take over the administrative part of the job. That's what I'm doing right now, gathering my stuff and moving to another office down the hall. Once she's settled back into the job, I'll just grab my fishing pole, ease on out of here and into the sunset."

Barnes gave him a pointed look. "So, as you can see, I'm really busy. No time for idle chitchat from a trouble magnet."

When Jim didn't respond, he continued. "That was a polite hint meaning what are you doing here? Since you signed the log, I assume it's some sort of official business. Maybe a complaint to lodge?"

"We need to talk." He raised his voice, turning toward the open door. "And that comment about crocodiles hurt my feelings."

Jim stared wide-eyed as Aunt Bea came stomping into the office. "You signed it 'your name' and wrote 'today' for the date."

Again, the heavy book made a painful drop into his lap.

"Do it right this time," she continued.

He signed correctly, thinking any more resistance and that book would injure potential heirs.

After she left, Barnes stifled a smile and raised his eyebrows in question. "You were saying?"

Looking out the window at trees starting to turn color and speeding cars on the highway that slowed down in front of the station only to speed up again, Jim continued. "I just wondered if you need help. Not much going on at the ranch. Alina is busy nesting and working in her fall garden. Pablo seems to have my dozen head of cows under control."

"So, read a book or something. Start a new building project." He smirked at Jim. "Count goats."

"Well, in no particular order—goats are uncountable, I only read after dark and I don't need anything else built." His building plans had been oriented toward an apocalyptic scenario that hadn't happened yet. Although, that dark cloud loomed closer every day.

"So, write something new in your Great American Novel."

"The GAN? I'd like to, but those mutinous characters stole a truck and left town." He took a pencil from the holder and tapped a single-drumstick solo on the tabletop.

Barnes sighed, running a hand through thinning hair before leaning forward and snatching the pencil away. "Look, Jim. This should not be difficult. Get a life. Find your place in it. There's not much going on right now. Boring is good. We have the Rona virus pretty well under control locally with a vaccine on the horizon, the stores are getting regular truck delivery—hell, most folks are ordering so much stuff online these days that even the USPS is breaking even. It's not a bad world right now."

"I met some folks that may change your mind. And I heard from Sally." He tried to interrupt, but Barnes was on a roll.

"Hey. Got the perfect job for you. Undercover. Someone is shooting at the blades on the new wind turbines in the southwest part of the county. How about you do a stakeout, unofficial of course. I can loan you a camera. We need evidence on that."

Jim rolled his eyes, having no doubt the turbines would get a lot of abuse. The wind farm project wasn't well received by the neighbors, they were noisy and unsightly, but it was easy money for the landowners, though only a few were actually in Limestone County.

"The wind turbine generators? No one could miss them from a mile away, even if it is a moving target. Those things are huge." He paused a moment. "And noisy."

Barnes wiggled his eyebrows. "In my position as Limestone County Sheriff—"

"Acting sheriff." Her voice came rolling down the hallway.

"—it's my sworn duty to inform you that it would be expensive shooting if the trespassers were caught."

Jim smirked at him. "You know I don't need that kind of target practice."

Deciding to jump in with both feet, Jim kept his voice low. "What about this new biker gang that's arrived?"

Wifey's voice was not diminished by distance. "What?"

The wall clock echoed on the wall to fill the silence until Barnes stood with a sigh and kicked his office door closed. "Dammit, Jim."

He took a few minutes and filled Barnes in on the

meeting with Red Dog Charles. With no response, he held his palms up. "Sorry, man. Your wife may not like me, but she deserves to know what's going on around the county. So do you."

"May not like you? She wouldn't piss in your mouth if your tongue was on fire." Barnes rolled his eyes. "She doesn't need to hear about everything. Besides, I've only seen a few bikers around. No more than usual. That does not constitute a wild gang intent on civil insurrection. It's still a semi-free country and people can go where they want."

Barnes continued, gazing at his friend. "Listen to me, Jim. Even if what you're worried about is true, you're not law enforcement. If we get into trouble here, we reach out to surrounding counties, and they'll send in help. That's the way it's done. And I meant it when I told you to retire and stay out of trouble. Rita will tell you the same thing when she gets back. We got this."

Shaking his head, Jim let out a long, exasperated sigh. "Well, I wouldn't count on help from outside the county, considering the riots and civil unrest going on." He did air quotes around riots and civil unrest. "In just about all the larger cities, your brothers in blue are pretty damned busy. Experience tells me you're on your own."

"As for the rest?" Jim continued. "I may not be an LEO, but I am your friend. It's my job to watch your back. And playing the Rita card? I wouldn't count on that. When she gets back, she won't speak to me at all unless polite decorum demands it."

"Polite...what? Since you started writing a book, your words are way too big. And why won't she speak to you?"

"She's been in Sally's clutches too long, and you know what that represents."

Barnes's eyebrows peaked while he shrugged. "Another conspiracy theory? Nope. Still not seeing it. You're imagining problems that don't exist."

He watched the shadow showing under the door shift, imagining an ear pressed to the flimsy, hollow-core door. Too bad they didn't have creaky floors. He knew Wifey's dislike of him was fueled by a rabid loyalty to her husband—didn't blame her at all.

Continuing, he tried to keep his voice low. "Yeah, well, I have a bad feeling about this. Let's hope things stay tranquil in your fantasy land. But that was not the impression I got from Red Dog Charles."

"Red who?"

"The apparent leader of the bikers. He's got a side-kick name of Boots. She's a real piece of work."

Barnes snorted. "I'll keep my eyes open. So, what did you hear from Sally One-Eye?"

Knowing Bea was listening, Jim decided to put the warning on hold. There wasn't much they could do about it at the moment so he shrugged and didn't answer.

Barnes continued. "I've already told her we were going to shove those federal badges deep in our pockets and not take them out. Ever. So, even though you're technically law enforcement...forget it."

In an effort to help with the legalities of busting a drug ring and the Good Old Boys, Sally had pulled strings to have Barnes and Jim appointed federal agents answerable only to a prosecutor in Washington, DC. Although requested, appointments for Alina and Pablo never came through. He also knew the legalities of those appointments were sketchy.

Jim nodded, realizing Barnes knew his wife was still

trying to listen in. "But you do expect to take that badge out sometime. You know that."

Barnes's gaze quickly found the door. "How do you figure?"

"No matter how deep you shove it, it's still in your pocket." He glanced around the room, changing the subject again. "You need help moving stuff?"

"Nope. Most of this is Rita's anyway. I was always temporary." Barnes gave him a grin. "So, when Rita gets back, will there be any fireworks between your old old lady and your new old lady?"

That gave him pause a moment. He didn't think there was a jealous bone in Alina's body, but on the other hand...she was a shooter. And Rita? A bad temper combined with impressive skills would not adequately describe her.

He refused to let his mind go down that rabbit hole. "I don't think so...doubt it. Rita was done with me anyway. I think we can all move on from that. At least, I hope so. We can still work together."

"Really? I was thinking more of public safety and avoiding a shootout at high noon. What a movie that'd make. Women with guns and some poor sap in the middle."

Barnes continued, shaking his head. "And again, with you thinking you are part of this team? You are not. You have to stop that. We're friends...hell, good friends. But you have to stay out of law enforcement business. After the stunts you've pulled, you're lucky not to be in prison. So, mind your own business." Barnes smiled, trying to take the bite out of the conversation. "Please?"

Jim gave his friend a short nod. "Fine. Whatever you

say. It's not like you don't tell me this every day. I can take a hint."

"Yeah, right. Sure you can. That's why we have to tell you every day. You have short-term memory loss."

When he got up to leave, Barnes stopped him. "Can you do me a favor? Remember that hardware store in Miller that sells all the guns? Next time you're down there looking around, you might give them a heads up on the bikers—just in case there actually is a problem. It never hurts to be aware."

"That's in another county. Why don't you reach out to their sheriff? Didn't you just tell me all you work together?"

Barnes shook his head. "That's a huge county south of us. You ever see one of their patrol cars north of Highway 96? There's kind of a seven-mile dead zone between our county line and ninety-six. There's nothing out there but cows and row crops."

Jim was tempted to tell his friend where to stick it, but he knew what a fine line the man was walking. The acting sheriff wasn't as strait-laced as he tried to appear. He nodded his acceptance of the task. Knowing Barnes, he meant forthwith, not sometime in the future.

"You should see the nice little Browning BDA .380 I found there. Sweet gun. They don't make them anymore and it's like new. We've been doing a lot of target practice trying to loosen up the spring in the slide, so we're going through ammo. Since they have the best prices around, I'll mention it next time I'm down that way."

"Make it soon. I'd appreciate it."

"Not a problem." He shrugged dismissively.

"You're not busy today, are you?"

Jim just stared at him a moment before shaking his

head. When he walked past the front counter on the way out the door, he waggled his fingers in a wave. "See ya later, Aunt Bea."

"Whatever. I'll sign you out."

He stopped and caught her smile when she thought he wasn't looking. "You know, you remind me of someone else sitting in your spot a couple of years ago. She liked me about as much as you. Brings me to tears."

A wadded-up ball of paper hit him in the back as he left.

ELEVEN

JIM LANE DROVE south on Highway 39 to the small town of Miller. Beyond the county line and a bit of a drive, it was still a gem of a find because of the hardware and gun store on its deserted main street. Other than the post office, there were few businesses left in the small, rural town. Entering the nondescript front door, his first impression was of a full-sized Home Depot jammed into a smallish building with narrow aisles full of merchandise. Tucked in the left corner was the gun department.

Every time he came in, he was amazed at the amount of new and used firearms on display. Coming into the building, he held the door open for a male and female police duo leaving, giving them a nod and wishing them a good morning. Arms loaded with packages, they returned his greeting with a friendly smile. He didn't see patches denoting their locality, so he figured they weren't local. This was a well-known store.

Finding his way to the glass-topped display counters, he looked at all the different models available. Although it wasn't his personal carry, he always admired the wheel guns. Revolvers were simple. They hardly ever jammed, and if you've loaded a dud, just hammer back and keep firing.

"Can I help you find anything?" A young man in his late twenties stopped in front of him and behind the glass case. "Name's Joel, by the way. I'm the owner here."

He wasn't sure why the name was important, but these were country folk, so he conceded. "I'm Jim. Looking for some .380 ACP and .40 cal, JHPs."

"We got 'em. Those jacketed hollow points are popular. What brand? We have everything from Winchester down to that Italian brand for cheap ammo."

Jim was a firm believer in clean shooting ammunition, it saved on jams. "Better stick with the 180-grain Federal Premium, although any of them will go bang."

"About sixty bucks and change for a box of fifty. Sorry, ammo prices are going through the roof. Do you like them better than the 165-grain? That lighter load is a little cheaper."

He looked at the young man a moment, seeing he was genuinely interested. "I do. The recoil on the heavier grain is more of a push than a snap. Seems to help to stay on target for the second or third shot."

That got a grin from the man. "What if you need more than three shots?"

Jim snorted and shook his head. "Gonna run like hell."

The young man laughed. "I hear that. How many boxes? I gotta tell you, supply is getting thin."

"Couple of boxes each should do for now."

They were interrupted by a young man who walked up next to them. "Could you show me a small frame .22

cal, double action revolver? My wife wants to learn to shoot, and I thought that would be a good pistol to start with."

Joel winked at him before turning toward the man. "Teddy, didn't you marry that Jackson girl about a year ago? The redhead with the temper? Seems like I remember her playing basketball and getting into some kind of ruckus just about every game."

Teddy nodded, smiling at them. "Yeah, that's her. Hell of a rebounder. She's a handful."

"That she was. We enjoyed watching her play." Joel paused a moment. "Is she mad at you? Better check her emails and Twitter account before doing anything drastic. Just suddenly wanting to learn how to shoot sounds kind of odd."

"Aw, hell. She's always mad about something. Since the benefits outweigh the downside, I've learned to live with it." The young man laughed. "Besides, a .22 cal won't hurt me much."

Eyebrows peaked, Joel started to disagree, but was interrupted by an older man farther down the counter. Dressed in overalls and a lightweight hooded jacket, he could have been any farmer in the country with a Vietnam Vet cap on.

"Now, son, you got that all wrong," the farmer said. "A time-honored rule is that nobody wants extra holes in them. They hurt like a bitch. A small caliber like that can mess you up plenty. Problem is, if it hits you in the chest or deflects on a big bone, it may come out your foot or your ass. There just ain't no telling what it will do. Nope, you listen to me. I got the age and experience to tell you. I bought my wife a .45 caliber pistol and loaded it with them G2Rs RIP rounds. I figure if she decides to shoot me, I won't suffer as long."

The young man gave him a puzzled look. "Rest in peace rounds? What's that mean?"

"Nah. RIP means radically invasive projectile. In plain English, that means the bullet will blow you to kingdom come and leave your insides on your outside. It ain't peaceful."

The young man just stared at the oldster while the others tried to stifle a snicker. They failed, and it turned into a full-blown laugh. Finally, he laughed, too. "Y'all are blowing smoke up my ass, but you might just have a point there."

"Of course we are, son. But there's a lesson to be learned. Puts a whole different perspective on keeping mama happy. A bigger gun is a lot more incentive."

"Yeah, I hear that."

Raised voices at another counter got the attention of Joel. After a quick glance, he reached below and seemed to be pushing a button. Once that was done, he put his hand on his sidearm and started drifting toward the altercation.

A young woman behind the counter was shaking her head, hands on hips. "Look, you can't buy a firearm, and you damned well know it. And it's a waste of time to fill out the paperwork. Everyone around here knows you served time for a shooting. We don't sell guns to felons, wannabe felons, accidental felons, thieves, known alcoholics, or raggedy-assed drug addicts."

"Now, you listen…" The man started to reach for her.

She put her hand on her pistol, slung low on her leg, and spoke in a calm, low-toned voice. "You need to step away."

Keeping eye contact with the young lady, Jim moved up next to the twitchy man, wrinkling his nose at the smell. Surprisingly, the old farmer had come up another aisle and moved into position on the other side. Together they boxed the man in, effectively pinning his arms to his sides.

"Hey, man. You stupid or something? Don't you see everyone in here is armed?" Jim tried to take Twitchy's attention away from the girl. "This is not going to end well for you."

"He's higher than a kite." The girl shook her head. "Watch him. If I ain't mistaken, he's got a switchblade in his back pocket."

The old man bumped Twitchy to get him off balance and then deftly pulled the knife out. "I always wanted one of these. They're handy cutting twine off hay bales when you only have one free hand."

"You give that back!"

Twitchy started to flail around when the two LEOs moved up next to them. "Hey, Joel. Lucky we were still outside looking at our new toys. This idiot causing a problem?"

"That old man stole my knife," Twitchy yelled at them, trying to get away from being pinned against the counter.

"Really?" The male officer did the talking while the female stood to the side with her taser in hand. "Lawrence, did you steal his knife?"

The old man snorted. "Actually, I relieved him of an illegal weapon...for his own protection, of course. You want it?"

"Nope." They grabbed Twitchy by his elbows. "Right now, we can just escort him out of town...

maybe drop him on the interstate and see how well he dodges the big rigs. If we were to find an illegal weapon on him, we'd have to arrest him...do all kinds of paperwork, that kind of shit. Ain't worth it. Besides, the wife has a roast in the oven, and I got a serious hankering for beef. I don't have time to waste."

The female LEO shook her head. "Maybe we better hang on to it for a few days, at least until we check out any unsolved cuttings in the area. Maybe do some DNA tests for blood. I'll do the papers on it. Damned druggies. We're losing this battle and don't know what in the hell to do about it."

Lawrence handed over the knife. "Damned if that wasn't the shortest amount of time I ever owned something."

———

WHEN THE OFFICERS left with Twitchy, Jim turned and shook the oldster's hand. "Jim Lane, from over in Limestone County."

Bright blue eyes not dimmed with age gave him a once over. "I've heard the name...thought you'd be meaner looking—maybe bigger. I'm Lawrence Dunn, gotta horse farm hereabouts. Nice to meet you."

Jim nodded toward the cap. "Thanks for your service."

The man laughed. "You're welcome. Hell, ain't like we had a choice. We had the draft back then. I should'a gone to Canada."

The young man behind the counter snorted. "What are you talking about, Lawrence? You don't like the winters around here—always complaining about the cold. What would you have done in Canada?"

Lawrence got a faraway look. "Dunno. Might could have stood it for a while." He grinned at them. "Maybe. Look, men, I gotta git. Don't want momma to start cleaning that pistol. Y'all have a good day, hear?"

When the man had left, he turned back to Joel. "Is everyone in your store armed?"

Joel nodded. "We all have our CCAs. Seems wise, considering."

Jim got to the main reason for his visit. "Josh Barnes is the Limestone County Sheriff and a friend of mine. He asked me to drop by. Since you're always nice enough to give a law enforcement discount, he thought you needed a heads-up. On top of all the general unrest going on around us, there's a biker gang trying to move into the area, and I expect they're pretty salty. Mostly they're staying around the lake, but that could change."

He paused and looked around. "You got a lot of guns here, plus ammo, camping gear—everything an itinerant biker might need."

"We sell to most anyone." Joel glanced at the girl. "We can take care of ourselves, but thanks for the warning. Appreciate it."

Holding his hand up, Jim continued. "I'm sure you can take care of things in most cases, one on one. I saw your poster for the Bad Guy Down Training. Since you're an instructor, I'm sure you have the skills."

He met the man's gaze. "But these bikers don't do anything unless there's twenty or thirty of them. They're like a pack of wild dogs on the Serengeti. I know you'd try hard, but I'm just thinking a pitched battle in close quarters would get your family hurt."

Jim could see the young man getting irritated as he continued. "Look around at where you are right now. It's crowded in here. In this corner of the store, there's no way out. You're boxed in, so it'd be wise to fix that. If they show up in numbers, it might be best to have a way to slip out the back."

He could see the man wasn't convinced, so he hesitated a moment and then played hardball. "That girl over there your wife?"

When he nodded, Jim continued. "She's beautiful."

She was listening, and that got him an impish smile from her that disappeared with his next comment. "What's she worth to you? You give that some thought. Those folks won't just take your merchandise, they'll take her, too—even if she's wounded. They just won't care."

"So with all your training," he continued. "What's your best advice about shooting situations? Or, any life-threatening situation?"

Joel grimaced, conceding the point while dropping his gaze from his wife. "Situational awareness. Don't be there. If you *are* there, get gone. Shooting is always a last resort. Or as some of our vets would say, un-ass yourself from your LZ."

"Abandon your landing zone. Get the hell out while your ass is intact." Jim laughed, thinking the vet would be Lawrence. "That's good advice, something I wish I'd taken a few times. I expect you're a very good instructor, and judging from the looks, you're getting a damned good husband. None of that will matter. It just won't. Look, all I'm saying is don't get caught in something you can't control. No matter what you have here, nothing in this store is worth that."

The man gave him a hopeful look. "Is there any way to control them if they show up? The biker gang?"

"I'm talking about any group of three or more. Not just the bikers. And the way things in general are looking right now?" He shrugged, giving the man a grim smile. "I'm not sure how your county sheriff would view this, but I'd change my routine and start screening people at the door. With the virus going on, you have a good excuse to start doing a door check...maybe a temperature check. You know most everyone around here. If you don't recognize someone or don't like their looks, deny access at the door. You already have a sign that reads 'No Shirt-No Shoes-No Service.' Just add 'If We Don't Like Your Looks' to it. That would have stopped the incident with Twitchy before it started."

Joel laughed. "Well, we actually know him. He's only dangerous to small animals." He gave Jim a long look. "What if they insist on coming in?"

"Just like I'm betting you teach in your class, and you've already said it. Situational awareness. If you've got twenty guys parked out front and some of them are trying to force their way in, you need to leave. You'll see and hear them pull up. Better yet, put up some security cameras. Don't be shy about it. Make your assessment and respond."

"What if I can't leave—get caught out or surprised?" He looked around a moment. "I can see that happening if we're busy."

"Look, I'm just a citizen, so any advice I give is strictly on me. But you need to do your level best to not let that happen. Make it a priority to *not* be surprised. But I know. Shit happens. If it does? That's when I'd start stacking bodies to block the door while all the friendlies in the store drift out the back or some other place out of harm's way. I'm going to assume you might have an M4 carbine or maybe an AK47 around? Maybe a Mini-14? Put it by the back door. While someone is stacking them up at the front door, I'd come around and take them from the back. Make a nice crossfire. Don't even think about fair play on this. There's no such thing in a fight." Jim paused a moment. "But you didn't hear that from me."

"Yeah, I've read that old saying. Maybe from Patton? If you're in a fair fight, it shows a lack of planning."

"Goes back a lot farther than that, but it's a fair assessment."

"The firearms you mentioned are illegal for me to own."

"I won't tell," Jim replied.

Joel seemed lost in thought as he turned away to wait on another customer while his wife tracked him with her gaze a moment.

Her voice was husky, a worried frown wrinkling her forehead. "You're serious about all this, aren't you?"

He sighed. It wasn't his intent to scare people but in this case, it might be appropriate. "Yes, ma'am. Dead serious. I'm not trying to scare you...well, maybe just a little bit. It pays to be informed. Look at it this way. I've noticed that everyone in this store is armed, at least all I've seen. That's not a bad thing and goes a long way to keep the amateurs from trying anything stupid."

"The problem is," he continued. "These thugs won't care if you're armed. The bosses in the gang won't care if some of their soldiers get killed—hell, half of them are high on the drug of the day anyway. The other half are psychopaths. They won't stop. They'll send in their newbies and wannabes first, because that's how they advance in the gang—killing people."

She gazed toward the front of the store, watching someone at the checkout register counting out over a thousand dollars for a plastic, nine-millimeter piece of junk. "We have a good relationship with the county sheriff, even the state police. When we hit the panic button, the call goes out and they're on their way."

He gave her a sad look, shaking his head. "I'm sure they are, and I'm sure they'll bust their britches getting here. You've used them before?"

When she nodded, he continued. "How long does that take on a typical day?"

"Anywhere from thirty minutes to an hour." Her gaze drifted away. "Shit."

"I'd say that's a damned good description of the problem." He smiled. These were good people.

Her gaze came slowly from the floor to meet his. "So, what do we do?"

"What about a vacation?" He paused a moment. "Look at it this way. You've seen the news. The world around us is slowly coming apart. From politicians calling anyone who don't vote their way insurrectionists, to virus lockdowns. People are mad and scared everywhere—in equal numbers, and that's a bad combination. Hell, there's rioting in Springfield, just fifty miles away. They're trying to burn it down. We're not insulated just because we're out in the country. Take your thinking to the endgame."

He waved his finger in a circle. "What do you do when all this goes away? How do you feed and protect your family? It goes way beyond owning guns and knowing how to use them. A gun is just a tool. Start thinking long term."

She gazed at him a moment, tears starting to well up in her eyes. "Well...aren't you just a ray of sunshine on a cloudy day."

Joel came back after waiting on his customer. His voice was a gruff warning. "You're upsetting my wife."

"Rather to be mad and aware of the problems than complacent." Jim nodded and shrugged. "Don't mean to ruffle your feathers. But think about it. If you prepare and nothing happens, what have you lost?"

The girl clutched her husband's arm. "Innocence?"

———

DRIVING BACK TO WHITE ROCK, Jim came up behind six bikers riding two across and three deep. Since the road was too hilly to safely go around them, he slowed to give them plenty of space. As they neared the entrance to Trader Jack's location, the bikers signaled and turned into the drive. He hadn't noticed on the trip out, but a new guardhouse had been built inside the fence. On impulse, he pulled in behind the bikers. The bikers were waved through. He was not. The gate dropped like a barrier of an East German border during the Cold War. The guard stared at Jim. It wasn't lost on him that the man was armed with an M-4 lookalike dropped on a one-point sling around his neck. His finger was inside the trigger guard. No words were spoken. Somehow he didn't think it was a lack of trigger discipline. Jim backed out on the highway and proceeded toward White Rock.

He knew Gomez had taken over the post as payment

for helping with the drug gang. Nobody cared at the time, and it was handy to have someplace to buy supplies.

That was good. But he hadn't seen Gomez in a long time, and those bikers just got easy entrance to what must be an armed camp.

That was not good.

––––––––

THE REST of the drive back to the Lazy J was done in pensive silence full of road noise and the moaning hiss of his air conditioner. Visiting the gun shop was a wake-up call for Jim. All the things he'd told them, he'd forgotten to tell himself. The world was unraveling at a furious pace. Every prepper site on the Internet that he visited had the same message. Bunker up. Hunker down. Bad times a comin'. Primarily the same as the cryptic message from Sally One-Eye.

There was a definite chasm between ideologies. Most conservative sites were preaching to have a week's worth of goods on hand—mostly food and water, still expecting government agencies to step up in times of emergency, after all that's their job. Progressives were solely reliant on government for all things, no need to prepare.

For the most part, America's population was concentrated in the cities. That was the biggest problem. If the economy crashed, there was no way to feed them. In a strange way, it was funny. Want to end the race war? Make everyone equally hungry. Shortages were already happening in some places and the rioting was starting. It was every man, every family for themselves, and who could blame them? You have to feed your family, and most hadn't thought more long-term than ordering pizza to go. So what happens when the shelves are empty? People leave. In droves. Like army ants in the jungle, devouring everything in their path—killing and dying on the way. Most won't know where they are going or what to do once they get there.

An area like Stockton Lake would be a target. In Springfield and its suburbs, there were over a million people. They wouldn't all head their way, they'd probably leave in all directions. Some would stay local to defend their homes and family, trying to survive by fishing the nearby recreational lake and streams and hunting. And he felt sorry for them, because the longer they put off leaving, the more danger they were in.

Stockton was a big lake, big enough to absorb a great number of people. Those weren't the problem. It was the desperate, hungry, and for the most part, lawless that would cause the problems. They didn't know how to get food except by taking what others had.

Barnes and his crew were law enforcement. It was in their DNA to try and keep a lid on things. Three people against hundreds, perhaps thousands? Wasn't going to work.

There was a medical term called triage. Basically, in times of disaster, you treat those most likely to survive first and send them on their way. You leave the least likely to survive for last, or not at all. That situation had not arrived yet. But it was coming. He could feel it in his bones.

He was ready for most things. Every week or so, Jacy would bring in an armload of medical supplies—simple things to keep you from dying...using more of her experience as a combat medic than of nursing. Food was laid by and Alina kept adding to the stores. He'd laughed when she bought toilet paper and tampons by the case. They had food on the hoof if need be, at least for a while. But his family was growing. Whether intentional or not, Pablo and his brood were family. Jacy and her kids were family. Barnes and Aunt Bea were family. And he wasn't sure he could stare into the children's eyes as they ate miniature goats for dinner.

And the biggest danger of all? He'd become complacent. Everyone telling him to stand down and to not meddle in other's affairs had a price.

Survival comes with rules of three. You can survive three minutes without air, three hours without shelter in extreme conditions, three days without drinking water, three weeks without food, and three months without hope. When those items aren't in play, the rules change to what is needed for survival. Security is first. Then it's food, water, and shelter. Everything else revolves around those. Short term, long term? It didn't matter. All things revolve around those basics. If you fail at any of those essentials, you're done. And the corollary to those rules? Back to security. The means to protect yourself and what you have, because if you have it—others will want it. If you fail on any of the basics, you're back to the beginning and that's a cycle you don't want to repeat.

Driving back to the ranch, he tried to compartmentalize. He knew what their assets were, both goods and people. There was enough food and supplies stored to last a year, if they were careful. The added people would put a strain on supply. His friends were solid and trustworthy, and that was important. But would they be able to isolate, even knowing the dangers?

There was no guarantee Barnes and his wife would come to safety. He might stay too long trying to control the situation, and she would never leave him. His deputies would try their best and fail.

Jacy was an unknown quantity...maybe. But he was sure the safety of her children would override any ideas of staying at the clinic. If he was any judge, they'd need her expertise desperately—they already had needed them.

The flip side of being prepared? Could they keep it? What were the dangers, aside from the zombie horde marching into their county? The bikers were an immediate danger. They would try to carve out a place of their own by taking what others had, and assuredly saw Jim Lane as an obstacle. That was the first and most immediate danger. It would get worse in the coming days.

He'd give Barnes his chance at taking care of the bikers and offer any help he could. He owed him that. And there would be pockets of resistance throughout the area that would whittle down the biker's numbers, but it wouldn't be enough. Should the law enforcement line of defense fail, and it would—he would have to try and take out the threat. Did he have allies that could help? All he could think of was Gomez, and for some reason, that gave him a queasy feeling. Gomez helped them before and then took over Trader Jack's—hadn't been seen since. The man seemed to go dark and disappear. He couldn't see any kind of alliance with Gomez ending well.

He sighed, watching the road winding into the landscape. In any event, war was coming, sure as God made little green apples. And like many before him had admonished...he was too old for this shit.

TWELVE

THE NEXT MORNING found Jim leaning against a post under his veranda, gazing to the south. He'd just finished his newly started morning workout, wondering how he'd gotten so far out of shape.

The screen door slammed, and Alina moved up behind him. Her voice was soft. "Lost in thought, my sweaty man?"

"Bird watching." He leaned against her, one arm around her shoulder, and kissed the top of her head. "Funny you should use the word lost. I seem to have a serious lack of motivation these days. I'm trying to jump-start it."

Moving deftly out from under his arm, she comments, "Well, you've jump-started your ode to sweat. You need a shower. And you also need a day job. You're getting bored."

She moved her sunglasses from the top of her head to her eyes. One hand moved in a sloppy salute while shading her eyes trying to see what held his interest. "You smeared my glasses. What kind of birds?"

"I'll try to improve my aim, but it takes practice. Anyway, they're turkey buzzards. Big, ugly mothers. Nature's cleanup crew."

"Ah. So there's a kettle of buzzards. Have they come to committee yet?" Losing interest, she moved her glasses back to their perch.

"What?"

She smirked at him. "A kettle is a group of buzzards or vultures in flight. When they land, it's called a committee."

He stared at her a moment, trying to see the joke and failing. "How do you know that?"

"Simple. I read and often remember what I read. Otherwise, it's just a waste of time. I know what buzzards are, but we're usually dodging them on the highway."

She echoed his concern. "That's a lot of birds for some roadkill. At least they're not holding a wake on our house."

"I'm impressed, sort of." He hugged her to him. "I've been meaning to do a walkabout up there to look for deer sign. I'd like to bag a couple for the freezer. I'd better check it out."

She relaxed against him. "Need help? We could take the four-wheeler."

He debated that a moment, knowing her aversion to stomping around the woods. She liked her nature experiences to be cut grass and raised bed farming. "Way too noisy. Besides, I need the exercise. You could walk with me?"

"Hiking? Through weeds and such?" She snorted. "I'll pass."

"Lazy." He poked her stomach, barely making a dent.

After extensive study, he'd never found an ounce of fat on her. "You could use the exercise, too."

"And again...no."

Laughing, he shook his head. "Okay, just keep the home fires burning."

"I will, if you keep feeding the flames. I've something in the oven anyway."

He glanced at her a moment, viewing his own personal forest fire in cutoff jeans and a thin, wife-beater tee shirt. She stared back at him with unblinking, clear-blue eyes. Flames indeed.

───────

AFTER AN HOUR of her impeding his changing into insect-repellent forest camo pants tucked into side-zipped boots and a T-shirt, he was on his way.

Moving toward the tree line, he watched the circling buzzards with trepidation. Wheeling in ever-lowering circles, their presence was an airborne finger pointing at something dead or dying. It wasn't abnormal to see buzzards every day. One or two carrion birds could be discounted since it didn't take many to clean up the occasional small dead animal or roadkill. But a dozen or so birds, with more riding the thermals and standing sentinel higher in the sky? Something large. They'd called in reinforcements.

From the higher elevation, he glanced at his small circle of paradise known as the Lazy J, or by Barnes's critique, the Fishhook. The valley resembled a bowl with very few access points. At least, easy ones. It was what attracted him to the property in the first place. Until you moved through the entrance, you couldn't see it from the road. The real estate lady had assured him that most were unaware of its presence.

The main gate was nestled between large limestone boulders and a metal pipe fence. A second approach to the valley was an area they called the maze, a no-man's land of jumbled boulders and brush dividing his land and Jacy Mane's horse farm. If you didn't know your way, it would take a couple of hours to navigate through it.

He'd climbed to the third way in, bordering his valley on the high side. He'd been planning to scout the area for deer rubs and bedding areas before the fall hunting season. It was government land next to Stockton Lake. The hardwood forest was the Ozark's version of triple canopy jungle. Brush, brambles, poison ivy, and sumac grew in the rocky ground—the small clearings covered in fescue grass. There were only a few game trails through it. Any other path required giving blood or risking a rash that would ruin your month and send you to the doctor for shots to relieve itching and swelling. The next level was populated by shade-loving small trees like dogwood and pear. The final layer topped out with an oak canopy, with a smattering of maple and sycamore along creek beds.

Beautiful country, but if they didn't start clearing brush soon, it would go the same way as the Southern California countryside. Conservation Department or not, he and his foreman had already done some controlled burns around the edge of his property to make sure any wildfire wouldn't progress too far into their valley. It was against the rules, but knowing it was needed, the local officials turned a blind eye to it.

Anything could be found in the hardwood forest. Discounting man, the apex predators that included black bear and cougar, fed on small deer and most anything else. That was a possibility for the buzzard convention, but he didn't think it likely. A predator could bring down a calf or foal, but they'd protect their kill until they were done with it. An occasional hiker could be killed—rare, but possible. Most hikers carried some kind of firearm for that reason.

With a sigh, he did a slow scissor over a flat-rock fence being mindful of copperheads and jumping spiders —the spiders being the scariest. Tarantulas were common but not feared. It was the fiddle-backs and fuzzy wolf spiders that made him wary. Or anything that put webs at face level—a cruel practice.

Some activists promoted the idea that the rock fences populating the hills were put together by slave labor. In a way, they were. Irish immigrants had often cleared fields, their indenture owned by those who bought them. Poor farmers were slaves to the land they worked, hauling rock by horse-pulled stoneboats as they cleared the fields. Often labor was provided by work crews from the county or state—prisoners earning their keep. The myth of slave walls were just that...a myth.

The silence of the forest is peculiar while the denizens decide if you are a threat. You can hear sounds in the distance...barking squirrels, the cry of an eagle or hawk, incessant chattering of Carolina wrens. But close to you, even the insects keep silent until you pass by. Only footfalls through rotting leaves signaled his passing.

The buzzard's quarry was in a small clearing just below the crest of the hill, a few hundred feet into the timber and dense undergrowth. They hadn't landed, though a few perched on lower limbs with a restless clenching of talons, unblinking eyes watching his every move. He stood quietly, every sense alert, in the shadow of an old oak whose base had to be four feet across. The sense of being in a scene from an Edgar Allan Poe story was strong. Their manner of watching his every move gave the birds an aura of intelligence they didn't have.

After a few moments, he decided anyone else in the area was either long gone or had more patience than he could muster. If waiting in ambush, they were damned good. One thought led to another, and he loosened the snap on his pistol, easing it in its smooth leather holster.

He'd never ventured to this particular neck of the woods, and idly wondered why not. His assumption was that the undergrowth was so dense it would keep people from coming into his valley from this direction. He was wrong. It would take some work, but a determined interloper could do it.

At first glance, the clearing seemed to be a camping spot. A fire pit was located close to the timber on one side of the clearing. A few beer cans populated the periphery along with a used, partially burned condom shriveled on the old ashes and charred sticks. A spot of grass close to the fire pit was crushed down, about the size of a queen-sized inflatable mattress. Curious, but not unheard of. Any fire or activity here would be hidden from his view from home because of the ridge. Smoke would be dispersed by the canopy of leaves. All told, not a bad spot to hang out.

Guttural squawking from above drew his attention. Barely visible through the foliage was a platform situated about twenty feet up the tree. A buzzard sat on it, peering down at him. He'd heard of them upchucking on people. Maybe true, maybe not. He moved.

A man lay spreadeagled on his back in the trampled

grass, eyes open to the canopy above, knees draped over a worn-smooth log used for a communal bench while roasting...whatever. The neat, small hole centered in what professionals would call the T-zone, that area you could mark by drawing a line up the bridge of the nose crossing a line drawn across the eyes. Only a thin trail of dried blood leaked toward his hairline. With this wound or at least incapacitation, death would have been instantaneous. Young, maybe late twenties. He couldn't figure out why the man was draped backward over the log. Anyone shot in the head would crumple like a puppet with its strings cut. This man was posed, arms spread wide in supplication...or acceptance? Or not. Dead bodies offered little interest to him, but this was...curious.

A few feet away, a young woman lay sprawled, a broken doll thrown away when its usefulness was over. At first glance, cause of death wasn't obvious. She seemed average in every way—nothing notable in weight, coloring, or size. She was in contrast with the man. Not posed, simply...fallen...crumpled, maybe tossed. It was not a peaceful ending.

Watching the ground so he didn't step on anything that might be considered evidence, he approached and felt for a pulse. It was an obligation, having little meaning. Her naked body was blotched in faded blue and white hues, half-lidded eyes dull and lifeless. She'd been there a while. Ants had found her.

Turning, he walked a reverse path to the same tree he'd first stood under. On impulse, he walked around the tree and discovered a ladder nailed into the bark. It was prefab, with stand-off metal corrugated steps, spiked to the tree for stability. His first thought was that it was an expensive ladder. Being sure to snap the strap on his pistol, he climbed to the platform. It was a bigger relief than he thought it would be when the buzzard flew away. Picturing himself hanging on a ladder with one hand while with the other trying to pull his pistol and fire at a screeching and flogging sharp-beaked bird was a nightmare in the making. He wasn't sure he could win that fight.

The climbing apparatus looked fairly new, but the platform was older. It blended with the foliage with a light sheen of green moss on the gray, weathered wood. Standing on the sturdy platform, avoiding a generous amount of bird crap, his gaze went to the scene below. Taking a picture with his cell camera, it still made no sense. From the higher vantage point, he did notice a slight trail going directly down the hill. Turning and looking to the north, two things became clear. This was not a deer stand, but an observation post. The platform was just high enough in the tree to give a clear line of sight over the ridge and to his cabin. He took two pictures from that vantage point, one regular and the other at full magnification.

Putting his phone away, he pulled a small high-power binocular from his pocket. Focusing on his place, his jaw clenched. Alina liked to catch some sun behind the cabin where she would be unseen from any angle—unless that angle were twenty feet up in a tree and under a mile away.

THIRTEEN

JIM SIGHED, standing with his back against the tree while looking at the attached safety belt—but didn't use it, thinking about fingerprints. It'd been a long time since he'd had to think this way. His ten years in the military police was a long time ago. At least he'd get good cell phone reception up here. It took another sigh and the rolling of tense, slumped shoulders before he woke up his smartphone and made the call. Discounting the soft litany of the carrion birds discussing an interrupted meal, or channeling a long-dead poet, he hated to break the peaceful silence.

The answer was immediate. "Talk to me."

"Barnes? Don't tell Aunt Bea, but you got some fresh trouble. I found a couple of bodies about a quarter mile south of my property line on government land. I'll babysit until you and the troops get here. You can thank me later."

He held the phone away from his ear when Barnes barked into the phone. "I thought we already had this conversation. Didn't I tell you to stay out of trouble?"

"Back off, Bubba. I was looking south from the porch and saw a boatload of buzzards. Thought I'd check it out." Jim gazed around the clearing. It still didn't make sense. "This is your problem, not mine."

Finally, Barnes continued in a more even tone. "I don't suppose they died of natural causes?"

He wasn't sure if Barnes's statement was sarcastic... knowing him, it was. "Well, I'm no medic, but I don't think so. It's a man and woman. He has a gunshot wound to the forehead. There's nothing obvious with her... except she's naked. My guess is the man was the lucky one, but you never know."

"Jesus. That's all I need." Barnes paused a moment. "So, where are you?"

"Not sure. It's behind my place on State land, but there's no access that I've seen. You'll have to use my phone's GPS. I'm betting you have it on speed dial. It's obvious there's a road somewhere or those bodies wouldn't be here. I just don't see it. If you have a map, there might be a fire lane down the hill. I don't get up here much."

Papers rustled in the background. "Funny. You've navigated places all around the world, but you can't find an outhouse in your own backyard."

"That's because I don't have one. You woke up cranky today. Aunt Bea got you on a short leash?"

Barnes's sigh of the downtrodden and put-upon was long and loud. "Alright, I have your little blinker on my screen. We'll head your way. Ambulance?"

Shaking his head, he realized only a curious blue jay could see him...and king buzzard with his Darth Vader cloak wrapped around his birdy body. "Long past that, brother. This is hours old."

It finally occurred to him. Where are her clothes? Climbing down the ladder and walking around the perimeter of the small clearing, he finally found a few scuff marks in the leaves. They were faint, but still there. Staying off to the side and dodging a clump of poison ivy, he followed the faint trail down the hill.

At the next level spot, Jim stared back at the ghost of a trail he'd followed. The marks ended here. No vehicle. No clothes. No tracks on the rocky, leaf-covered ground. Why would someone take them up the hill to kill them? Knowing the simplest answer was often the most correct, he accepted it. They wouldn't.

It was a half-hour before Barnes's patrol SUV labored up the hill and stopped within a few feet of him. Barnes exited and came to stand next to him, gazing around the forest. "I didn't figure you'd stay put. Glad you stayed. What's the story, Jim?"

"Apparently there's a meeting spot or campsite about fifty paces up the hill. Looks like something kids would use, although it takes a hike to get there. There are two bodies. She's naked, no wedding ring, and no obvious cause of death. And curiously, no clothes or vehicle here. There's a male in the clearing and obviously killed up there judging by the blood tracks on the body."

Nodding, Barnes gazed up the hill. The low grind of a couple more vehicles traversing the fire lane came to them. "So? What's your take?"

"No telling how many people were up there. The ground is hard. The grass is tall, but there's a packed down spot, maybe from a mattress or blanket. Someone took them there or followed them there and did the deed. I didn't see a weapon, but you might do a metal detector search for brass. Never can tell. Maybe someone took both of them there, did whatever to the woman while they made him watch, and then killed him. Why they chose this spot is pure guesswork. It's a puzzle inside a puzzle. Possibilities are endless."

Barnes gave him a steady look. "Do you believe that, Detective?"

Jim rolled his eyes, pulled out his phone, and sent his pictures to Barnes, except for the ones of home, from the platform. "This is all I have."

"And if I was writing the story?" Jim continued. "It almost looks like two different scenes up there. Might be someone came for a rescue, was too late and just did the guy."

"Wedding ring on the man? Any ID?" Barnes watched his deputies come up the hill.

"Wedding ring, yes. ID? I didn't move the body to look. Maybe they were doing something they shouldn't have been doing. Someone caught them." He thought a moment, gazing up the trail toward the clearing. "And then sanitized the area. Curious. Kinda blows up the anger scenario."

Barnes shook his head, shrugging. "Your personal history notwithstanding, there's not always a love triangle."

Jim pantomimed pulling an arrow from his chest. "Ouch, that hurt."

"Just for the record, what are you carrying?" His friend smirked at him.

"My Glock .40 and Shield EZ."

"What caliber?" Barnes seemed to like the momentary distraction.

"380. Nice little gun," Jim replied. "Accurate all the way out to ten feet."

"A senior citizen's gun. Happens to all of us." Barnes nodded, gazing up the hill. "What's the wound on the guy look like?"

Jim paused a moment, knowing where his friend would go with the answer. "Probably a .22, definitely small caliber. It could be a .25, but I doubt it."

They stared at each other a moment.

With an expression turning serious, Barnes continued. "You know that I have to ask. Has anyone pissed off Alina lately? I know what she carries. She's not exactly a stranger to this kind of action."

"No, she's maniacally serene these days. And she's done with that. Of course, when those bikers came by for a parley, there wasn't much love lost there. I doubt the folks in the clearing qualify as bikers, but I could be wrong."

When Barnes started to speak, Jim held up his hand. "And there's only a few thousand .22 caliber firearms around, and that's just in this county. But I'll give you a pass on that one...I know you have to ask. For the record, I don't know those people in the clearing. I doubt if Alina does, but you can show her pictures if you want. Actually, I'll do that anyway. I can't see her doing this."

Shrugging, Barnes changed the subject. "I don't suppose you heard shots fired? Anything helpful?"

"Sorry, can't help pinpoint the time for you. No shots, no campfires. No screaming perps fleeing through the woods dropping clues from their pockets. Just buzzards."

Barnes snorted back a laugh, offered his hand, and the friends shook. "Alright. We've got it from here. If you'd go in and type out a report, I wouldn't even have to go up there. You're a good investigator. You should come work for the county and wear a white hat for once."

Jim took off his old bushman hat, often wadded up and stuffed in his pocket only to be taken out and beaten back into shape, and examined it. "Couldn't pass the background check. Stole some Twinkies from a gas station once. It's on my record. Felony Twinkie."

Dripping with sarcasm, Barnes responded, "Well, since you're a felon, stay out of the way. For now, you can go back to skulking around the woods or whatever you were doing."

He gave his friend an innocent look. "Bird watching and scouting for deer sign."

"Right." The word was drawn out, and if possible, laced with even more sarcasm. "Just a thought. You'd have heard the gunfire, wouldn't you? Even that small caliber round pops pretty loud." He gave Jim a pointed look. "Unless it's suppressed."

"Nice try, Detective. Just kind of sneaking that in there? Not buying it." Holding up his hand to stop the reply, he continued. "And just food for thought, not trying to change the subject, I followed some bikers on the way back from the gun shop yesterday. They turned into Trader Jack's. Someone has built a new guardhouse by the entrance. I'm guessing Gomez is branching out from his plumbing business."

"Well," Barnes said. "His business is his business."

"Until it isn't. Seems to be a lot going on behind the scenes, brother."

Barnes scowled at him. "Thanks a lot. It was a nice day until you called."

He could feel Barnes's gaze burning into his back as he walked away, giving his friend a little waggly finger wave over his shoulder.

FOURTEEN

SHORTLY AFTER LEAVING BARNES, Jim walked into the cabin and found Alina stretched out on the couch thumbing through a gardening and seed catalog. She turned her face up for a kiss. Trying not to get distracted, he noticed there were no tan lines. No matter how she tried, her genetic pool guaranteed a tan was beyond her capabilities.

Fulfilling his duties and savoring the slight peppermint taste, he turned and gazed out the window toward the forest to the south. "I'm surprised you're sticking around today. You're usually out and about. Already planning next year's garden?"

"Nah. These are just dream books. And you know I get bored with you being gone a lot or buried in your laptop. I drive. I shop. I keep busy." She waved the catalog, making the pages flop. "All this is too overpriced. It's cheaper to get everything from the local growers—just can't get all the really neat stuff."

"Like money is a problem for you?" He didn't know the depth of her bank account, but anytime she needed something, money seemed to be available. Not that he was complaining. The money that came their way from her father to make amends for their previous little dust-up was generous. He wasn't too proud to take it.

She smirked at him. "I'm frugal. It's why I have money."

He nodded, not looking at her, trying to be casual—hard to do when thinking of the observation post. "I didn't see you put on any sunblock. With your skin, you shouldn't forget that."

She bounced off the couch with a smile. "Were you spying on me? Why, you old letch, you. Aren't closeups good enough?"

"Never enough." He put his arm around her. "We may have a small problem."

She stepped away. "How small?"

After relating everything he'd found and showing her the pictures, she paced the hardwood floor, bare feet padding cadence with her breathing.

Her gaze snapped toward him. This was not the warm and cuddly Alina he'd grown used to seeing. "The wound looked like a .22 cal?"

"Maybe." He nodded, remembering the wounds. "Probably."

"Single penetration or exit wound?"

"Both." He described in detail what he saw and then showed her the pictures again.

She took his phone and magnified the picture. "Looks like he was shot after he fell backward. Probably pushed backward and then finished off. I don't think he was posed like you think. His arms were out to break his fall. If he was shot while standing, he would have gone straight down. I'm thinking there was a second shooter.

The one doing the pushing wouldn't have had the good straight-in angle."

"Crap. I didn't think of that." Sometimes he forgot what she used to do for her family. Or, more accurately, he didn't want to think about it. Killing in the heat of battle was one thing. But in cold blood?

She continued in a musing tone. "So, full load standard Long Rifle, maybe a stinger. Probably a jacketed round since it punched through. Not a hollow point or soft nose, so definitely not a pro shooter. There are millions of those rounds out there."

Alina stopped a moment and then resumed pacing. "Shit. I bet Barnes was all over this."

"Well." With a rueful glance, he nodded. "He did bring up the subject, but not in a real serious way. He's a friend...hell, a good friend. But he'll be a bulldog on this. You know Barnes, he won't make any hasty assumptions."

Her eyes locked onto his with an intense gaze. "Aren't you going to ask?"

Giving a slow headshake, he didn't break eye contact. "Nope. Neither of us are virgins. I figure if you have skeletons in your closet, you'll trot them out sooner or later. But I did think about it, and I can't see that this fits your profile."

"I have a profile?" Her lips started a smile but stopped as she waited for an answer.

He grinned at her. "Oh, yeah. And it's all mine."

Watching her start pacing again, he continued. "You're going to hyperventilate if you keep doing that."

Her gaze settled on him. "Did you destroy it?"

He made the mental leap. "The platform? No. It's in the middle of a crime scene. And it was a little too well made to be someone getting their kicks spying on a beautiful woman, and it's too high for a deer stand. It was an observation post. And I'm betting they're really pissed at the killings done right under their platform. The only thing worth watching in this direction is us, or the ranch in general. Our best bet is to find out who it is. If we do that, we'll know why."

"I'm beautiful? You don't tell me that enough." She slowed her pacing, giving him an intense stare. "How will you find out about our voyeur?"

"Now that I know where the OP is, I can use a spotter scope to look back at them. We'll check it a few times a day and at night. The scope has a camera function, although the night pictures suck. We can always put up a trail cam."

He thought a moment, trying to think of all the scenarios that would put someone on the platform spying on them. "Now that there's traffic around that tree, it may be a few days before whoever it is resumes. I doubt it's a regular thing."

"Do you think the murder and platform are connected?"

"Now, that's a thought." He'd often wondered if she would make a good investigator for someone. Maybe in the private sector. She'd have connections for that. Which led to another thought. Private eye service? It would fight the boredom...if the world didn't go belly up first.

She came over and leaned against him. "Why don't we just sabotage the platform so they fall and break their damned necks?"

He nodded. "Well, I did think of that. But there is the off chance it could be lusty teenagers ogling your body.

They don't really deserve to die because of their out-of-control hormones. Right?"

"Maybe." She relaxed in his arms, shaking her head. "Ogling?"

"I do it all the time." Smiling at her fake glare, he continued. "But there's just the one thing."

Her question came in the form of a raised eyebrow.

"You may have to start wearing clothes."

"Or?" She grinned at him, hands on hips. "I could put on a show?"

"Um. Please don't. I'm not into sharing, even from afar. Not my thing." He gave the window a musing glance. "Besides, I suspect you already have."

FIFTEEN

THE DAY after discovering the bodies next to his land,
a visitor arrived. Surprise wouldn't describe it. After
acquiescing to Alina's suggestion that he talk to someone,
he thought it would take months to happen and expected
travel to an undisclosed high-priced den of mind-melding
shamans. Or at least a decent witch doctor. Visions of a
dark, subdued room with rich leather furniture and soft
background music came to mind. Part of his expectations
were correct—the shrink could have been from central
casting on a movie set.

Her dark hair was pulled back in a severe headache-
producing bun, showing a few strands of white. Obviously not vain enough to supplement with color, she was
a studied vision of "all business." He wondered if a
particularly coarse joke would break that veneer.

Once she was settled, the woman's voice was soft and
well-modulated, eyes brown and gentle as her spoken
word. "Why did you leave the Shepherds, Mr. Lane?"

"Which time?" If her projection of gentleness was an
act on her part, it was a good one. He had to admit, if

only to himself, he was trying to poke the bear to get a response—any kind, just to get her bubble off center.

Her stare was calm, unperturbed...not someone to be sidetracked—a teacher with a recalcitrant student. The corner of her mouth started to lift, then was brought under control. If she'd had a ruler, he would have hidden his knuckles behind his back.

"Don't be difficult," she replied. "The last time. The most important time. The reason we're gathered here...time."

They were sitting at the kitchen table. Dr. Tricia Bartol and Jim...Alina leaning against the kitchen counter, arms folded above her stomach, trying to be unobtrusive—body language showing defensive full alert. Her thin tee shirt and tight jeans were distracting, but he suspected she knew that. Judging from the guarded glances, she must have been distracting to the doctor as well—hovering like a protective lioness.

Dr. Bartol had shown up unannounced driving a black SUV the size of a small tank. The shine was bright enough to attract a murder of crow's intent on bombing practice, along with a slight dust storm following the vehicle's journey up the gravel drive. The luxury conveyance would not leave in pristine condition.

She introduced herself and requested to talk to Jim alone. He disagreed and asked Alina to stay. If she were to understand, she needed to hear it all. The doctor didn't like it but nodded acceptance. His house, his rules.

"There were many factors contributing to my exit," he replied, returning to her question.

Staring past Alina and through the kitchen window, he watched the ever-growing miniature goat herd trotting relentlessly toward her raised beds, led by a black-and-white buck not much larger than a fat cat and sporting a malicious grin on his snout.

"I was pushing forty. Getting too old for that kind of life, and it was physically demanding. But mainly I left the Shepherds because of my last assignment. The results got to me...more than I expected, more than anything I ever did. In the past, I could disassociate—often did—you know, just do the job and forget about it. Put my feelings in a box, locked away in a room with the key thrown away. Not this one. I tried, but it won't go away. It's like all my mental boxes are full and keep spilling over."

The doctor was a twiddler—her gold-plated pen constantly tap-tap-tapping like Poe's raven on the requisite yellow, lined tablet taken methodically from her vintage briefcase bag. The soft leather accouterment probably cost more than the average monthly salary of any working stiff in flyover country.

Her smooth voice held all the emotion of a recording from the latest AI inventions threatening to take over the world. "And now you're having trouble sleeping? Night sweats? Irritable?"

He nodded his admission. "Not just at night. I get triggered other times."

A quick glance at Alina found her holding up her palms before he asked the doctor. "How'd you know those specific symptoms?"

"I'm a doctor. It's what I do." Smiling, she paused a moment. "Besides, your lady friend told me."

He wondered at that. More than a lover, marriage hadn't been discussed. He needed to nail that down—have the talk. Alina was a constant surprise. When she came back to him, she was all in and made her intentions known right up front. It wasn't easy, but she'd breached his anger and sacked his castle. He turned and grinned at her, shaking his head.

"That figures. Domestication is a surprising fit for her. She told me the other night we were equally yoked—whatever that means."

"I'm sorry?" Bartol gave a confused smile and glanced at Alina before returning her attention to him. "Oh, yes. She seems nice, although I can't speak for her domestication. So, if we can get back on track? What happened?"

He stared at her a moment. Nice was not a description he'd ever associated with Alina, at least with her attitude toward other people. She was more the dominant female wolf protecting her pack. "Wait. Are you talking about Alina Ivanov?"

The doctor looked startled. "No, of course not. I'm speaking of Jacy Mane. She's a nurse in one of my classes. A very good one, I might add. Definitely doctor material. In some areas, I sometimes think she's teaching me."

"Ah." He nodded, ignoring the mock anger being projected at him from his resident assassin. "Alina talks to Jacy. Jacy calls you, and here I am."

"Yes. And here you are...dodging all my questions. I didn't realize you were so detail oriented, or I would have explained all that. You're not objecting much, so your presence must be voluntary. Please understand. People are trying to help you. You should be encouraged by that. So, if you don't mind, I'd like to hear your story. What's going on?"

SIXTEEN

JIM SHRUGGED, shaking his head a moment before meeting her gaze. "I killed a woman."

"Surely not the first person you've killed?" The doctor held up her hand. "Sorry. Remember, I know your history. Sally told me of her personal rescue. It sounded impressive, like the heroes we see on the silver screen. You pulled it off and saved the day."

"A long time ago." Drifting into memory, he came back with a direct gaze and light banter. "It was a lesson in how audacity can sometimes win the prize, along with a fair amount of luck."

Sally One-Eye, the current head of the Shepherds, was an agent at the time of her rescue, and both of them were ten years younger. When he heard she'd been captured and that the higher-ups were sitting on their collective asses wondering what to do, he'd squeezed an informant for intel and waltzed into a warehouse full of terrorists of unknown allegiance and saved her—shot his way in and shot his way out. By any reasonable account, they both should have been dead. Sally lost an eye from the ordeal.

The doctor brought him back to present time. "So, this woman you killed was special in some way?"

"I think all mothers are special, but she wasn't unique in any way. I'm sure in her circumstance and locale, she was perfectly normal. Things just turned out different. I suppose it was more of what was happening in my world than hers. She was the one I was supposed to rescue...an innocent with an equally innocent child."

"Doesn't sound very traumatic." She looked disappointed. "There has to be more to the story."

"There always is." His friend Josh Barnes would be proud of him using one of his favorite comebacks. Josh was a man used to hearing sad stories.

Hands folded in her lap, one eyebrow raised in expectation, she gave him a half-smile and nod to continue.

"You talked to Sally, so I suppose you know what being a Shepherd entails?"

She sighed. "Ah. Back to details. Yes, I talked to Josh Barnes. He had me reach out to someone called Sally, whom I presume runs an organization called Shepherds. You'll be happy to know she put me through security hell before she'd talk to me. It was worse than trying to get through all the AI respondents in a large company and finally talk to a human. I was up all night in that endeavor. She's pissed at you, by the way."

After a pencil-tapping stare, she continued. "You can be assured I do my homework, Mr. Lane. Please continue."

He grinned. "One of the few successful and continuing missions in my life that I'm proud of is keeping Sally pissed at me."

When he didn't get a response from the doctor, he sighed before continuing. "As you know, we specialized in high-risk extractions or rescue. A woman on the periphery of a drug cartel had information someone on our side wanted, reasons unknown. In exchange, the informer would get a new life in the USA, probably a dream come true for her. It was a simple mission with several agencies being involved. Everything was provided, including the dusty old car I drove and a small puddle-jumper airplane for extraction sitting in a clearing a mile away. All I had to do was pick her up and escort her to the extraction site, and take care of any unforeseen problems that might happen. My job was to keep her safe until extraction. Another agency would handle it from there. It was a simple in-and-out operation. Easy-peasy."

The images wouldn't go away. "It's funny how memory works. I can't remember what I had for lunch yesterday—"

"Spaghetti," Alina interjected, and then held a hand over her mouth.

"—but this is in full color...every detail. I don't even have to close my eyes. Going in, I remember thinking it was too easy. There was one guard by the front door, and he wasn't all that alert. That was my first clue that things weren't right. There should not have been a guard unless the pickup was compromised. Once he was eliminated, I walked into the house."

"Eliminated?"

His voice was flat. "I killed him, Doctor. And then hid the body behind a rosebush for organic fertilizer."

From her shocked expression, he wondered at the futility of talking to a non-combatant. If you've never had blood on your hands, how can you judge?

"Anyway, they were waiting in the center of the room, tied to chairs—the mother and a small child. The little girl was already dead with a single gunshot wound to her forehead. There was blood soaked through her dress, so no telling what they did to her before she died. Although atrocities are commonplace for the cartels, it was needless. The mother would have broken and started talking long before they harmed her daughter, so it was pure sadism with the child. Her killing might have been a mercy shot, or simply what happens when usefulness is at an end."

He paused a moment, seeing her gaze settling on his hands. Relaxing his fists, he continued. "The mother was still alive, at least what was left of her. Someone took a lot of time, fixed her cuts and wounds with what looked like super glue to stop the bleeding, and then started all over again. Have you ever put that stuff on even a little cut? The pain can take your breath away."

Taking a deep breath and glancing at Alina, he continued. "I remember turning away. Maybe I was just going to leave—probably should have, I don't know. But the vision was already playing in a loop—I've never gotten rid of it. She was naked but covered in too many cuts and slices to count. Everything they did added to her pain. The dried blood looked like a poor job of body paint. Some of the things they did to her—"

Bartol raised her hand, dropping her pen and pad in the process. "I don't need the fine details."

Taking a moment to drink a glass of water, he glanced at the doctor. Her gaze tracked his every move. "At first, I thought she was dead, but when I turned back, she was watching me. The sounds she made...her tongue was clipped so she couldn't talk, but I could see the pleading in her eyes."

He met the doctor's gaze. "I knew what she wanted. Her child was dead, tortured by monsters. She was... done. Used up. If I took her with me, judging by the amount of blood loss, she'd never survive the trip. If I left her in place, they'd be back to continue their fun. I thought about waiting for them...I did...but it'd be like turning over a beehive. I'd be outnumbered in a heartbeat. Every day I wonder if I should have waited, just to go out in a final blaze and taking as many of the bastards with me as I could."

His hands were clenched again, shaking with the strain. Taking a breath, he relaxed his fingers. "But I didn't. I nodded to the woman and told her I was sorry— that I understood. She nodded back and mouthed *por favor*, at least I think so, before closing her eyes. My hope was that she was dreaming of better times with her daughter. I used a pillow to muffle the shot. After that, it was like I'd taken Novocaine to the brain. I put out the fire on the pillow, left tracks in the blood so they could follow, and left out the back door. No one followed. I was disappointed in that."

"The old timers, if they live long enough to share experience, will tell you never to look someone in the face when you kill them. There's a reason for that." He took a ragged breath, seeing tears on Alina's cheeks. He'd never seen her cry. "As far as I know, she was the only innocent I've ever killed."

SEVENTEEN

THE DOCTOR'S eyeliner was not waterproof. Sighing, shaking her head, she stood, and after Alina pointed the way, walked into the mudroom by the back door. It had a half-bath. He heard water running, and then she blew her nose with a loud snort before returning.

"That's gotta be the worst story I've heard in a long time and I've heard some doozies. I'll confess that I was looking for some kind of battle fatigue, body count piling up, all the acronyms that we throw drugs at, that sort of thing. Now I may need a brain-picker of my own to get rid of the imagery. You should be a writer."

"So, what happens now?" He didn't feel cathartic for having unloaded his burden. Mostly, he didn't feel anything at all. Just kinda numb.

"If you're looking for an instant cure, there's no such thing." She glanced at Alina and back to him. "If you're looking for forgiveness, I think you already have it. The woman gave it to you. The mistakes, assuming there were any, were on her and the bastards that caught her. Her child was dead because she reached out to the wrong people. She was at death's door and in agony...inevitable, as I understand it. Death was merciful at that point."

"If I'd gotten to her sooner...if I'd—"

"And now we get to the heart of the matter," she interrupted. "You're what we call a knight, wrapped in the chivalry of good versus evil."

The doctor paused a moment. "Look. It was out of your control. There was nothing you could do. In my opinion, you made all the right decisions but one."

He gave her a curious look. "Which was?"

"You pulled away from the reality of the situation. Instead of dealing with it, you walked away from everything. I imagine you've had this ability to disconnect for a long time. Maybe since childhood?"

"So I'm a sociopath, like a serial killer?"

"Oh no...well, mostly no. We all have a little of that in us." She glanced at Alina. "Some more than others. From what I have found in the short amount of time on your case, you would never go on the offensive against anyone unless provoked. Am I right?"

"So a defensive serial killer." He shook his head, glancing at a clearly upset Alina.

Bartol gave a small laugh, not losing eye contact. "Actually that's quite good...but, no. What are you looking for? Are you looking for atonement? Some sort of sackcloth and ashes remedy? Self-flagellation?"

She shook her head, still matching his stare. "Face up to it. You left and acted like a pouting child—someone took away your perfect record. I think what you actually felt, and still feel, was anger because someone took control away from you."

"A pouting child? You...?"

She grinned, holding up her hand. "Just seeing if anyone was alive in there."

Before he could say anything, she continued. "Even though you were running away from the violence, it's still all around you. You ever wonder about that? Situations keep arising that need someone to step up and stand in the way of evil. The conflict in your mind, the one you're not forgiving yourself for, is that you didn't stay. Not from anger, but to right the wrong and dish out justice. You're confusing the roles of being a shepherd, as opposed to being a knight. Being a reluctant hero just leads to confusion. I think that's what you're feeling, and it's messing up your mind."

He almost laughed. "Is that your medical prognosis? My mind is messed up? I'm a defensive serial killer?"

"It's as good as any. Your reluctance needs to end. Mr. Lane, you cannot change who you are. More importantly, you can't change what you are—what your life and sum total of experiences have made you."

"And what am I? Or the better question, since you seem to be in bed with Sally One-Eye, what do you and the Shepherds think I am?"

"I think you know the answer to that question. Think about it. Didn't you find it odd they didn't give you extensive training when you got out of the military...something to prepare you for the high-risk rescue business? They didn't have to. You were a natural—just throw you into a situation and let you figure it out."

She glanced at Alina again. "Both of you are playing with fire. And yes, I mean both of you. Reformation is fine. Mending your ways is a good thing if you can. But don't forget who you are."

Clearing her throat and taking a drink of her lukewarm tea, she continued. "It's kind of like the fable of the farmer and the snake. On a cold spring day, a farmer finds a beautiful snake that's too cold to move. The snake looks at him and says, 'Help me. I'm dying.' The farmer puts it inside his shirt to warm it up. When the snake revives enough, it bites him. Before the farmer dies, he asks the snake, 'Why? I saved your life. Why did you bite me?' The snake replies, 'You should have known better. I'm a snake. It's what I do.'"

"So to you, we're snakes?"

The doctor reached out and touched his arm. "Now you're being obtuse. The snake represents evil or evil-doers. You're trying to make sense of what some evil people did. You shouldn't. It's what they do. And to stand in their way? To right those wrongs? That's what you do."

"Alina, too? She used to right a lot of wrongs."

The doctor flinched, her expression guarded as she gave Alina a long look. "The jury is out on her. That would have to be a whole new field of study."

Jim nodded and then laughed. "And what would the farmer call us?"

"Makes no difference. The farmer was a sheep taken in by evil. Beautiful, but still deadly and evil. A shepherd would keep him from taking the snake to his bosom. You're a shepherd."

He shook his head. "You went a long way to work that word in."

She smiled. "It's what I do."

The silence stretched a moment. Jim finally shook his head with a grim smile. "Alina? I don't think the good doctor likes us very much."

"Not true," Dr. Bartol interjected quickly. "I'm not against what you have done. Well...maybe Alina a little bit, but that's not for me to judge. Things happen. After a quick study, which I'd like to do more, I actually admire both of you. You have completely different backgrounds, and yet you're both very similar in thought and action—at least that's what your records indicate. And yes, Alina. You've been pretty well documented and are not quite as anonymous as you think. Sally One-Eye is very thorough."

Alina shrugged, giving a small smile. "As long as she thinks I'm useful, she will be my biggest fan. When that usefulness is over, she'll try and have me killed. It's the way of the world. In that sense, she's no different than the bosses in crime families. However, that's not my concern."

She nodded toward Jim. "He is."

The doctor stared at her a moment. The statement about the Shepherd's boss may have given her pause. She recovered quickly. "I understand. And in that sense, I sincerely hope I can remain useful to you. Aside from that, anyone can see your concern for Jim. That's a big plus in your favor. I mean that. But back to the problem. Jim, I think the solution actually comes from your old boss. Maybe it would be a good question for both of you. She wants to know one thing. When did you stop being a shepherd and become a sheep?"

He nodded. It was what he expected. He and Alina were assets, and by default, his small group of friends. His biggest worry was—to what end? Were they being pushed toward some unknown ending? Who herds the shepherds?

"So you think I have a conflict of interest between what I should do and what I want to do? Don't we all have that problem?"

"Perhaps." She shrugged, slowly shaking her head with a small smile. "If someone knows they're crazy and embraces it—lives with it...there's a school of thought that says they are not crazy at all, but a rational being. Sociopaths are rational, after all. Just not in a common way."

"And sooner or later, evil will be consumed by the fire it loves," he quoted, fingers tapping the table, mimicking her pencil. "I read that somewhere."

After his statement, the silence in the kitchen drew out as both women stared at him. The doctor with a wry smile, Alina with a hand over her mouth. Her need for speech was palpable.

"So, all this comes down to one thing." His sigh was expressive, giving more meaning than words. "A leopard can't change its spots."

The doctor shrugged. "Takes a lot of bleach, and it's not so good for the cat."

Standing on the porch, they watched the good doctor leave in a trail of dust, guiding her less-than-pristine battle cruiser directly through the potholes.

In a wry voice, he said. "Well, that was interesting."

Alina stood with her arms wrapped around herself. Protectively? "I don't like her."

"No matter," he replied, pulling her close. "We'll likely never see her again. She was here to deliver a not-so-subtle message. That's all."

"Still..." Alina spoke softly. "I do not like her."

EIGHTEEN

THIS WAS A FISHING DAY, and Alina knew it.
When he awoke the next morning, she was gone, leaving
a note that she had things to do. This was happening
more lately. He was curious but didn't pry. She'd been
moody after the head doctor left, and he wondered if the
shrink had pushed some buttons better left untouched.
Then he wondered if the doctor was legit or some kind of
aberration sent by Sally One-Eye. That was a possibility.
The more he contemplated, the more it became clear his
friends liked to push him in certain directions...for his
own good, of course.

In one way, he and his resident assassin were alike.
Having a wealth of experience dealing with people, both
were quick to judge. The rules were simple. You either
like someone or not. There is no middle ground. If someone's personality has to grow on you, that endeavor is
usually a waste of time. First impressions are nearly
always right, along with the simplest answer being most
always correct, and Murphy's Law is, in fact, the law of

the land along with every corollary thought up by the wizards of thought.

Often thoughts and contemplations while fishing carry the same weight as dreams that disappear at the break of day—weighty, profound, and nebulous as rising smoke from a fire. Intelligence might be measured by the ability to harness those thoughts before they drift away.

With the sun high in the sky creating enough heat in the water that only a starving fish would accidentally get tangled with his hook, he quietly drifted his pontoon boat into the shade generated by a tree-covered limestone bluff on Lake Stockton. His live well was full of crappie and channel catfish. He'd snagged a couple of large walleyes but threw them back, not liking their bland flavor. Popping open his cooler, he was ready for a relaxing lunch before heading home. He'd just unwrapped his baloney and grape jelly sandwich, and popped open a refreshing green tea and citrus drink when his cell phone lit up.

Barnes precluded a witty answer and was talking when the connection was made. "Hey, Jim. You busy?"

Looking around his tranquil surroundings, he took a bite from his sandwich. "Define busy."

"What? Sounds like you're eating something. You have time for lunch? I never have time for lunch."

He thought of all the times his friend, the ex-law dog, had admonished him to stay out of other people's business. "Every time I see you, I'm reminded not to poke my nose in where it doesn't belong. So, yes. I do have time for lunch. I'm a simple man of leisure with a small, let's say, minuscule ranch to run. Not a care in the world, with nothing else to do but enjoy the fruits of nature. As a point of order, I sent you a text this morning to invite you to come along. You never answered."

"Yeah...yeah, sure you did." Barnes laughed. "I never got it. Maybe you sent it to the wrong number. Any strange people show up from the invite?"

He thought of a blue-haired couple standing, arms entwined, watching the sun rise over the water when he boarded his boat. The man's scraggly beard was dyed to match his hair. The woman was colored the same—no beard. "There are always strange people, but they don't want to fish. They just want me to give them fish. What's going on, Barnes?"

"We have a trailer truck coming in from the Food Harvest in Springfield. It's supposed to show up at the Baptist Church parking lot in about an hour. I'm thinking I may need some extra security."

"I know about it. Alina and Jacy are supposed to help distribute, so they'll already be there. We'll be donating frozen fish at the marina sometime later. I'm cleaning out my freezer at home—out with the old and in with the new."

"Oh, you poor child...having to go fishing so you can feed the masses. You have bread, too?"

"Careful you don't get struck by lightning." Jim gave a loud yawn. "Okay. I guess I can show up. Do I have to wear a mask?"

"Not unless you're going to rob the place. Wearing a mask is not mandatory in Limestone County. At least not yet. We've hardly had any COVID cases."

"I'm sure that will change, given time." Jim started the outboards and maneuvered away from the bluff. He couldn't resist a dig at Barnes. "I thought you wanted me to retire. I'm remembering several long and semi-eloquent speeches about that subject."

"Come on, Jim. I'm not asking for a crew-served fifty-caliber machine gun and a kill zone. I just need some bodies to stand around. All you have to do is look official and keep people moving along with your scary smile."

The wind was gusting hard across his bow, so he had to keep adjusting his heading. "You're not thinking of a certain biker gang that may be looking for a handout, are you?"

"Jesus, Jim. Turn away from the wind or stop to talk. It sounds like you're in a wind tunnel and I can barely hear you. Did you say something about the bikers?"

"I thought we already had this discussion." He ducked down behind the windscreen. "I think they're called the Sons of Unknown Progeny or something like that. I told you about meeting the head cheese and his sidekick. He seemed to have an inflated opinion of himself. I'm on my way in."

"I doubt they'll be trouble. Those guys are generally more bark than bite."

Jim shook his head before realizing no one could see the gesture. His friend must have woken up in fantasy land. "I hope you're right, Barnes. But don't turn your back on them. I'm not far away. See you in thirty."

———

EARLY THAT MORNING when Jim had settled in front of his laptop, he'd punched up the Drudge Report. Admittedly it was a website that leaned toward sensationalism in headlines, but the articles were simply taken from an aggregate of news sources—liberal, conservative, no matter. Of all the things going on in the world, three headlines leaped off his screen.

- SUPPLY CHAIN WORKERS WARN OF SYSTEM COLLAPSE...
- WORLD FOOD COSTS AT RISK OF SOARING AS CHINA FACES TOUGH HARVEST...
- BACKLOG OF CARGO SHIPS AT PORT OF LA REACHES BOILING POINT: 500,000 CONTAINERS...

Those headlines hadn't left his mind all morning.

Thirty minutes turned into forty-five, and things were already in progress when he arrived. Jim was amazed at the number of cars lined up in the parking lot waiting for an allotment of food. At one box per car, he was sure some of the families had several cars and could milk the system for all it was worth, and the truck's cargo would be depleted in a short time.

The city of White Rock had one grocery and one fast-food convenience store. After the hoarding and panic buying at the first announcement of the pandemic, both stores started checking IDs for purchases. That might be a smart procedure for these food handouts, although it would be hard to turn away people in need. With the crisis of businesses being shut down inducing a COVID-trashed economy and the possibility of more problems looming on the horizon, it might be a good idea to implement here. It says in the Bible there are always rumors of war, but it was getting closer to fact every day.

He waved to Alina standing inside the trailer, clad in her customary T-shirt and jeans, and stopped in front of Barnes. His sheriff's uniform was ironed and creased, looking sharp as always. The man's normally jocular expression was grim as he took off his hat and rubbed his forehead.

Jim gave Barnes a nod and quizzical expression. "What's up, brother?"

"My assessment of the bikers may have been premature. You can see about twenty of them parked on the south end of the parking lot." He shook his head at Jim's eye roll. "They came in a few minutes ago and already tried to cut in line, so I need to stay here by the truck to prevent that."

"How can they carry these boxes?" Each person was being given a large cardboard box of canned goods and fresh vegetables that looked to weigh about forty pounds. Some boxes looked fragile.

"Jesus." Barnes's frustration came leaking out. "That's your take on all this? Where do they put the boxes?"

"It's a fair question."

A calming breath seemed to put Barnes back on track. "What they're trying now is over by the exit. A couple have tried to stop cars from leaving, just to take their boxes. I've got PJ directing traffic at that end and the Energizer at the entrance, so they're tied up with traffic control. I need you to try and discourage the bikers."

There were two deputies helping to work the county. PJ Rails was their steroid pumper, a man whose rich parents must have spent a ton in political donations for him to pass the police academy. Allison Crewes was their ex-gymnast Energizer Bunny and class clown, all five feet of her.

"So, you want me to go over there and read to them from the book? Preach a little gospel? Teach them the error of their ways? Stand there and look pretty? What are my rules of engagement?"

"Your ROE?" Barnes closed his eyes a moment, giving a long sigh. "You do remember that you're turning over a new leaf, don't you? No shooting. If you brought your badge, hang it on your belt."

"I never leave home without it."

Sally One-Eye, his ex-handler at the Shepherds, had pulled strings and awarded them federal agent status, complete with a shiny new badge. It wasn't worth much around country folk who had a real aversion for the feds, but it was certainly an impressive-looking piece of metal.

"Don't worry." He patted Barnes on the shoulder. "I see my buddy Charles over there. I'll go talk to him."

As he approached the end of the line of vehicles waiting to exit the parking lot onto the highway, Red Dog Charles and Boots were standing by an older model white minivan. Pastor Tanner was the driver and was lowering his window.

Jim shouldered by the surprised biker to stand at the driver's side window. "Hey, Pastor. Nice to see you again."

"Mr. Lane? Good to see you. It's been a while. Sorry you never took me up on the invite to Sunday services."

"I've still got it on my bucket list. What are you doing in this neck of the woods?"

The pastor gestured over his shoulder with his thumb. "The Food Harvest is a county-wide thing. We just come over to pick up some boxes for our own food pantry. It's a great thing the Food Harvest is doing, don't you think? There are many people in need right now."

"Yes, sir. There certainly are." Limestone County was designated agricultural by the COVID powers that be and considered essential, so most businesses were still open.

The only places closed were a couple of factories and bank lobbies. Masks were optional, and social distancing encouraged, so most people weren't too affected by the shutdown mandated by the state. The problem was in resupply of goods—namely food for the grocery shelves.

He continued, glancing over his shoulder at the bikers. "But we still have people here who'd rather take a handout instead of a hand up."

Pastor Tanner laughed. "Still cynical, I see."

"Just a product of the world situation, Pastor." He paused a moment. "Say, whatever happened to that Mrs. Hyatt—the one that lost her husband? Did she make it to Kansas City?"

The pastor's expression turned bland. "No. She's still local. The last I heard, she was working at a local bar. I guess she makes more in tips than with any other job on wages."

"Huh. I guess I'll have to look her up...maybe point her in the right direction. That's not a good career choice, especially when raising a little girl."

He nodded to Pastor Tanner and then turned to address the bikers. "Well, if it isn't Red Dog Charles and his little sidekick Boots. How the hell are you? And speaking of handouts. I'm sure y'all have plenty of money. You don't need to be bothering this man or anyone else around here."

"Well, that's not very hospitable." Dog glowered at him. "We're running a little short right now."

"Then sell your bike. It's worth plenty. Or, here's a shocker, get a job." He talked to Dog, but his attention was on Boots. He vowed to never let that woman out of his sight.

"Job market's not too open right now." The biker

feigned a hurt expression. "And I can't sell my wheels, man. How do I get where I'm going?"

"That's the point, Mean Dog. People like you"—he risked a glance at Dog before returning his gaze to Boots —"and your merry little gang, are never going anywhere meaningful. Your *'ride til ya die'* attitude only gets you dead. Every place you stop becomes a blighted community. There's no future for you around these parts."

The biker's forced smile faded. "Now there you go disrespecting me again. Somehow I don't think you take me seriously."

Boots had been beckoning at someone and was now grinning at Jim. He shrugged, seeing another biker approach and wondering why the world wasn't shaking with small earthquakes with each step the man took.

"Charles, you should understand," Jim continued. "I've got a live and let live attitude. Where you call home is none of my business, providing you do it somewhere else. We already had this conversation, and here I am repeating it again. You need to be gone from here."

Red Dog pointed with his thumb over his shoulder. "This is Mongo, one of our enforcers. He took that name from his favorite character in a movie he saw once."

One of Jim's favorite authors had written a line about a character whose face was insentient as a bowl of oatmeal, and he'd vowed to try to use that expression one day. He was facing that character now. The face was dead from hairline to chin, eyes included.

"How?" Jim asked, searching the man's eyes for some sign of life.

It was a full two seconds before Mongo replied in a deep rumble. "How what?"

"How did you watch a movie? Did you stand in the

back of the theater? I can't imagine you fitting in one of their chairs."

Jim glanced toward the row of motorcycles a few hundred feet away. "Do you have to ride one of those Harley tricycles to carry your weight?"

After another two seconds to process, Mongo took another step forward. "Don't ride no tricycle."

Dog's smile was splitting his cheeks. "As you may have guessed, Mongo has a very singular attention span. He's our insurance that we get to stay where we want and do what we want."

He never took his eyes off Mongo while talking to Dog. "Well, as much as I'd like to cancel your insurance policy, I did take a vow of peacefulness with the local sheriff. But what I told you stands. Stop harassing people and hit the trail."

Seeing Pastor Tanner had used discretion and vacated, along with most of the line of cars, Jim stood facing the trio as more bikers started drifting their way. He didn't want to spare a glance at the food truck and possible help, but he was feeling a little like Custer at the Battle of Greasy Grass.

When Mongo advanced another step, Jim swept his shirt tail away from his Glock. "Dog, you need to disengage. I'll not be ganged up on, and for damned sure, I'm not going to play patty cake with your trained gorilla."

Boots stepped out from behind Dog, hand on her pistol. "Well, I never took you for being yella. I can smell the fear on you from here."

"Is this what you want, Dog?" He pulled his attention from the behemoth Mongo and gazed at her a moment. "I've killed one woman in my life and regret it to this day. I don't want to do that again, but I can manage it."

"Knock it off!" Barnes strode between them. "Jim, back up. I've got this."

Jim glanced to the sides and saw both deputies standing with shotguns pointed at the bikers. He took his hand off the Glock, still wary of the bikers. They seemed to want to push something, he just didn't know why.

"Alright, Sheriff," he replied. "It's your call."

Barnes stood too close to the bikers, and it was a tactical error. The deputies couldn't fire without hitting friendlies. Seeing his chance, Mongo started a slow rush toward the sheriff, arms opened for a crushing bear hug. Jim intercepted the man in mid-stride, and they both went down in a rolling tangle that ended with Jim on top, mostly because he weighed less. Pulling his pistol, it took three slaps to Mongo's head before the man slumped unconscious.

Breathing heavily, Jim stood with blood streaming from a cut to his forehead.

"Sorry." Barnes eyed him critically. "I've never been real good at crowd control."

"Ya think?"

He flinched as Alina came rushing to him and held a piece of cloth to his bleeding head. Glancing down, he realized she'd torn it from the tail of her T-shirt. It was a piece of cloth she could ill afford to lose. "Tear another strip from that, and you'll have to leave the church grounds."

"I still have more clothes on than that Boots bitch."

He smiled and tried to nod his head.

"Stop moving. That's the same spot you got cut before. You need to stop leading with your head."

They watched the main group of retreating bikers

abandoning Boots and Dog while they talked. "Where's Jacy?"

"She left to fill in at the clinic about the time you arrived. They've lost some people to sickness, so they're shorthanded." Taking the cloth away a moment, she grabbed some hair and pulled his head down to look at the cut. "Which is where you're going. That cut is down to the bone and needs irrigation and stitches. How did you do that?"

"Bastard bit me."

She shook her head, re-folding the cloth to a reasonably clean spot and applying pressure again. "So now we're looking at tetanus...maybe rabies or COVID?"

"What about Bigfoot? I hit him pretty hard."

She glanced over her shoulder. "He's stirring around, but I don't think you ruffled his feathers much. He probably won't even show a bruise."

"Swell."

Barnes had his pistol out and pointed at Boots. He'd figured out she was the instigator. "Alina, go ahead and take him to the clinic. As soon as the dummy on the ground gets up, the rest of us will escort this trash out of the county."

Dog strode forward. "You got no right..."

The sheriff fired a round between the man's feet, splattering gravel and dirt. The ricochet hit something metal, and they could hear yelling in the distance.

"The citizens of Limestone County say different."

As they left, Boots stopped and looked back at them. "So, your name is Alina? You and I are going to have some fun. I'll come visit later."

The woman made a kissy noise before she turned and left. It was the same thing Alina had done at their first meeting. Jim was sure he didn't want to be present at a third meeting.

Alina was hissing and stepping forward when Jim caught her around the waist. "Not now. I need stitches, remember?"

NINETEEN

TRAVELING THROUGH TOWN WAS EERIE.
Hardly any businesses were open, the direct opposite of
what he thought would happen. The most cars parked
anywhere were at the clinic. Gone were the days of
walking into a clinic and requesting care. Walk-ins were
acceptable but not under the new COVID protocols. Once
they'd called and checked in, they had to stay in the
vehicle.

They waited a half-hour before they were called to
come into the clinic. After having their temperature
taken when they stepped through the double doors and
asked a dozen questions about symptoms or trips out of
the country, the nurse asked about masks. Everyone they
could see was wearing one.

"Are they required?" Jim asked.

"So far it's optional but recommended. This is a clinic
and there are sick people here."

"Then no."

They were taken back to an exam room to wait. After

another thirty-minute wait, Dr. Bartelli and Jacy breezed in.

As she washed her hands, Jacy glanced over her shoulder and mumbled something.

"What?"

She lifted the bottom of her mask. "Sorry. We get that a lot. I asked what happened?"

Bartelli was already examining Jim's forehead. "Well, at least you're not shot this time or cut."

Alina snorted. "He got bit by a giant biker. For a moment, it looked like mating season between a gorilla and a monkey."

"Ow!" He swatted at Bartelli's hand. "You're poking my brain."

Jim glanced at Alina. "Mating season aside, I got tangled up with a biker named Mongo who's the size of an NFL lineman. He bit me. I'm just hoping he didn't have rabies. Or scabies. Or anything else ending in *ies*."

"My oh my, aren't we cranky today?" Irrigating the wound with saline, Jacy swabbed his forehead with Beta-dine before trying to pinch the edges together. "Probably need some help here, Doc. It's going to take a heavy stitch to hold this together, maybe some skin glue."

Jim rolled his eyes. "You're going to use Elmer's Glue?"

The doctor chuckled. "Well, wood glue might work best for your head. But no, wise ass. Cyanoacrylate."

After deadening the edges, which hurt more than the bite, Bartelli pinched the edges together after applying the glue. Jacy started stitching.

Bartelli commented, his face uncomfortably close. "Put them close together..."

A scream from outside the room startled them, then a

blast from a gun put an exclamation point to it. Jim was first out the exam room door and faced a cavernous barrel. No matter the caliber, a barrel opening always looked big when it's pointed right at you. Especially by a man with a shaky finger on the trigger.

"I'd appreciate it if you'd take your finger away from the trigger and safe that weapon." Jim held his hands out to the side.

The man stared at him over the barrel, both eyes open. "You got string hanging from your forehead, son."

"I'm lucky I wasn't killed. You scared the snot out of my nurse." He glanced over his shoulder knowing the old man was moments from death. "Alina? Jacy? Stand down. If this man wanted to kill anyone, he wouldn't have shot that ceiling tile."

"Mister, I don't know who you think you are, butting into something like this. All I want is that doctor standing behind you. I shot the ceiling just to get everyone's attention. You best get out of the way so I can get on with it."

The man had dead eyes and a grim expression, but there was something there...he wasn't a killer. Jim took a step closer. "First, let me apologize. I can see there's no safety on that weapon. That's a beautiful antique. Looks like an old 1897 Winchester. I know because I had one once. That model served well in both World Wars and Vietnam. I love that gun. It never jams, even when it's covered in mud. I'm betting you have to use low-powered shells for it, though. Modern shells might blow out the barrel. Am I right?"

"Mister? I ain't here for the antique road show. Step out of the way."

Jim shook his head. "Now, I can't do that, and you

know it. It's too late for that. If you were going to shoot someone, you'd just walk in and do it without all the fanfare. So I know, deep down, that you don't want to do that. What's your beef with the doctor? I know he's ugly, with no sense of humor, but he's still a good man."

"Mister, I'm not real experienced at this, nor am I up on all the proper ways to do it, but I'm a fast learner. This is personal, and I ain't telling you again. Move aside."

Arms spread wide, Jim replied. "And this isn't personal? There are innocent people all around you. Nurses, moms with sick kids, and doctors. I know you don't want to hurt them. If you fire that weapon again, it's going to happen. And even worse? What happens if you don't, and the police break in here to take you out? People will get hurt...people you don't want harmed. So, how about we come up with some solution that doesn't end with people dying? Your ending to this story isn't worth a crap. And I think we both have the time to explore that."

The barrel of the shotgun wavered a moment and then steadied. "I ain't interested in a conversation. That doctor killed my wife, and he's going to pay for it."

"I can't imagine that's true. There's got to be more to it than that. Look, I'm sorry your wife died." He cast a quick, puzzled glance at Dr. Bartelli before turning his attention back to the man with the shotgun. "Look. That thing is heavy. The longer we stand here, the more likely we're going to do something stupid. You, me, and everyone around us are going to try to do something, and it'll end up like a circular firing squad."

He sighed a moment, keeping eye contact with the man. "Now, I gotta tell you. After you killed that ceiling tile, I didn't hear you rack a fresh shell—didn't hear the empty hit the floor. I can see the top of the hammer, so that reinforces my notion that you don't have a shell in the chamber. I'm armed. People behind me are armed. What do you think your chances are of getting what you want?"

With every word and hand gesture, he'd been inching closer. When the shooter's gaze dropped to the hammer, the barrel went offline a fraction. Jim leaped toward the distracted man and pulled the shotgun from his grasp, first pointing it upward in case the man's finger caught on the trigger and then away. Once he had it and still keeping eye contact with the man, he handed the shotgun behind him. Alina must have taken it because it went away.

"Christ, Jim," Alina said. "He chambered a round. You're crazy."

With the sound of the weapon being pumped until it was empty coming from behind him, he put his hand on the man's shoulder. "What's your name?"

"His name is Bill Friedman." The voice came from behind him.

"That's amazing. I didn't see your lips move, Bill. How'd you do that?" He glanced behind at the doctor. "How about from now on, you answer for yourself. What's this all about?"

The man stood with tears coursing down his cheeks. "Damned doctors is what it's all about. They're all a bunch of killers and don't care about anyone, not really. My wife fell at home and hurt her ribs. I brought her here to make sure she was okay and maybe get some pain pills. That doc standing behind you sent her to the hospital in an ambulance. Thanks to this damned virus, I couldn't go along. When I got to the hospital, it was the same thing. They wouldn't let me go in—couldn't talk to her, couldn't see her. All I could do was go and sit in the parking lot. Three weeks later, I get a box delivered to my house. The delivery guy just set it on my porch and left. It was her ashes, delivered with no more fanfare than a toaster. That's the story. How do I square that?"

Jim stared at the man, shaking his head. "I could have gone all day without hearing that. It's a terrible story with a god-awful ending."

Turning to look behind him, he continued. "Doc, I think you need to take this man to your office and have a long talk. Don't you think?"

Bartelli came forward, taking the man by the arm. "He's right, Bill. Let's go talk this out."

After they disappeared down the hall, one of the nurses asked, "Should we call the sheriff?"

Jim reached into his pocket and pulled out the federal badge holder, and held it up. "I got this."

Once back on the exam table, Jacy fussed at him while tapping on the partially closed cut. "When we deadened that cut, it must have got into your brain."

"That can't be a problem. I'm thinking there's nothing in there," Alina piped in, leaning against the counter. "He's been doing some crazy stuff lately."

Jim broke into their conversation. "Hey now, I thought that went pretty well, considering how it could have ended. No one got hurt."

"We all could have gotten hurt," Alina grumbled. "One round at that range could have fixed that."

"Both of you stop." Jacy then glared at Alina. "You'd have shot him? In a crowded clinic? Jim just risked his life against a loaded shotgun to avoid that. Killing people isn't always the answer, Alina. Try to remember that."

Alina snorted and shook her head but didn't answer.

Jacy finished the stitches, and none too gently, cleaned up his forehead. After placing a large adhesive patch on the wound, she continued. "Try and keep that clean. Use a topical antibiotic on it. I'll be over tomorrow to check on you. Don't do any other stupid shit until I get there. Please."

She turned to face them both, leaning against the door. "And another thing. You need to take this virus seriously. It's mutating. There are at least seventeen strains that we know of, and some are deadly. It's mostly taking the older generation, grandma and grandpa, but you can't count on that. I'm talking four days from first symptoms to death. That's why the hospitals are locked down. That's why *we're* going to be locked down soon."

"What should we do?" Jim glanced at Alina.

"Isolate as best you can. If you're around people, wear masks. If you have them, use the N-95s. The others are pretty much useless against a virus but might help a little. Most important, if you're out in public—stores and whatnot, disinfect and wash your hands. Keep clean and no hands to the face until you know you're clean."

"It's that serious?" Alina asked.

Jacy warned them one more time before leaving. "This one is troubling. So yes, it's that serious. Now would be a good time to start using the supplies from your basement. Try to stay out of the public until this thing blows over." She paused a moment before saying softly. "If it does."

Holding the door open, she continued. "Now, I want you to leave by the back door. I'll see you tomorrow at the ranch. Double up on your vitamins, especially B12 and D. As far as disinfecting? I want you to absorb so much sanitizer through your hands that when you take a piss, you sterilize the toilet bowl."

Jim grimaced, glancing at them both. "That's gonna burn."

"I can't stress this enough." Jacy stared at them a moment, not responding to the attempt at humor. "About the only way you can get it through the air is if someone comes up and spits, yells, or coughs in your face. That's why separation is important. In this way, it's like the flu. Prevention is all on your hands...hands to mouth, hands to eyes, fingers to nose." She handed them both small bottles of hand sanitizer. "Stay clean."

After leaving by the back door and walking around to his truck, they both sat and stared out the front windshield while vigorously applying hand sanitizer.

Jim finally spoke. "Well, that scared the hell out of me."

She glanced at his forehead. "Let's hope Mongo wasn't sick."

"Doubt it. He didn't seem to be sick, and if he was, I'd hate to tangle with him when he's well."

"You don't need to tangle with him anyway." She put her hand on his arm and squeezed, making sure she had his attention. "Regardless of what Jacy says, if you see him, either shoot him or run away."

He glanced at her. "I guess we don't stop for pizza?"

She gave him a shocked look. "It's a pandemic, not the end of the world. Casey's is just up the street."

TWENTY

LIMESTONE COUNTY SHERIFF Rita Morris stood admiring her new ride. She'd just deplaned from an old C-23 Sherpa at the Springfield-Branson National Airport with a contingent of Missouri National Guard members. One of the troops had joked it was a mighty big name for such a small airport, and Rita laughed with all the rest. They had a point.

Being a VIP in the cockpit and hooked up to the radio system, she'd been listening on the headphones when the pilot informed Springfield Tower in no uncertain terms that they were landing and to clear the pattern. The combat pilot sounded as if she wasn't used to disagreements. She didn't get any. Looking out from one of the few windows of the aircraft, it looked like the city was burning. Several fires in the downtown area sent huge billows of smoke towering above the city, flattening into a haze at the first thermal layer.

The transport landed with barely a bump and taxied to an unmarked building. The spinning of the twin turboprops made sure no one would hear well for the next few minutes—maybe never. Mixed in with the people, no one would have noticed her, not that she knew of anyone who would be looking. Her entry back into the world she'd left so abruptly would be low-key, and that's the way she wanted it. The most amazing fact was that she was still alive.

That anonymity would be gone the minute she jumped in the new GMC Tahoe, stylish in all black with no chrome anywhere, decked out with low-profile light bars and enough antenna to resemble a mobile communication center—which it was. Limestone County Sheriff stenciled all around just sealed the deal. Sally One-Eye spared no expense. The question was, why? She didn't need shock and awe to roll into the small town of White Rock, and most of the county denizens would be less than impressed.

The soldiers gave her curious glances as she opened the driver's side door, stripped off her shirt, and then stripped out of the light body armor she'd been forced to wear. Standing in jeans and bra, she got light applause from some as they passed. From her own military service, she knew the type as they moved past in loose formation. Battle-hardened, men and women alike. Green troops would have tried harder to look military. These folks didn't care. They'd just unloaded a few crates from the Sherpa in record time. Another unanswered question to her list was—why were they in Springfield? There were already members of the Guard in the city protecting their armory and facilities at the airport. These soldiers were different. On mission came to mind.

As she watched, the last soldier in line abruptly changed direction and walked toward her. She could only see part of the woman's face, the rest hidden behind wrap-around sunglasses, but what she could see was seriously black—and seriously devoid of expression. From her tactical bump helmet down to desert camo zip-up boots, she put a new definition on wired tight.

The woman shifted her M4 around to her back and unsnapped the chin guard of her face protection. Lifting off the helmet, she vigorously ran her fingers through her short hair, giving a long, drawn-out sigh.

Her voice was Louisiana southern. "Damn, those things are hot."

"Thank God," Rita said, holding a hand over her chest. "I thought you were a stormtrooper from *Star Wars*, converted to battle rattle."

"No, ma'am. I hit what I shoot at."

Both laughed a moment at the *Star Wars* joke.

"From what I've heard," the woman continued. "So do you, Sheriff Rita."

"So," Rita asked. "What can I do for you? You seem to know me, but I'm detecting a lack of insignia, patches, or even what country you are from. That's kind of non-regulation, don't you think? What uniform is that? Maybe you are a stormtrooper."

The soldier snorted. "Anyone who needs to know is fully aware of who I am. And this little old thing? The DOD designed a uniform just for us women. You know, since we're the weaker sex. I've got a blast gauge on my collar, a smart sensor on my ballistic plates, and..." She held up her wrist. "I have a status monitor so they know if I'm alive or dead. It's a lot more like *Alien* than *Star Wars*."

"Well, let's hope for a better ending than *Alien*."

"Copy that."

Rita's gaze took in the woman and the other soldiers

walking away. "Jeez. I bet you'd kill for shorts and a tank top." She shook her head a moment. "So, again. What's up?"

"I'm Captain Hawkins." They shook hands for a moment. "What you've seen us unloading are Predator drones with a full load out of munitions—armor piercing to anti-personnel. In true military fashion, I don't even know why we are here. For all I know, we're assisting a pack of beagles at a fox hunt. My orders are to stand by at this airport, secure my area of operations, and await instructions."

"That's interesting, but—"

"I was also told by someone named Sally to introduce myself to you. With the current stateside situation, of which I think you've been briefed, she thought we should be battle buddies."

Rita gazed around the tarmac, taking in the beehive of activity. A sandbagged defensive point was already in view, complete with a belt-fed and crew-served M230 machine gun. What in hell was going on?

"Um..." She pinned the captain with a calm glance. "I know what that means, but the application escapes me— at least, with my personal circumstances."

"You have a sat phone in your SUV. I'm not on the contacts list, but if you press 6-6-6, my phone will ring. It's always monitored."

Rita glanced inside the SUV. "Isn't that a little satanic?"

Hawkins inclined her head with a small smile. "Well, it is hell, ma'am. We have AGM-114s. Hellfire missiles. I think the number is a little Sally humor."

Since she'd just graduated from Sally One-Eye's accelerated school for wounded sheriffs who might be close to her favorite Shepherd, that made perfect, twisted sense. "Alright, Hawkins. I'll keep that in mind. We might need one of those for traffic stops on a Saturday night."

All traces of humor gone, the soldier nodded curtly and came to attention. Rita exclaimed. "Don't you dare salute me."

A brilliant grin painted the woman's face a moment. "I'd never salute someone standing in a black-lace, demi-cup bra, ma'am. Other things maybe, but no saluting."

Shit. Rita's arms came up to cover her chest. It didn't bother her that the soldiers had seen her from a distance. But this? She wasn't sure exactly what this was.

"I bet you would salute if I had oak leaves pinned to the straps." Rita grinned at her, trying to cover her confusion.

Hawkins grinned at her again and extended her hand, forcing Rita to uncover and shake. "I like you, Sheriff."

"Thank God for that," she muttered as she watched the soldier striding away, helmet in one hand and rifle in the other. She'd hate to see what would happen to someone that woman didn't like. Hellfire, indeed. Expelling a long sigh, she turned back to her ride. That was one scary woman.

———

RITA SAT in the Tahoe and cranked the AC on high with her blouse unbuttoned. If she'd had a towel, she'd have been mopping and blotting. Spying the sat phone on the charging pad, she picked it up, tapped Contacts, and called the only entry.

"Hey, Barnes. There was an entry on my contacts list

of my brand new cell phone that read 'old retired broken-down lawman,' so I pressed it. What's up in your world?"

"Rita? I've been expecting to hear from you. Where are you, and how soon can you take your old job back?"

"You sound anxious to get rid of it." She waited for denial but didn't get it. "I'm wheels down in Springfield, fixin' to head your way. Anything I need to know? You're not having any parades, right? I don't need to stop and buy candy to throw to the crowd as I pass by?"

Barnes gave an obligatory laugh before continuing. "Yeah, well...there's plenty you need to know, but it can wait for you to get here. There's one thing, though—what the hell is that noise?"

"That's my ride trying to beat the air into submission so it can leave." She waited for the noise from the C-23 to die down, wondering why the transport wasn't sticking around longer. "All right. Go ahead."

"Here's the deal. Don't come in from the south. There are probably unfriendlies around Trader Jack's. It might be better to do Highway 160 and come in from the east. Are you in a marked vehicle?"

The new ride wasn't what she expected, and she seriously thought about renting an old beater car. "Yup. Stands out like a Christmas parade in July."

"In that case, take Highway 215 and come in from the north."

In the time she'd been gone, the Shepherds had preached that she needed to start thinking less like law enforcement and more like a survivalist. Judging by the looks of Springfield as they flew over it, she wondered if resisting that idea had been smart. She'd actually laughed at some of their suggestions. Now, she wished she hadn't. Things were happening.

It had turned into a dichotomous world. Any place there might be a camera, there were riots and civil unrest for the next news cycle. So far, it seemed the countryside had been spared. So far.

"Is this precautionary?" she asked. "Or are things getting that bad?"

"Well, it's not bad for us...yet. I'd say the potential is here. It's like if you're about to dive into the ocean and suddenly hear the theme music to *Jaws*. Pays to be careful. One of your favorite people says the world is full of cattle and they're about to stampede. It's not like law enforcement has anyone outnumbered around here."

She sat quiet a moment, the air conditioning finally overcoming the sweat. "So, how is he?"

"Who?"

"You know damned well who." She could almost see his innocent look.

It was Barnes's turn to hesitate. Finally... "I'm worried. It's like he's got trip-wires all around him, and we don't know where they are. He's acting okay. Well, pretty much. But..."

She sighed, curious about a beehive of activity around the National Guard hangar. "Shit. Nothing's changed, then. Seeing me probably won't help. What's the situation with him and Alina?"

"Sorry. They're tight, for now."

It took her a moment to comment. She hated parroting conversation, but had to know. "For now? You sound like a perp about to lawyer up."

"Did you know a Sally-approved shrink has been out to see Jim?"

"Yeah." She drew the word out. "But *you're* not supposed to know that."

"Well, she stopped in to see me on her way out of town. She couldn't talk about Jim since he's a patient, but she sure had a lot to say about Alina. She said the warning signs around her were like cowbells flapping in a hurricane."

He paused and then continued. "I think she's into something she's not telling him about. There's been a few killings in the area that just don't add up, some disappearances. Strangers, not local residents. The mechanics are all the same. Not too many around here use a .22 caliber against people with perfectly centered T-zone shots. I've seen Alina snap-shoot—never aims, never misses. Her accuracy is uncanny."

"That was taught by the Israeli, and then cowboy action shooting. You should know that. One of the western writers that Jim likes to quote explains how it's the most accurate way of shooting, at least for short range. Point and shoot." She paused a moment. "Could be a setup?"

"Maybe. I haven't told Jim, but we're kind of watching her when we can. A couple of people were killed practically on his doorstep, and then two more that he did find were next to his property line. He says it can't be her, but then there is Occam's Razor."

She sighed while maneuvering the snaps closed on her western blouse. "The simplest answer. Boy, he can really pick 'em. He wouldn't know a good woman if he saw one."

Barnes snorted. "Seems to me he picked a good woman, and she threw him away."

Rita's heart hammered a moment, and then she took a calming breath. "Yeah, there's always that. Thanks for bringing that up, Barnes. It wasn't exactly my finest hour."

She started the engine, looking for an open gate to exit the tarmac, she continued. "I know you're best buds and all that. I get it. Didn't mean to rub you the wrong way. We all have our little problems. Alright. I'm outta here. You can catch me up when I get there. Depending on the state of the populace, it should be an hour, or two...or three."

———

NAVIGATING a couple of farm-to-market roads out of the airport took her to westbound 160. Once settled into the drive, her mind went on autopilot as she remembered her last few months and exposure with Sally One-Eye and the Shepherds.

Thanks to some experimental surgery procedures and drugs, she convalesced in record time with two dimples in her belly and a couple of larger scars on her back. Physically, she felt better than anyone in their forties had a right to feel.

Now she was back and had her head on straight. She was clear-eyed and bushy-tailed, ready to go to work. Unfortunately, knowing exactly what she wanted in her personal life and getting it might be two different things.

Driving through the first of several small towns, she almost ran into a couple of Greene County patrol cars with open doors. Beyond the vehicles were two deputies fighting with a handful of people at the convenience store.

"Aw, hell no." She screeched to a stop in the parking lot, grabbed her Talon ASP, and waded into the fray.

Within a couple of minutes, five men and a couple of women were laid out on the blacktop.

Breathing heavily, one of the deputies turned to her. "Wow, that was..." He shook his head. "Thanks." His eyes wandered to the lettering on her SUV. "We appreciate the help, Sheriff."

"What happened here?" She collapsed the baton, gazing around the parking lot as she clipped it to her belt.

He shrugged. "Same thing all over the county. People just walking into stores and stealing what they want. The store owner objected and called 9-1-1. We were close by and took the call. The owners are damned lucky they weren't shot. These people are crazy."

She stood with hands on hips, watching a few customers leaving the store with their purchases— presumably paid for. "So, what now?"

Shaking his head, he turned to his patrol car. "Now, nothing. We'll haul them off a ways and turn them loose. I'm not sure we have a jail left in town or even a court system to try them. Thanks to the virus, judges won't leave their homes. They want to do everything virtual, and then only important stuff. We're told to turn everyone loose except for major crimes."

The deputy stopped a moment, gazing toward a smoke-filled horizon. "I'm not sure what they call a major crime anymore. If you came out of Springfield, you saw what's happening there. Hell, we can see the smoke from here. Springfield PD and the National Guard are trying to put a lid on that. The rest of us are staying out of town."

"Do you think they can handle it in the city?" She watched one of the men she'd whacked across the thighs stumble around on one leg, trying to put weight on the other.

"I know what you're thinking. We should be helping out in town." The deputy's expression was grim. "There's no way in hell a few more warm bodies will help that situation. All this? What you're seeing here? People are going nuts. It has to be some kind of mass psychosis."

He waved his hand in a circle above his head. "We're kinda making this up as we go along. Don't know what else to do."

Rita gazed toward the columns of smoke rising from Springfield. There was no way of knowing if only a few blocks were involved or if it involved the whole downtown area. And what of her county? She had a sudden urge to end the conversation and get gone. How long would it take for the civil unrest to happen there? Limestone County had the smallest permanent population in the state, but it also had a nice lake area. She couldn't imagine a wave of people bent on destruction. What would be left in their wake?

Ending her mental gymnastics, she asked. "What do you hear from your sheriff?"

"We haven't heard anything in hours. All our radios went dead. We got the 9-1-1 call over our cell phones. The dispatcher said he's about ready to bug out. I heard shots fired in the background noise while we were talking."

"Jesus." She shook her head. "Well, good luck. I'm not your boss, and don't pretend to be, but I will tell you this. If things get worse—and you'll know when that is—take care of your families. Do not stay on the job past the point that you can't leave and see to their safety. Take it from an officer that got gunned down in her own home. There's a point you have to call it a day."

She reached out and shook his hand, waving at the other officer. "You boys be safe, hear?"

"You, too, ma'am."

Hitting the road again, her drive was more sedate, her thoughts introspective as she scanned the road in front of her—wondering what was around every bend and curve and what had happened to the world.

TWENTY-ONE

ROLLING INTO HIS DRIVE, Jim tried the remote for the iron gate. Nothing. Tossing it back into the cup holder, he sighed again—sighing was becoming a habit lately. The fancy gate was a waste of money. Once he'd made it through the opening and washboard drive and parked in front of the house, he moved up the steps. Alina stopped him at the top step to give him a quick kiss and hug.

Her gasp was unexpected as he watched her. "What?"

She turned him by his shoulders toward the southeast. "Look toward Springfield."

Their elevation was enough that trees didn't obscure the view. A column of smoke rose in the distance, rising a few thousand feet. It could have been a cloud, except unlike cumulus towers, this one flattened off at the first thermal layer before being carried off by the winds aloft like a giant flat-top carrier. It had to be big to be seen from this distance.

After a few moments of looking around his grass kingdom, he joined her at the kitchen counter.

Her voice was soft as she held his gaze. "Talk radio said there was a huge explosion downtown and reports of the National Guard Armory being attacked out by the airport. Police and firefighters are being shot at when they try to respond. I was in Springfield shopping and didn't see a thing. What do you think is going on?"

His shoulders slumped while shaking his head. Well, what else could go wrong? "Same thing as the rest of the country. It just took longer to get to us. The Northwest has been under attack for months, the same as New York, Chicago, and other big cities. But this is worrisome. More than you might think."

"Why?"

"Springfield is one of the largest truck shipping hubs in this part of the country, along with Joplin." Hand in hand, they walked to the top of the hill behind their house, looking toward Joplin's identical column of smoke. "Well, shit."

Alina gave him a curious look. "Meaning?"

"Remember when I told you about all the shipping containers not being offloaded because of COVID protocols and the rest of the supply chain problems?"

Nodding, she looked perplexed. He'd be the first to admit she seldom listened when he mentioned something on the news. Judging by the content, he couldn't really blame her. At least, until that same subject matter came back to bite you on the ass.

"I'd bet someone is interrupting the shipping lines in this region. That means this whole thing is coordinated. All the stores that use 'just in time' inventory will have about a week's worth of food left on the shelves. And it's not just food. It's everything from light bulbs to toilet paper."

She leaned against him. "Jim, you're scaring me."

"Got kind of a pucker factor myself."

———

JIM WAS TRYING to call Barnes when he heard Alina gasp. She stood staring at a news channel video feed, paused to show a group of men firing on a police line. Her finger tapped on the screen. When he looked closer, he could see what she was upset about. Several of the faces looked familiar, especially one. Gomez. Most had masks on, but some did not.

"Why aren't they wearing masks?" Alina asked quietly.

He shook his head. "Beats me."

Nudging her with his hip, he quipped. "I'm not sure what the protocols are for rioting. But masks outside are cosmetic for COVID, so it's not that. I'm thinking it's because the gloves are off now, and it doesn't matter if we know who they are. Whatever they wanted to achieve has been done. With that in mind, more than likely, the rioters will crawl back into the holes they came out of."

Giving up on Barnes, he placed another call. "Pablo? Do you have any photos of Gomez from when you were traveling in the same circles?"

"Maybe. Let me check my phone. Hang on." A couple of minutes passed before Jim's phone notified him a message had arrived. Pablo came back on the line. "It ain't too clear. He didn't like pictures. The only way you get a picture of Gomez is if you're taking a picture of something else, and he happens to be there. Kinda like you. What's up, boss?"

"Alina was watching a news feed on the computer.

Gomez was caught on video shooting at a line of riot-control police in Springfield. Know anything about that?"

"Hell, no. I ain't seen much of him since we took down Trader Jack's."

"Okay." He rubbed his hand down his face, thinking a moment while Alina watched. "I think it's time we got a little more proactive with the homestead. I'd like you to move enough limestone boulders to block off the entrance to the valley. Just leave enough space to get one vehicle through the opening. We'll still need to get in and out for a while."

Pablo's clipped response was all business. "Got it. Anything else?"

"Do you still have the charges set to blow out the cattle guard? If not, I need you to check and make sure that's going to be operational."

"Juanita has been glued to the TV and is filling me in on the news. It ain't good, I know. We got this, boss. We're a lot better prepared than most folks around here."

Pablo was right, and conversely, he hoped most people didn't know it. Murphy's Law lurked around every decision. "We need to be able to block access quickly, so you might as well leave the loader down there with the rocks."

Jim could hear Pablo trying to shush the kids in the background, and he could envision them hanging all over him. "Got one better, boss. There are some of those concrete dividers just a quarter mile down the road that the highway department seems to have forgotten about. They used them while working on the bridge. Those will work better."

Those dividers weighed tons and were particularly

useful dividing traffic. "That's good thinking. I guess were thinking alike."

"Boss. You forgetting? I was a Marine, remember? Break things and blow shit up? We know how to bunker up and protect ourselves."

"Yeah, well, let's hope we don't have to. When you get that little chore done, we need to move the travel trailers close to the house and get them hooked up to water and sewer. I expect Jacy and Barnes to be coming in with their tails on fire one of these days."

"Yeah. Maybe sooner than later. Anything else, boss? I only got two hands."

"Driveway access today, trailers tomorrow. Sorry, Pablo. I haven't been paying attention. Now I'm playing catch up."

Pablo laughed. "Hey. This is my home, too. Ain't nobody coming in that we don't want. If things get bad, we have the cave behind the house fixed up for Juanita and the girls. It's dry, got supplies and everything they need."

"Not for you?" He knew the answer even as he asked. First and foremost, Pablo was a warrior.

"You know the answer to that. It gets to that point, we'll be putting the hurt on some folks."

"Good enough. Remind me to give you a raise. One thing, though. Family first—remember that. Everything else is secondary. I'll be out and about, so stay frosty."

"You got it, boss."

Alina leaned against the counter, arms folded as she stared at him. "You're not going to start doing stupid stuff, are you?"

He didn't reply right away, forwarding the picture of Gomez to Sally's number. "Not sure yet. Depends on your definition of stupid. I need to see what Barnes is doing and go from there."

"Will you need to help, Barnes?"

His gaze was level and serious. "Yes, I will. I'm not sure he's aware of it yet, but he's going to need it."

"So much for your retirement." Her hands were held up in surrender.

She didn't seem to be catching the 'let's get things done' fever. "I'm going to see if Aunt Bea will move out here. That will take one worry away from Barnes. You might reach out to Jacy and see what she's doing. I'm sure she's aware, but you might let her know what's going on and that she and the kids are welcome to a travel trailer. If she's real busy at the clinic, she might not have the big picture. We don't want our medic caught out in harm's way."

Before they could move, the Darth Vader theme started playing on his phone. Surprised, he looked at Alina and put it on speaker. "Sally. How's it shaking?"

Clipped and hurried conversations seemed to be the tone of the day. "That picture you sent. He's local?"

He rolled his eyes at Alina. "I'm fine, thanks for asking. Alina is fine, too."

"Cut the crap and answer the question." It was curious that she was on a radio. Her transmission was voice actuated, and he could hear muted noise in the background as she spoke, then nothing.

Already knowing where this was going, his stomach knotted. "Yes, I'm afraid he is."

"He's a bad actor. You need to roll on him right now."

Going out on an operation wasn't on the top of his 'to-do' list. "Slow down, Rambo. Bad actor? That's kind of obvious, given what the news video shows. Given the state of things now...what's the hurry?"

"I didn't see any video and don't need to. He's on our list."

"Your list?" He felt like he was playing catch-up again. "List of what?"

"Dammit, Jim. He's a known terrorist. We've been looking for him. How do you know him?"

"Well, he's a good plumber, and my foreman knew him. He also helped us take down Trader Jack's the first time. When that was over, he moved into the place. Now he lives in a prepper's paradise, out in the boonies, with a sizable arsenal. Thinking of that, it's a perfect base of operations for him."

"How'd that happen?" Her rapid speech and background noise made him think she was doing several things at once.

"Well..." He paused. "It was quid pro quo. He helped us take out some bad people, and then we helped him. If he hadn't decided to help blow up Springfield, we'd never have known he was bad."

He could hear a soft conversation happening away from the phone. "Alright. Hang tight. I just may have a solution for this. If things come together, we'll get this taken care of. I may need the GPS for this Trader Jack's."

"With all that's going on, is this something we need to worry about? It may be past making a special effort for retribution. The way things are winding up, the problem may take care of itself."

"We need to drop this guy, Jim. He's a bad apple."

"A bad apple?"

He didn't know how she could make a cell phone slam when she hung up, but she did it. Must be an app for that. Rolling his neck around his shoulders, he hoped the popping and cracking wasn't a bad sign.

"You doing anything special tonight?"

Alina stood and gave him a wary glance. "Not really. What do you have in mind?"

Jim gazed out the window a moment before answering. "I'm thinking we need to make sure all our toys are cleaned and operational and load all the extra magazines. There may not be time later."

TWENTY-TWO

RITA ARRIVED at the sheriff's office after an uneventful drive from Springfield. Well, almost. Aiding the deputies in Green County was hardly a blip on her radar. Her mind was busy with things she wanted to talk to Barnes about, how to start a conversation with Jim if he just happened to come by, and what in holy hell Captain Hawkins was doing in Springfield with her Predator drones and Hellfire missiles.

Her first surprise was Bea meeting her at the door with a big hug. She didn't remember seeing her before, so there must be some underlying motive going on. The woman read her mind.

"I'm sorry to be so excited, but you're my savior. As soon as you're settled in, my husband is out of here."

She stared at the woman a moment before continuing to her office. Barnes walked around the desk and shook hands as she entered.

"It's good to see you, Rita. How are you feeling?" He glanced past her and spoke. "Bea, can you close the door on your way out?"

"Wow. You're living dangerously." She glanced back at Bea. "I don't mind her being a part of this. Why don't you stay, Bea?"

They spent the next hour getting her caught up on the goings on around the county.

"What about COVID protocols?" she asked. "Looks like some things are still open."

"We're not in bad shape. It's only banks and government that's closed. Last I looked, we only had seven cases. That's not bad at all. Early on, we lost some folks from the nursing homes, and then a few outlying older people. I think about thirty-one out of a county of eight thousand. Other than that, the symptoms are bad colds with full recoveries."

Barnes watched her a moment. "Okay. So what's up with you and Sally? Are you a Shepherd now?"

"No," she replied. "I'm the Limestone County Sheriff. But I have a few more options now than before. What about you? Can I keep you on?"

He thought a moment. "I'm thinking it's going to take all of us in the short term. I'm going to move Bea out to the Fishhook."

Rita gave him the raised eyebrow look.

"Jim's new place. It's a small ranch. Calls it the Lazy J, but do me a favor and call it the Fishhook. It really puts a burr under his blanket when you do that. But he's got a good place to defend, if it comes to that. There's a lot of new things you need to catch up on with his situation."

"I can imagine, some I already know. Anything coming apart here that we need to address right away, fires to put out...zombie hordes...anything?"

"Not yet, but there's a feel to the air I don't like. Call it a gut feeling. We have a biker gang wanting to take over the lake. They're from the St. Louis area and I don't think they quite understand the local citizenry. If it weren't so serious, it'd be funny."

"So, how are you doing this?" Rita asked. "Thanks to COVID, the courthouse is closed. The judges and lawyers are from out of town anyway. All the public services are closed. Limestone County is not innocent and I distinctly remember keeping the courts busy."

Barnes snorted. "We just ask everyone to be nice." They shared a laugh for a moment before he continued. "Actually, I've leaned on Jim and his federal badge a little. Most everyone knows him."

"I don't remember him having that many friends."

"Friends might be a stretch, but word travels, and he does have a reputation as a straight shooter...in more ways than one. If I see trouble brewing, I can send him around to sniff it out and maybe head it off. He has more trouble on his own doorstep than he knows, but there's not much we can do about that for now."

"Alina?"

Concern colored his response. "In spades. Jim can't see it."

"Well, you're right. We can't stick our noses into that...unless something happens, and I do remember a certain stubbornness with Jim."

After another hour of talking, she was ready to leave. "I understand my house has been fixed up and is ready?"

"Yeah. You sure you want to go back there? I mean, after the shooting?"

She shrugged. "I don't think of the bad things, just of lessons learned. I'll be fine."

He stood to see her out the door. "So, bright and early tomorrow?"

"With bells on."

TWENTY-THREE

DEPUTY ALLISON CREWES'S day started at five a.m. with two people who, according to the neighbors, had been drinking for days and arguing all night. When she arrived on scene, the man and woman were outside their trailer and engaging in the ancient art of wobbly, stumbling fisticuffs, screeching and cursing at each other, tripping over discarded wine bottles and beer cans—thus disturbing the neighbors. She was pretty sure the woman was winning, although the prize would be an obscure victory.

When she left an hour later, sporting scuff marks on her cheek and forehead, the neighbors were mollified, and the two combatants were sleeping it off...one on the couch, the other in a lawn chair—both outside. The skeeters would have a feast, and she didn't want to think about what could be lurking under those sofa cushions.

There were times when she wished she'd get a call out to see normal people—hey, we're just sitting on the porch having a beer, want one? When all you see are problems and problematic people all day long, it eats on your soul.

Downshifting her Dodge Charger to take a ninety-degree curve, she squalled her tires, standing on both the brake pedal and emergency brake pedal, and not clutching, which killed the engine. All three procedures resulted in a near-instant stop.

Standing in the road was a young girl, holding an over-stuffed bunny by one ear, eyes wide at the sudden noise and now near silence broken only by the ticking of the rapidly cooling engine.

Allison jumped out of the car in time to see the Batman backpack, with the girl under it, break for the woods. She was fast, but the ex-gymnast deputy caught her within a few steps, avoiding a tackle by grabbing the girl's collar. That was only a penalty in football.

Breathing hard, both stared at the other a moment.

"What's your name, young lady?" She let go of the girl's shirt, checking her out for obvious injuries. Although scratched and dirty, the girl seemed to be physically sound, given her speedy flight over rough terrain.

"Come on," the deputy tried again. "You have to have a name."

The girl just shrugged, staring past her at the road and starting to lean away.

The deputy grabbed her arm. "Do you live around here, sweetie? Where are your folks?"

Still mute, the girl shrugged out of her pack while giving the deputy an exasperated look. Unzipping the top and pulling out a small bottle of water, she chugged the whole thing while engaging in a staring match. Finally, she reached into a side pocket and produced a business card.

Allison stared at the card a moment, wide-eyed and shaking her head. "Do you know this man?"

The young girl nodded.

"Alright." Allison's gaze flicked between the girl's face and the business card. "Will you come with me? I'll see what I can do to help you. Okay?"

The girl hesitated.

"Hey." She leaned close to the girl, making sure she had eye contact. "It beats walking."

The girl, definitely a tween and nearly as tall as the vertically challenged deputy, nodded and walked to the patrol car. Glancing at the seat on the passenger side filled with books and paper, she waited patiently for the officer to open the back door to the Charger.

Once the girl was safely inside, Allison looked at the card again before scooting inside the car. She glanced through the mesh divider. "Are you alright, sweetie?"

Allison was rewarded with a single nod.

Starting the engine, she dropped the transmission into low. Chirping the tires as she worked through the gears and glancing at the rearview, she caught a small smile from the girl. Maybe there was hope for her. Special girls like hot cars...and stuffed bunnies.

RITA AND BARNES gazed at the precarious-looking mound of paperwork piled on the desk. It was amazing the number of forms that were involved with the transition of bringing Rita back into being the sheriff and moving Barnes out of the position. Grateful for an interruption, they swiveled toward the door at a commotion in the front office.

"What the...?" The exclamation from Barnes's wife at the front desk was loud and then quickly stifled.

Deputy Crewes walked in carrying a girl nearly as tall as she, whose feet were close to dragging on the floor. Breathing heavily, she deposited the girl none too gently into a chair. Pointing an angry finger at her, she growled. "Stay. You try to run again, and I'll cuff you to that chair. Upside down. And backward. With gummy bears stuffed in your nose."

Rita stared at them until Allison continued in a mild voice. "Welcome back, Sheriff. You're going to love this. I can't wait."

Stepping past her, Rita said. "Aren't you Janie Hyatt?"

The girl hesitated a moment before giving a quick nod.

"She refuses to talk," the deputy said. "I was coming back from a call when I about ran over her standing in the road. She had on her Batman backpack and..." Her voice broke a moment. "She was holding her stuffed rabbit by one ear. I've never seen anything so pitiful."

"Oscar." The voice was barely heard.

"Oh, now she talks," Allison said as all eyes turned to the girl. "She and Oscar the Rabbit look so sweet. But looks are deceiving." She gave the girl a menacing look. "She also likes to run."

"Alright," Rita spoke sharply to her deputy but watched the girl closely. "Why don't you go get us some jelly donuts..." No reaction from the girl. "Or maybe some pizza slices?"

Janie's expression perked up at that.

"On my way. Oh, one other thing." The deputy reached into her shirt pocket. "Just to make things interesting. She gave me this card...we're gonna need to sell tickets for this one."

Taking the card, Rita's heart skipped a beat.

The Lazy J Ranch - Jim Lane.

She dropped to her knees in front of the girl. "Okay. It's time to stop fooling around. Please talk to me. Where did you get this card?"

Tears tracked through dirty cheeks. "Momma gave it to me. She put it in my backpack along with the water bottles and some food—said it was for emergencies."

Questions were tumbling over each other in Rita's mind before the most important came out. "Why? Did you have an emergency?"

The blond hair bobbed a couple of times. "Momma didn't come home. She works at night, but she always comes home to fix my breakfast and put me on the bus for school...well, used to. We home school now 'cause of the 'rona. But she didn't come home."

Rita gazed at the girl. "Do you have any idea why she wouldn't come home?"

"I don't know." The girl shrugged. "Mr. Lane helped us once. I like him. Momma said he'd take care of me if something bad happened." The girl took a deep, shuddering breath. "If she couldn't."

Close to tears of her own, it didn't help when she heard a sob from the receptionist. "Do you know where your mom works?"

The girl shook her head. "No. She just started there. It was something about a hangman?"

"A hangman." Rita thought a moment. "Maybe a gallows?"

Another shrug. "Maybe?" Janie held her stomach. "I don't feel good."

"How long since you've eaten?"

"Not counting beef jerky?" She counted on her fingers. "Four."

"Four days?" Rita gasped.

Without looking, Rita snapped her fingers and pointed toward the door. "Barnes? No more retirement. The Gallows Bar and Grill. You're looking for Jana Hyatt."

Barnes headed for the door. "On it."

A few minutes later, Janie was wolfing down her third slice of pizza under the watchful eyes of the sheriff and her deputy, plus a dewy-eyed receptionist.

"Slow down, honey. You'll give yourself a belly ache."

The girl's voice was low and sarcastic. "Already hurts."

Deputy Crewes snorted. "Oh, she'll get along with Lane just fine."

After giving the deputy a dirty look, she asked. "Janie? Why don't you stay here with us until we can find out about your mom?"

The girl stopped chewing, swallowed a huge amount of pizza, and then wiped her mouth with a napkin. Her gaze was a thousand years old. "Take me to Mr. Lane. Momma said."

"But..." Rita shook her head, amazed at the presence of the young girl. "Look, you're a minor. I can't just hand you off to anyone you say."

"Is he a bad man?" For the first time, she looked uncertain.

"Well, um...no, not usually." How many definitions of bad could there be? Maybe the old western explanation was best. A bad man to tangle with, a bad man to have mad at you, with morals no better or worse than those around him or that situations dictated.

Janie clenched her eyes with a shudder, trying to get control of her emotions. "Something bad has happened to Momma. I just know it. She always comes home. Always."

"She left you alone while she went to work?"

"I'm old enough." The girl's expression hardened as she reached toward her pack sitting on the floor with one hand, the other grabbing Oscar the Rabbit by the ear. "Thank you for the food. Please let me go."

"Alright," Rita relented, knowing child services wouldn't be much help due to COVID, along with the rest of county government cowering in their respective basements. It was her first day back and time to put on her big-girl panties and take control. She suspected if she tried to hand off this girl to anyone but Jim, it would be a blowup of epic proportions. Sometimes the easiest solution is the best.

She patted the girl's hand. "I'll do as you ask, but this is going to get real complicated. But before we do any of that, we need to go to your home and get you some clothes."

Rita gave her deputy a pointed look. "We can do some looking around while we're there. Maybe we can figure out where your mother has gone. Okay? Sound like a plan?"

The girl glanced between the two women and seemed to be thinking a moment. "And then you'll take me to Mr. Jim?"

"Yes." Rita smiled at the little girl, thinking Deputy Crewes was right. It might be a good idea to record that meeting. The look on his face... "Once we get your things, we'll take you to Mr. Jim."

TWENTY-FOUR

CURTIS THOMPSON WAS SITTING with his family at the breakfast table enjoying his last cup of coffee before heading off to work. The sun was just peeking over the tops of the trees, and he wasn't in any great hurry. All he had to do for the day was clean out creek gravel from under the bridge over by Hulston's Mill. And it wouldn't go to waste. As soon as he had it piled up, folks would show up in pickups or pulling wagons to be loaded. The extra gravel would be gone before noon and likely spread on driveways and barn lots by the end of the day.

His small farm was about six miles northeast of White Rock and was his pride and joy. He did enough odd jobs to earn extra money that helped in lean times, but mostly his wife and two children helped him work the homestead.

A couple of heated greenhouses kept the family in produce year-round. The wood-burning heaters were large enough to walk into when they needed cleaning out and burned planks up to seven feet long. Chickens, goats, sheep, and a few beef cattle gave them everything else. He even had a family of llamas to watch for coyotes and foxes. Once that long-necked sentry established his territory, predators had a hard time sneaking in for an easy meal.

Their pantry was full, along with the smokehouse and root cellar. It was rustic but wasn't a bad life. Before the COVID outbreak, both his children had been in college on academic scholarships. Now they were home—and bored.

He was lacing up his boots when the early-morning peacefulness was interrupted by the window-rattling cacophony of motorcycles. Fingernails on a chalkboard wouldn't have been any worse. ATVs and dirt bikes were common sounds. Each has their own distinctive sound. This was different.

"Y'all expecting anybody?" He glanced around the table.

All he received were headshakes as his family watched him expectantly. His son was already half out of his chair.

"Okay, then. We've been hearing some bad things from around the county about a biker gang. They're bad dudes. It's probably nothing. I know a lot of good folks who ride motorcycles, but let's not take chances and do this like we've practiced."

He finished tying his boots and stood. "Cathy, I want you upstairs in the window that overlooks the front lot. Marcie, you're by the front window on the left side of the living room. Jeff, go out the back door, come around to the side, and use the woodpile for cover. Should make for a nice crossfire if we need it. It doesn't matter who this is.

If they are armed and put their hands on a weapon... well, you know what to do."

The kids responded wordlessly like they were running off to play a game. He watched them leave, worry wrinkling his brow. They were good kids. They'd learn soon enough that this was no game.

His wife, Cathy, took a moment. "You sure about this, Curtis?"

He shook his head and then hugged her as the sounds grew louder. "No, I'm not. But it's better to be prepared. Maybe they're just tourists looking for directions." He swatted her behind to move her on her way to the stairs.

They'd practiced this scenario, although doing things to make it fun. He knew his family was ready, with loaded rifles at their designated places. The kneeboards under the windows were reinforced with sheet metal. Sending his son to the woodpile was chancy but worth the risk. Spaces between the chunks of wood weren't much of a deterrent.

Most of their guns were old, bought before the prices went out of sight—the same for ammunition. But it was all in perfect condition. They preferred the Ruger Ranch Rifles or Mini-14s, which had the same firepower as all the AR-15 variants, but with less political blowback. They weren't made from scary black plastic. Well, they weren't scary if you discounted the twenty-round magazines and suppressors. He likes to call them functional.

Propping the front door open, in case he needed to fall back through it in a hurry, he walked out on the front porch. His shotgun, a semi-automatic loaded with zombie shells, a slug surrounded by 00 buckshot, rested easy in the crook of his arm. He wished he could spit the dryness from his mouth. Practice is one thing, real life another.

Three men rolled up close to the porch and came to a stop, shutting down their Harleys and flipping out the kickstands. It looked like a practiced move. Two of the men had sandstone-colored machine pistols strapped into scabbards attached to their gas tanks. The other had an AR-15 clone fastened in a clip on his handlebar forks. He was going to have a hell of a time getting that into play. It would take precious seconds he wouldn't have.

"Help you men with something? You look to have escaped from an old *Mad Max* movie. Somebody shooting a few scenes around here I don't know about?"

"You're trying to be funny. *Mad Max*. I like that. Unfortunately for you, we're the real thing."

The bikers grinned at each other. The one doing the speaking was an obnoxious-sounding redhead with a woolly beard. "You got a nice place here. We'll be taking it off your hands."

"Really?" Curtis spoke in a calm voice. "That's what you came here for? Just like that? We're supposed to leave? Move out on your say-so?"

"Oh, no." Red snickered. "You got this all wrong. Ain't nobody leaving. Especially your women. I hear you got a couple of fine lookers here. And don't even think of using that shotgun. You'll be way too slow."

They stared at each other a moment while Curtis waited patiently. He'd let them play it out. Finally Red couldn't take the silence. "Ain't you gonna ask us to leave? Plead your case? Offer to buy us off? Something? You could at least make it interesting. We love it when people beg. It won't do any good, but I'd like to hear it."

Without looking, Curtis checked the safety on the

shotgun. He hadn't walked outside with the safety on, but it never hurts to check. "If you boys get your jollies by making people afraid of you, then you're in for a disappointing day. Why don't you just hustle your butts on out of here? We'll call it your last chance for a reasonable ending."

The bikers had pistols strapped to their belts. When they reached for them, Curtis didn't have to move. The moment their hands touched the butts of their pistols, the men were cut down in a fusillade of rifle fire. One of the rounds sliced through a gas tank and Curtis flinched, expecting it to explode. It did not. They always did in the movies.

Curtis leaned his shotgun against the wall of the house. "Well, that made a mess."

His two ladies exited the house and came to stand beside him, staring at the bikers, his wife clutching his arm. They could hear Jeff throwing up behind the woodpile before he came strolling up, wiping his mouth on the sleeve of his shirt. The youngster of the family, he was pale but carried a determined expression.

"It's alright, Jeff." He put an arm around his son, and then they all did a group hug. "Everybody knows that women have stronger stomachs than men."

That comment netted him a couple of blows to his shoulders, but it broke the ice as he intended.

"It's not like the movies or a video game, is it? Killing is never a good thing, and it's never easy. But they called the shots...so to speak."

He continued. "And it's not pretty."

"It stinks," his wife said, wrinkling her nose as the breeze shifted in their direction. "In more ways than one."

Curtis nodded, arms still around his family. "I'm sorry, y'all. I wish this hadn't happened. But it did, and I'm proud of you."

He stood looking at the mess in his yard, the smell of gasoline a constant worry. "Alright, y'all go back inside. Clean those weapons and top off the magazines. It's hard telling if there will be more coming to visit. I can't believe scum like this would be missed, but they might. We'll have to move fast if that happens."

"And Cathy? Look up that list for our neighborhood watch. We need to get folks up to speed on this. And make a note of those that don't answer. Some of these peckerwoods may have already paid them a visit."

"Anything else you want me to do, master?" she quipped as she stepped from him.

A quick glance saw she was still armed. "Please?"

After they'd gone inside, he pressed a number on his cell phone. "Hey, Jerome? Didn't I see you still had your backhoe and front-end loader on the trailer? Good. I need a favor."

He paused to look at the motorcycles. "Yeah, I need to bury some hogs. I'll explain when you get here. We need to get them into the ground before they start to smell."

While his family was inside, Curtis went about collecting the biker's guns, knives, and what money they had. They wouldn't be needing them where they were going, and he knew Jerome would take them for payment.

He chuckled a moment in comic relief watching chickens walking all over the llama bull. The large animal appeared half-asleep, unperturbed by the gunfire, staring across the field at the goat herd. In the middle of the herd, the female stared back.

His next call was to Jim Lane.

"Hey Curtis," Jim answered. "I'm out of the fight game, buddy. Have you healed up yet?"

He smiled before answering, the post-fight adrenalin jitters making his voice quiver. "Yeah, I'm doing alright. My back still hurts some. I just called to give you a head's up. We had a visit at the farm from some bikers. They were armed, and apparently moving into our house was a real high priority for them."

"You sound a little shaken up. What can I do? Are they still there? I'm just headed into town, so it'll be a few minutes."

"That's alright." Curtis looked around at his front lot. "We got it handled. You know anything about these guys? I've never seen them before."

"I've met a few of them. They have a bunch of Hollywood names and bad attitudes, like Dog and Boots. But they are dangerous. I think they're mostly out of St. Louis. Did they cause trouble? Family okay?"

Curtis took a deep breath while looking around. "Well, they didn't cause as much trouble as they intended and weren't very good at what they tried. You can scratch these three. After they went for their weapons, they got dusted. The family is a little shaken up, but we'll be fine. I'm putting our neighborhood watch on high alert."

"You did the right thing, Curtis. The world is not a pretty place right now. Take care of your own."

"Well one big question, since you're friends with Barnes, I'm wondering if I need to involve the sheriff in this rodeo?"

"Barnes is a good man, so I don't think you have much concern there. It's always been this way, Curtis. If you have an immediate problem, calling 9-1-1 isn't always your best option. And it's not their fault. They can't be sitting on everyone's doorstep."

"Understood," Curtis said. "We'll keep a low profile and not offer anything unless asked. I'm worried more bikers will show up."

"Curtis, I have no clue what they're up to. Just keep your head on a swivel and have your neighbors do the same."

When he ended the call, Curtis had a moment of self-doubt. Was this the best path to take? Should he have called 911 and then forted up with his family to wait for law enforcement to show up? At best, they would have been a half hour away. Like most places, his wood-frame home would not stop bullets, except for his reinforcements under the windows.

Real life wasn't like they show on TV, where the good guy hides behind a door jamb holding his trusty pistol and then defeats the bad guy who is firing an automatic weapon at him. The old joke, seated in a lot of truth, is that if you fire a .45 caliber in your house, the bullet goes through your walls, your neighbor's walls, and kills the burglar hiding behind his refrigerator. Hollow-point ammo would alleviate that somewhat, but the analogy was valid.

He scuffed the dirt with the toe of his boot a moment before casting a hard look at the bikers. No. Hesitating would have resulted in injury or death to his family. That was unacceptable. Sometimes you just do what you gotta do.

From this moment forward, they would go armed.

TWENTY-FIVE

THE GALLOWS BAR AND GRILL didn't open for business until eleven a.m., but the front door was propped open when Barnes arrived. Nighttime hangouts could always use some fresh air and the light of day. Walking into the gloom, he paused a moment to let his eyes adjust, stepping away from the door so he wouldn't be silhouetted by the light.

He wasn't sure fresh air would drive out the spilled beer and sweat aroma that assaulted his nose and permeated the place. The last time he'd been here, the place seemed a whole lot cleaner. Releasing the safety on his pistol, he had a momentary thought of a sheriff in the Old West going into a saloon—maybe the analogy wasn't far off. This was definitely going into harm's way.

All sound stopped like an old door closing on a rusty hinge. His soft-soled boots barely whispered as he moved toward a woman standing behind the long bar. She avoided his gaze while holding up her hand. Her voice was louder than needed in the abrupt silence, as her gaze slid to a table at the back of the room.

"I don't know anything about anything."

"What's your name?" He threw that comment out just for fun, already knowing the answer.

"Don't remember that either, cowboy."

Barnes continued walking toward the last table, not needing the bartender's hint. He stood a moment, letting the silence stretch out. "I thought I told you folks to clear out of Limestone County?"

Dog held his hand up to stop a response from Boots. "It's still a free country, Sheriff. Live free or die, you know? As long as we don't break the law, we go where we want and do what we want."

Starting to speak, he was interrupted by a high-pitched squeal and then men laughing from upstairs.

Dog shrugged with a benign smile. "Adults at play, Sheriff. No biggie."

"Yeah, sure." Nodding, Barnes decided to get to the matter at hand. "I'm looking for a woman that works here, Jana Hyatt. Have you seen her?"

"That bitch?"

Dog whirled to look at Boots. "Shut up."

Turning back toward the front, Dog yelled. "Hazel. You know anything about some chick named Hyatt? Maybe works here?"

The woman behind the bar shook her head. "I don't know anything. Never heard of her. People come and go around here."

Barnes nodded. "Why would you ask her? She can't remember her own name."

He didn't expect anything different. If there were a book written about criminal evasive responses, these phrases would all be there. But they'd already given up what he wanted to know. If the Hyatt woman was alright, they would know her and admit it.

Hand on his pistol and staring at Boots, he commented. "So, does the fact that her car is sitting in the parking lot ring any bells?"

"No idea," Dog responded with a smirk. "It's a public lot. Goes along with a free country."

"Alright. How about y'all take me upstairs to see if she's there?"

Dog grinned at him. "Well, see...that's where we live now, so it's a private abode. You'd need a warrant for that. Anything else we can help you with, Sheriff?"

There was no way he wanted to go upstairs with these two at his back. He thought of all the ways to do it. Maybe a fire safety inspection, flooding the place with volunteer firemen? Or a welfare check on the woman upstairs...all on shaky ground. Especially without backup. His gut was telling him that she wasn't upstairs, but he had to know for sure. He could call for help and take the place apart, but what would it gain him? The sheriff and Deputy Crewes were busy with the little girl and who knew where the other deputy was—generally as far away from actual police work as possible. So, he was out of options.

On the other hand... While enduring the baleful stares of the duo in front of him, he placed the call.

Jim Lane answered on the first ring. "Hey. I was just thinking of you."

"I'm touched." Barnes backed a couple of steps, turning so he could watch the duo at the table and the bartender. "Are you in town?"

"Yeah, just stocking up on doughnuts...want some?"

"I could use a little help at The Gallows." He smiled at Dog. "I'm kind of in a pickle."

It must have been his tone of voice. His friend didn't hesitate. "Three minutes."

He glanced at his watch as Dog started to get up. "Sit your ass down."

"Now, look here..." Dog's voice trailed off as he watched someone come in the front door.

Jim walked up beside him, staring at the bikers at the table. "Why...hello, Dog. And your trusty sidekick is here. How they hanging, Boots?"

Ignoring the growls and dirty looks, Jim turned to Barnes. "What's up, brother?"

Barnes didn't look away from the table as he spoke or move his hand from his pistol. "You remember Jana Hyatt?"

"Yeah, I do. Nice lady that had some hard times. I always figured her for settling the score with Little Dickie."

"Well, be that as it may...she's missing. More to the point, we know she works here, but the local fauna aren't talking. Do you have your shiny new federal badge with you?"

"I do."

"Cool." Barnes's voice was noncommittal, just passing the time of day. "A few minutes ago, I heard a woman scream upstairs. I don't have a warrant to go up to the living quarters, but I'm thinking we have probable cause. And we really need to make sure she's not up there..."

Jim was already moving up the stairs. It was easy to track his progress. They heard a hoarse yell and then a body came piling down the stairs, followed by another. The silence stretched a moment while they could hear conversation going on. Finally, Jim came back down, stepping on one of the men when they didn't get out of the way.

"It's all clear up there, except for being a pigsty. How do people live like that? The lady, and I use that term loosely, doesn't want to come down—says everything happening up there is consensual. She also said she doesn't know Hyatt. I'm thinking she wouldn't admit it anyway."

"Yeah, you wouldn't believe how much people don't know around here." Barnes nodded. "Thanks, brother. I appreciate your help. Why don't you head on out? I'll catch up later."

"Maybe I should stick around. Given the history of this place, it needs to catch on fire."

"I'll be out later." Barnes gave him a pointed look. "Save me some doughnuts."

Jim stared at him a moment and then walked away. "Stubborn ass."

Stopping abruptly, Jim turned back. "Dog, I hear you're branching out. A little birdie told me you're trying to take over some local homes to house those jackals you call bikers. You'd better call them back before you lose them all. This ain't the city."

He paused a moment. "I'm also headed down to Miller. I got a call that said the gun shop got burned down. If my friends tell me they saw even one biker in the area, I'm coming back to nail your balls to the wall."

After Jim left, Barnes turned his attention to the bikers.

"We about done here?" Dog asked. "I think my guys need a doctor."

"What guys? Do you mean those men who rushed

down the stairs hoping to do their civic duty and help local law enforcement with an investigation but then tripped and fell? Tell them I appreciate their enthusiasm and thank you for your—" He paused a moment while looking at all their faces. "Cooperation. But just like Jim Lane said, once I get all my ducks in a row, I will be back."

Glancing at the bartender on the way out, she met his gaze and then lowered her eyes. Thinking of the little girl, he was getting a bad feeling.

He was almost to his car when his cell phone rang. His shoulders slumped when he saw the caller ID. "Barnes."

"Barnes?"

Responding to the shaky voice, he sighed into his phone, "Didn't I just say that, PJ?"

Wind noise carried through the microphone of the cell phone. "Yeah, sorry. Hey, we got a dead body on the beach out here at Twin Bridges."

He sighed, glancing back at The Gallows. Boots was standing in the door watching. Like any officer, he didn't believe in coincidence. "Gender?"

There was a short, muffled snort. "You know we can't ask that."

He couldn't believe Rita had hired this man. Dealing with him was death by a thousand cuts. This was no time for bubble-headed humor. He'd been told PJ just acted stupid so people would underestimate him. To Barnes, that would take a level of intelligence the man didn't possess. "Is the body male or female, PJ?"

"It's definitely female."

"Alright. Take care of it." He took a deep breath of clean air, purging his lungs after being in The Gallows.

"You know the routine. Rope off the scene. Keep any spectators away. Call the coroner. Work the scene."

Silence permeated the airways until PJ cleared his throat before responding, "You need to see this."

Sighing, Barnes pinched the bridge of his nose. There was no use arguing. "On my way."

He speed dialed Rita. "PJ found a female body out at Twin Bridges beach. I got a bad feeling."

"Shit." Rita paused a moment. "Okay. Let me know if you can ID. If you need help, I can get Bea to babysit and be there in twenty."

He didn't want to pull her away from the young girl. "No need. I'll handle it until we know more. Thanks, Rita."

"No problem." She gave a short laugh. "I'm not sure if all three of us in the office can handle this innocent young thing anyway. I may have to put her in the holding cell."

"Understood." He tried to hold back a laugh, knowing it wasn't appropriate for the situation. He wasn't successful. "Welcome back to Limestone."

"Yeah. Thanks a lot, Barnes."

––––––––

AFTER BARNES LEFT THE GALLOWS, Dog stood abruptly, making his chair slam against the wall. Boots came back from the door to stand with him.

"I need to kill that man." Boots's voice was a low hiss. "I need it."

"Which one?" Hands on hips, Dog's gaze settled on his men struggling to their feet.

"Both. Barnes, and especially Jim Lane." Her breathing was heavy.

Dog replied mildly, "You'll get your chance. We just have to wait for the right moment."

"Boss?" One of the bikers from upstairs walked toward them. "I gotta broke arm here."

"Alright," Dog answered calmly, frowning at the man. "I'm sorry as hell about that. Tell you what. Why don't both of you go out the back door? We'll take care of you on the back patio. There's more light out there and easier access. I'll call the medics."

His men wordlessly traipsed out the back. Watching them a moment, he turned to Boots.

"We need to clean house a bit." He met her fevered gaze. "You want to go take care of those boys?"

"Be glad to." She followed the men out, her knife sliding into her hand.

Dog walked over to the woman behind the bar. Without warning, he grabbed her hair and slammed her face into the bar top. She rebounded and fell into a heap behind the bar.

Leaning over the bar to look at her, he growled, "Next time I tell you to keep the door closed, you do it."

When the woman didn't answer, he palmed his cell phone. Pressing a speed dial number, the answer was immediate. "Hey, Mongo. Have you heard from any of the teams we sent out? No? Well, keep on top of that. We may need another place to stay soon. I think we're wearing this one out."

He paused a moment, listening.

"Soon as you hear anything, let me know. And have someone bring the van in and park in the back of The Gallows. We got some trash to take out. Oh, and Mongo.

It's time we took care of that other problem. Yeah, Jim Lane. That problem needs to go away. Make it happen."

Gazing toward the back door, he shook his head. Boots wouldn't like it, but things were coming to a head. Any opposition in Limestone County needed to disappear.

TWENTY-SIX

AFTER A FIFTEEN-MINUTE DRIVE, Barnes pulled into the public access sand beach area of Twin Bridges. There was no sign of life except for a black and white SUV patrol car. A bird-spotted and dusty black Cadillac SUV was parked on the far side of the lot. Maybe the victims?

PJ was standing at the edge of the sand. Just beyond, a stark-white body lay twisted like a discarded toy.

This was a bad day getting worse, but it was still better than the victim's day. "Why didn't you spread some crime scene tape around here? I told you to rope this off."

"What for? Ain't nobody here but us." PJ sounded offended.

"Well, for one thing, PJ, it was an order from your superior, not a request." Barnes was giving serious thought to going home and climbing into bed, just to get up and start the day over.

After a pause, he tried again. "You could have covered her. Shown a little respect?"

PJ snorted and rolled his eyes. "Are you having a bad day, Acting Sheriff?" He emphasized the word acting.

Barnes whirled and stared at the man a moment. "Are we having issues, Deputy? I can have your resignation processed pretty damned quick."

When the man didn't answer, Barnes continued. "Any ID?"

"No." PJ's response was unenthusiastic. "There are no clothes around, and I looked. Nothing, really."

"Any clothes in that car over there?" He pointed with his thumb at the SUV.

PJ gazed at the vehicle for a moment. "I didn't check yet. It's pretty far from the crime scene."

"It's a damned short walk, PJ." With a long sigh, Barnes turned toward the body on the beach. "Well, let's go see."

The woman was partially on her side. She was medium-sized and thin, with blond hair. Lividity was already showing, although from the number of cuts showing and obvious blood loss, he didn't see how there could have been any extra blood for gravity to pool. She'd been there a while, and judging by the lack of any blood on the ground, more than likely dumped. Taking a picture of the face, he suddenly wished he'd had Jim Lane come with him. The man could track a skeeter across a mud hole.

"PJ, when you walked up here, were there any tracks going to the body?"

"Didn't see any." The man's voice was gruff, and Barnes had to wonder how many dead bodies the deputy had seen.

"Well, think about it," Barnes said. "Did you think she

fell straight down from the sky? Maybe from an airplane?"

PJ made a motion to look up, but stopped himself. A flush was starting to show around his collar.

"When was the last rain?" Barnes continued pressing the man.

"Dunno. I ain't no detective." PJ's voice was sullen as he looked around at everything but the body.

"Are all these footprints yours?" It looked like a herd of cattle had wandered through—all with size ten hooves.

The deputy made a show of looking around the area. "Yeah, I reckon so."

"Who called this in?" Barnes tried to hold his temper in check. "C'mon, PJ, give me something to work with."

"Nobody. I was crossing the bridge and glanced over here—always check out the beach. Something didn't look right. Came down here and saw this. Called you. That's it."

"In other words, you saw someone naked and thought you'd check it out." Hands on hips, Barnes looked the scene over. If there were anything there, any actionable clues, they were too inept and undermanned to find it. Welcome to Limestone County.

There was one possibility. Although no drag marks were apparent, and with a hundred-pound body, there wouldn't be, but she could have been tossed. He was picturing a certain biker, one of the biggest men he'd ever seen. Someone who could throw a body like a bag of trash, or like his namesake in a movie, knock out a horse.

"Alright. Wrap this up and call the undertaker." Barnes made sure he had PJ's full attention. "You haven't done that either, right? And if you don't mind, cover that body. It might keep the seagulls off."

Barnes walked the beach before heading back to his vehicle. Other than Zebra Mussel shells and a few discarded condoms washing up on the shore, making him wonder about eating the fish from the lake, there was nothing remarkable to be found. It'd rained hard the night before, and he knew the cool morning would have kept anyone from visiting the beach. There were no tire marks in the sand and nothing on the blacktop but puddles in the low spots.

He walked to the SUV and tried to look inside, but the dark tinted windows prevented that. He put on a pair of latex gloves and tried the door. It was unlocked, so he checked out the car. The glove box didn't have any paperwork for ownership. That wasn't too unusual. He took out his cell phone and took a picture of the license plate and the VIN number showing at the bottom of the windshield. It was too expensive of a vehicle to be left unattended.

On a whim, he walked up to the government-approved close-to-a-watershed unisex outhouse that used to be the men's and looked inside. Pulling his flashlight, he flipped up the lids. The top of the affluent was about six feet down. He was inordinately relieved when there were no clothes or anything else unusual down there, although that retrieval would have been a good job for PJ.

Several feet away and protected by a privacy wall was what used to be called the women's restroom. It was a large space with a dressing area. Instead of a door, it had a left-turn and right-turn baffle. His nose told him the story before he went inside. A fully dressed woman was sitting on a bench, sightless eyes staring at him. A neat, round bullet hole was in the T-zone, exactly at the bridge of the nose and between her eyes. Her arms were at her sides, palms up like she'd held them in supplication only to have them fall limp with instantaneous death. He'd learned over the years this was the sweet spot for snipers...and assassins.

He gently moved her head forward to see no exit wound. Swell. Now they'd have the bullet. A quick search found no identification, but he had a gut feeling. He'd only talked to the woman on the phone. He'd never seen any female in Limestone County dressed in full business attire that screamed professional. This was not going to end well.

He made a quick call to Rita. "Are you still in the building?"

"Yep."

"Okay. You need to separate yourself from your young lady." He heard her talking to Deputy Crewes in a low voice and then footsteps as she walked away.

"I'm going to send you two pictures to see if you can identify them." Hearing the notification on her phone, he only had to wait a moment.

Rita gasped and answered in a low tone. "The blond is Jana Hyatt. Dammit, this sucks! How do I tell that little girl that her mother is dead? I don't know the other person."

He sighed and played a hunch. "There was a head doctor that Sally commissioned to talk to Jim. He's been having some issues. Her name was Tricia Bartol. Look her up on the Internet and see if we get a match."

After a few moments of typing sounds, she came back. "Confirmed. Jesus. You don't think...?"

"The body has a classic T-zone wound, I'd guess .22

cal. No exit wound, so probably a subsonic round. You know what that means. Rita, we need to keep this under wraps for the moment. If we go rushing in, circumstantial evidence or not, it could be a shootout of epic proportions with a lot of collateral damage. I can't stress that enough. I've seen that girl shoot. She could take us all out before we pulled leather."

"I agree. Okay. I'll let you handle that part of it for now, and we'll get our heads together later. We can't move on speculation. We may think we know who did it, but I doubt we can prove it. We'd have to kill her just to get her pistol for a ballistics match. And with the condition Springfield is in right now, I doubt they have a lab working." She paused a moment. "Dammit. I don't know about taking Janie out to the ranch now."

"I wouldn't worry about that," Barnes said as he exited the dressing room. "I'll bet you a brand-new Benjamin she won't be there. The doctor may have spooked her for some reason."

"Shit." Rita sighed. "This is not a good day."

"Well, it's better than the day these two women had."

"Do you have any idea who might be responsible for killing Jana Hyatt?"

Barnes sighed. "Yeah. I got good ideas on both. One is a giant, and the other an assassin. We just need to fill in the blanks."

"Sorry, Barnes. I guess your retirement is postponed."

The bodies would be picked up by the local undertaker. Notifications would be made when possible. They didn't have crime scene people like on television. That was a big city thing. A call would be made for a coroner and technicians from Highway Patrol, but he was sure they wouldn't come. From what he could see, the Springfield area was a war zone—their crime scene people would be swamped if working at all. Limestone County's problems would stay in-house. As usual.

He disconnected, and with one more look around, turned to go to his patrol car. Catching a glint of reflection on the floor, he nearly tripped with his sudden stop. No...could it be that easy? A shiny brass .22 caliber shell casing was embedded in a clump of mud, probably turned over when he hit it with his shoe. After taking a picture with his cell, he bent down and picked it up, mud and all. Hopefully it would all hang together until he could get a zip-lock plastic baggie from his car.

He could imagine the frustration of the shooter, looking frantically around for the spent casing, not wanting to leave any evidence—obsessive about it. But there was mud on the sole of their shoe, and they'd stepped on the casing. It was just their bad luck that the little chunk of mud came loose when they left. They'd not pay attention to a little mud on the floor.

Thinking of Jim Lane, he suddenly felt a hundred years old.

TWENTY-SEVEN

RITA LED the two-vehicle parade to the farmhouse of Jana Hyatt. Janie had opted to ride in the Charger with Deputy Crewes, helping clear out the passenger seat of all the junk and toss it into the back seat. They strapped her in with her backpack between her feet and big-ear bunny by her side.

The old farmhouse was neat as a pin, easy to do when almost bare of furnishings. It was an easy assumption that times were hard for the two of them and money scarce.

She knew most of the story. Last year this had been the Hyatt's farm. When Dan Hyatt was killed, Jana sold the small farm. Once the debts were paid, it was a net zero, which happened often. Most small farms looked good on paper, but the cost of operation often exceeded income.

Apparently, they now rented the house they used to own. That in itself would be depressing. Now, both parents were dead, and the world was left with a hollow-eyed and gritty little girl putting up a strong front for show. Somehow, she had to make sure this girl's run of bad luck ended right here, right now.

Janie was slump-shouldered as she looked around the house. "I know my momma's gone. I can feel it." She paused a moment, looking at Rita. "Can you tell me?"

Rita's gaze met with her deputy's. They were both cowards for the moment, unwilling to break the news, not knowing how—neither wanting to break this little girl's heart.

In a rough and tight voice, the price of pushing down tears, Rita said, "Let's get you some clothes."

As they passed the bedroom that must have been Jana's, the daughter darted into the room. On the night-stand was a pistol.

The two LEOs watched in horror as the girl picked up the large-framed, semi-automatic, staring at it a moment. Rita yelled, "Don't touch that." At the same time, Allison yelled, "Put that down."

Janie, the pistol pointed out a window, gave them a look of disdain, released the magazine, and stuck it in the front pocket of her jeans. In a practiced move, she pulled the slide of the pistol back and caught the ejected round in her palm, snatching it from the air before it hit the floor. Placing the pistol on the stand a moment, she reloaded the round in the magazine, picked up the pistol, and slapped the magazine home. She handed the pistol to Rita, butt first.

"Momma always took this with her. Always." The girl's voice was listless. "She must have forgotten it."

It took a moment for Rita to speak. "How do you...?"

This young lady clearly knew her way around firearms. That her mother would teach her was another sign of how alone the two had been. Then an innocuous piece of information stored in the back of her brain jumped forward as she remembered the solid thunk when Janie dropped her backpack to the floor. Thinking it was full of snack bars and stuffed bunny rabbits was an idea that went out the proverbial window.

"Allison." Her voice was quiet. "Would you do me a favor and check out this little munchkin's backpack? See if there's a quick access panel on the bottom, probably Velcro and not a zipper."

She wasn't gone long. "Son of a…" Deputy Crewes came back, holding a small-framed Smith and Wesson M&P EZ, 9 mil.

Rita knelt before the girl. "That's your gun, isn't it?"

"Of course." Her voice was indignant. "Momma liked it because of all the safety stuff on it, and it's easy to pull the slide."

Jesus, take the wheel. Rita's gaze traced the fly-spotted ceiling tiles a moment before coming back to the girl. "Why did you carry it with you?"

The girl gave them an incredulous look. "I might have needed it."

How bad could their world have gotten when a little girl thinks she needs protection? "For what?"

The girl shrugged. "Bears."

"Bears?" Rita's expression was deadpan as she glanced at her deputy. Turning back to the girl, she continued. "If you don't mind, we'll keep these for now. Any other guns we need to know about?"

She paused, knowing how literal children could be. "Strike that. Any other guns here in the house? Hidden outside? Anywhere at all?"

Her gaze was hollow. "Just these. Is my momma dead?"

Crap. Kids can be so damned perceptive. She pulled the girl into a hug. "Yes, she is, sweetie. I'm so sorry."

The girl didn't cry, and that worried Rita more than anything going on in the world. Rita teared up some, and Deputy Crewes suddenly had allergy problems. The poor girl had lost her father. Now she'd been told her mother was dead. With all that on her preteen plate, all she did was stare at them, watchful and curious about what was going on. This girl was wired way too tight.

After they'd gathered her clothes, and as they were leaving, Rita spoke to Deputy Crewes. "Allison, I want you to stay here. Turn this place inside out and upside down. Check the attic and crawl spaces, hen house, outhouse, and any other place you can think of. We need to know who in the hell Jana Hyatt was, and I need it yesterday."

The deputy gave her a big-eyed look. "Got it, boss."

Rita turned to Janie. "Okay, grab your bunny and backpack. You're now my honorary deputy, and we'll do a ride around."

"Are we going to see Mr. Jim?"

Mr. Jim. Rita hadn't seen him yet, and that was supposed to be first on her homecoming agenda. She'd hoped for a private meeting. It didn't look like that was going to happen. At least, not right away. Hopefully, it wouldn't be during a confrontation with Alina. Tears misted her vision for a moment. Again. They were coming too easy now. How in the hell had he fallen into that trap again? Dammit, Jim.

"Eventually." She gave the girl a smile, catching up to the conversation. Maybe they could pretend to be normal for a while, anything to keep the girl from thinking about her mother. "We'll have to check to see if he's home. He's out and about a lot. First, I thought we'd go by the drive-in and get some burgers and fries, maybe a milkshake to go with it?"

"I could eat, I guess." The girl perked up a little. "Does your car run like the Charger?"

"God, I hope not."

———

AN HOUR LATER, Rita and Janie were sitting at a picnic table with their lunch. She watched the girl dump her fries on the spread-out wrapper and then line them up like little soldiers. Ketchup was plopped onto one corner, and the methodical consumption began. First a small bite from the cheeseburger deluxe, then grab a fry and dip the end in ketchup, put the whole thing in her mouth at once—chew and swallow. A sip from her Dr Pepper, and the sequence started again.

Janie looked at her. "What?"

Rita snorted. "Oh, nothing. I've just never witnessed method eating before."

"We all have our talents." She shrugged and returned to eating.

How old was this girl? But then she realized she'd probably been treated as an adult for a long time. Adult conversations. Adult responsibilities.

The process started again. They were halfway through.

Her phone buzzed with a text notification from Deputy Crewes.

Nothing here. She's a ghost.

She returned the text while Janie watched curiously, munching on a fry.

Very funny.

I'm serious. Nothing here.

Rita thought a moment. There was nothing to be gained by staying there.

Alright. RTB.

K, Returning to base.

Crewes acknowledged.

They were wrapping up their trash when Barnes pulled in next to her SUV. He exited the vehicle and sat with them.

"Jim reached out to me just now. Seems our biker friends—"

She interrupted. "Little ears."

"—have been visiting isolated farms on our side of the lake."

Janie gave them an exasperated look. "I'm not a child."

"Actually, you are. Enjoy it while you can." She turned back to Barnes. "So, the message?"

"Well..." He glanced at Jamie first and then back to her. "It seems the local residents are handling the situation in-house, so to speak. At least so far."

Nothing unusual there. "Has anyone reached out to us for help?"

"Not that I know of."

Rita gave him a thoughtful glance. Last year she'd have been all up in everyone's face about law and order, threatening to arrest both sides and insisting they let law enforcement handle things. That was last year.

"Well, that may be the best solution for now. We might want to figure out who'd be more likely to need help and offer it to them."

Barnes snorted. "I can't think of any right off hand. That's a pretty independent bunch in those hills. I understand they have their own 9-1-1 system, and the response is a little more abrupt than ours."

"Agreed." While she'd never seen it in action, the rumor was there. Certain parts of Limestone County were covered in proverbial layers of fog. If you were a friend, the fog lifted. If not? You go through one layer only to find another, and another.

She glanced at Janie, nodding at the girl's expectant gaze. "I guess we'll head out to the Lazy J and talk to Mr. Jim."

"You might want to wait on that." Barnes shrugged. "He got a call from a friend and is headed down to Miller. Mutual aid says half the downtown is on fire. Mostly, they're just watching it burn."

She stared into the distance for a moment. "Let me guess. Someone hit the gun shop?"

"That's my guess, too. Anyway, a few days ago, I sent Jim down there to warn them about the biker gang, so he knows the folks."

"Swell." She had visions of a pissed-off Jim Lane stalking amid the ruins. What would he do now? Hell, she knew what he'd do now. In her mind, she could hear klaxon horns blaring and then the announcement over the intercom of *Battle Stations Nuclear—this is not a drill.*

Barnes continued. "Some advice, at least for the short term? Jim has a foreman for the ranch. Pablo and his wife have kids about Janie's age. Juana homeschools them, plus Jacy Mane's two kids. This young lady would fit right in. Janie might learn most of it in Spanish, but that's not a bad thing."

Rita nodded, anxious to be rid of babysitting duties. "That's a good idea. What do you think, Janie?"

"I don't much feel like playing with little kids." The girl busied herself building a little house with her excess french fries. At the rate she was devouring the fries, she'd run out of supplies soon.

Barnes picked up the conversation. "Juana makes really good cookies. Keeps everyone fat as little butter balls." He looked the girl up and down. "Of course, you probably like being skinny."

"I'm not skinny! See?" Janie flexed the muscles on one arm. She paused a moment, watching Barnes carefully. "What kind of cookies?"

Rubbing his chin, Barnes pretended to think a moment. "It's usually those chocolate chip oatmeal ones, or maybe peanut butter—saw some chocolate coconut ones once."

She turned her gaze to Rita. "I could eat."

"How?" Rita exclaimed, thinking of the large burger and fries the girl had just inhaled. "You just ate half a cow."

Barnes shook his head at them. "There's always room for a cookie, maybe a little ice cream thrown in. As a professional investigator, you should know that, Rita. I'll call her."

TWENTY-EIGHT

JIM STOOD WELL BACK from the crowd of spectators who seemed to be mesmerized by the smoking ruins of several buildings in downtown Miller. The central focus seemed to be the remains of the hardware store and watching the volunteer firemen pull bodies from the rubble. He remembered the narrow aisles and merchandise stacked nearly to the ceiling that would make the search a nightmare.

A quiet voice broke into his thoughts. "It's a bad day around here."

He turned to find Lawrence Dunn at his elbow. If anyone would know what happened, he would. Although he wasn't sure he wanted answers to the questions. "I guess the obvious happened?"

The man sighed, taking off his cap and running his hand over his head before answering. "Yeah, it did."

Jim's thoughts were on the young owners and his conversations with them. He'd hoped the husband took the warning as seriously as the wife. They were good people, but often good people were victims of thinking other people held the same restraint, the same values. "Did the family get out?"

"Yeah, most of them." The old vet paused a moment and then answered with anger coloring his voice. "Joel stayed back...held them off while the others got away out the back door."

Jim nodded. Not much else needed to be said. He could picture it—the fear and gut-wrenching anguish of kissing your wife goodbye if there was time, tongue stuck to the top of a dry mouth, and then the resolve of knowing what had to be done to save the others. He'd hoped the ending would be different for them. In a way, he was responsible because he'd often thought that he should have shot Red Dog Charles that first day. It would have been murder. But then, when you find a rattler on the trail in front of you ready to strike...you kill it.

He finally continued. "Well, I guess I've seen all I need to. Where are the survivors? Are they cared for?"

The old man took off his cap again and ran fingers through thinning white hair. It looked like a habit born of stress. "Got them all out at my place for now. They'll be taken care of...not sure about Anna, Joel's wife. She's around here somewhere, waiting for them to find his body."

Jim winced and turned away a moment. "That's got to be hard. If you need donations...?"

"No need. They'll be taken care of." The man's voice hardened. "Me and some of the boys are thinking about coming north. We figure you have a vermin problem that needs to be cleaned up."

Jim gazed at the man a moment. "I'd take it as a favor if you'd hold off on that a bit. Our sheriff takes a dim view of civilians taking the law into their own hands." He grimaced, thinking of his own situation and then shrugged. "I have some personal experience with that."

They were interrupted by Joel's wife coming up and leaning against the old farmer. "Anna, you shouldn't be here. Let me take you home," Lawrence gently scolded her.

Her voice was tired, lacking any kind of emotion. "No place else I can be, at least until they bring him out."

"You remember Mr. Lane?"

"Sure." She offered her hand. "I remember. I need to thank you. We made plans after you left. We were in good shape until Joel went back inside. Then there was an explosion." Her voice caught. "We didn't expect that. He didn't come out."

Jim didn't know what to say, tried anyway. "It's always that way. You never know the result of an impulsive act. We all make decisions on the spur of the moment. And then there's the X factor, something unknown—unplanned for. Sometimes it works out, sometimes not."

He paused, matching her gaze. "I'm really sorry."

She sighed. "Thank you. I'm in kind of a brain fog right now. I don't know what I'll do after this. You got any words of wisdom, Mr. Lane?"

He almost laughed. "I've been short of wisdom for a long time. One thing to consider. You're a warrior. I can see that. If your husband is dead, then you mourn him. But get on with your life. You have a lot going for you."

When she shook her head, he reached out and gently lifted her chin a little. "You're a strong young woman— beautiful, smart, and not afraid to work. That's a combination that will get you anywhere you want to go. I'm betting Joel would want that. Besides, the way the world is going, we're going to need strong people. My bet is on you."

Anymore conversation was cut off by a huge front-end loader roaring up the street. It was rock quarry sized and would make short work of moving debris.

Anna moved off toward the store.

When the noise level dropped enough, Lawrence commented, "That girl is a pistol. So, what's going to happen in Limestone County? Do you think your sheriff can handle this?"

Jim stood with hands on hips, watching the loader work. His sigh was long, drawn out. "Sheriff or not, this will get handled."

"So I'm guessing you're going to lend a hand?" The man gave him a quizzical look.

"I have to. Like it or not, those bikers have made it personal." Hands in pockets, Jim softly continued. "The sheriff made me promise to take a vow of no violence. He's adamant about that. I'm good friends with both the sheriff and the acting sheriff. They both still think that only law enforcement should handle problems like this."

"Yeah, right," the old man snorted, giving Jim a side glance. "How's that working out for you?"

"It's one of those things that are good in theory but doesn't work well in practice. They can't be everywhere at once." He gave the oldster a level glance. "I'm thinking the wheels are coming off that train in a big hurry."

The look Lawrence Dunn returned put a cold sweat down Jim's spine. "You tell that sheriff of yours to get it handled. Otherwise, me and the boys will be coming north. We don't allow this kind of shit to go unanswered."

Jim watched the oldster march away with a firm step.

He wondered just how many vets the man could muster and bet it would be a large number. This part of the country ran long on patriots who'd served. And if they came north, could they tell the saints from the sinners? In no circumstance would that end well. It would be a bloodbath.

Hands on hips, he gazed to the east. Springfield was burning with civil unrest, the same for Joplin to the west. Maybe sanity would prevail, maybe not. Everywhere he looked, people were mad and upset. Families were split down the middle. As far as he could tell, that included the whole country. Strings were being pulled that people couldn't see, and wouldn't believe it if they could.

Overseas wasn't any better. Europe was girding for war, the Mideast was rattling their sabers, and China was fanning the flames, hoping to pick up the pieces. There wasn't anything he could do about the world. But he could work on stabilizing Limestone County. It was time.

He hit the speed dial for Barnes. "Brother, we need to talk."

His friend's reply puzzled him. "You have no idea."

TWENTY-NINE

TRAVELING north from the gun shop massacre, Jim had time to reflect on the situation. Things could be worse, but he was hard put to figure out how. The bikers were sinking their fangs in Limestone County and needed to be eradicated like the nest of snakes they were. Or vermin, as Lawrence Dunn called them. He still chided himself for not taking out the head snake on their first visit—promise of non-violence notwithstanding.

His first need was to talk to Barnes so they wouldn't be stepping on each other's toes. His friend wouldn't like it. Passing the entrance to Trader Jack's, or whatever Gomez called it since he took over, he almost pulled in to start that ball rolling. The only reason he didn't was he knew that without good planning beforehand, he wouldn't survive that mission. From what he knew of Gomez, Jim was sure that was a hard target.

Jim rolled into the Lazy J with a cloud of dust chasing him like an angry whirlwind. The only vehicle he could see was a sheriff's patrol SUV, with Barnes sitting on the porch.

Exiting his truck, Jim envisioned an ominous black cloud waiting to rain on him. As he approached the front steps, the premonition was confirmed when Barnes reached into a small cooler and brought out two bottles of beer.

Clinking long-necks, Barnes said, "Better times."

After a couple of ice-cold swallows, Jim stared out at the fields, enjoying the quiet for a moment. He sighed while his friend waited patiently. Finally, he relented. "Tell me."

Barnes's voice was quiet, like reciting a memorized piece he didn't want to do. "After you left The Gallows, I got a call from PJ about a body found on the beach at Twin Bridges. We've identified that body as Jana Hyatt."

Jim flinched, staring at his friend. "What...?"

"We have no idea why. She was working at The Gallows," Barnes interrupted. "I figure she got crosswise with someone there. My best bet, can't prove it yet, is Red Dog and Boots. The body was broken pretty bad."

"Broken?"

Barnes nodded. "As in rib bones sticking out, back probably broken."

He started to stand, but Barnes pulled him back down. "There's more."

Jim stared into the distance a moment. "Of course there is."

Barnes continued. "I found one more body that we've identified as Patricia Bartol."

Going rigid for a moment, Jim settled with a long sigh. "The shrink."

Barnes nodded. "She was T-Zoned, Jim. Small caliber, probably hollow point or soft-nosed and sub-sonic. There was no exit wound. I did find a .22 cal casing stuck in some mud dropped from a shoe. With what we have, there's really no way of tying the casing to the bullet, but it is circumstantial. Her body was in the dressing room building at the same beach as Hyatt, her SUV in the parking lot. I'm guessing she was meeting someone there."

"I don't think the two events are related," Barnes continued.

"You're probably right." Jim stood, hands clenched. "Far as I know, Bartol only knew two people in this county."

"How long since you've seen Alina?" Barnes watched his friend a moment. "You know where this is going, Jim."

"Yeah, I know. The doctor asked some questions that made Alina uncomfortable. At times, the doctor seemed more interested in Alina than me." He glanced at Barnes. "She was approved by Sally One-Eye and was only sent to tell me to get off my ass and quit watching the world go by from my porch."

"Figured that. Given the circumstances, I'm not sure that's the best course of action right now."

"I'm not real sure what to do, Barnes. Alina has been gone a couple of days. I don't keep track of her that much. She's always out and about." Jim was still standing, feeling like he'd been cut adrift—no paddles, no sails.

"There's more."

"Well shit, Barnes."

"This one is kind of funny. You believe in Murphy's Law, right?"

"I do."

"Then hang on to your hat."

They both turned and watched another patrol SUV

coming up the drive. It was coming slow, dodging potholes and washboards, but seemed threatening by the measured ascent to the house.

Jim watched through narrowed eyes. "Who's this?"

"Rita and a friend."

"Rita? Well shit, Barnes."

Barnes chuckled. "You've really got to work on your vocabulary, brother. I'm guessing you'll have to clean it up a lot in the future."

Jim gave his friend a puzzled look before turning and watching Rita exit the vehicle. What surprised him was the little blond-haired girl that clambered out, running toward him with her arms out and crying. He stood, and she stopped in front of him, staring at him with a trembling lip. She seemed suddenly unsure of herself.

"Janie, what are you...?"

"Momma's dead." The girl suddenly hugged him tight, and her thin arms wouldn't let go.

His arms automatically wrapped around her, one hand smoothing her hair. Looking up, he saw tears coursing down Rita's cheeks, and Barnes was making coughing noises while staring off into the distance. "I just heard about that, and I'm really sorry. I told you once before, anything I can do..."

The girl looked up at him. "Momma always told me if anything happened to her, I was supposed to come to you. You're supposed to take care of me."

"Me?" His gaze pinned Rita. "How?"

"It's you or the system, Jim." Rita's voice was soft. "As far as we can tell, she has no one else."

He sat on the steps, eye level with Janie. "Is that what you want, Janie? To stay with me?"

The girl nodded, suddenly finding the ground under her feet interesting.

"Okay then, it's settled." He had no idea what to do now. Everything flooded his mind—clothes, food, where to sleep. He wiped unexpected tears from his eyes. Some kind of service for her mother. Maybe that closure would break the tough facade she was hiding behind.

His desperation must have been clear because Barnes rescued him. "Here comes Juana and her tribe. I called her earlier and thought maybe the kids could play."

They were suddenly surrounded by a flurry of children piling out of the electric golf cart, all wanting Janie to play.

Rita stepped in. "Janie, it's alright if you want to go with Juana and the kids. There are even a couple more children about your age to get to know. You might even get a sleepover."

Janie looked at Jim with a question in her eyes. He nodded, wondering if the girl could have fun given the circumstances. "It's okay, Janie. It's good to be with other people, even if you don't feel like it. I've got some things I have to do to make things better for you. It might take a couple of days, but I'll never be far away. You can call me anytime."

She looked undecided until the miniature goats trotted around the house, and the chase was on, adults being ignored completely. It was a raucous avalanche of goats, calico cats, and children that drifted down the valley. Some might have thought it cruel for the kids to be chasing the goat kids, but if the children stopped for whatever reason, the little goats would come bounding back and the chase would be on again. The cats just tagged along so they could ignore everything.

Closing his eyes a moment, Jim slumped and sighed. "What in the hell do I do now?"

Barnes grinned at him. "Hello, daddy."

That broke Rita and Barnes down into guffaws and giggles for a moment before they realized Jim wasn't amused.

As they retreated inside the house, Rita was the first to speak. "So, to the more serious matter at hand. Where's Alina?"

"I don't know." Jim sat on a three-legged stool by the kitchen island, drumming his fingers and looking out the window. "You can check the house if you want."

Hand on her holstered pistol, Rita said. "Oh, I'm absolutely going to do that."

Rita wandered off as Barnes spoke. "The way I see it, we got two major problems. I don't know what's up with Alina or if we'll ever see her again, but Red Dog and Boots have got to go."

Jim sat up straight with a big breath, slowly expelling it. He was only slightly surprised at the ex-highway patrolman's attitude. "I agree, although both those problems may be self-limiting. If Alina killed the shrink, although I don't know why in the hell she would, she might leave and never come back. I feel like an idiot. One minute she's concerned about my sleepless nights...the next, she's missing."

"Can't argue there," said Barnes with a headshake. "It's one of your talents to be duped by women. How's the motorcycle gang self-limiting?"

"I'm sure they feel the same—that I need to be eliminated, so they'll probably come hunting. I'm surprised they haven't shown up already."

Walking into the room and sitting on the stool next to

Jim, Rita broke in. "I don't see any girlie stuff in the bath-room, some drawers are pulled out with some mighty fine underwear left on the floor. I think she left in a hurry and is in the wind. While I'm not surprised at that—sorry, Jim."

"I'm not sure you're right, but thanks anyway." He sighed, trying to marshal his thoughts. "Now, along with our two problems, we have problem number three. Remember Gomez that helped us out? We've seen pictures of him involved in the fire-bombings in Spring-field, plus firing at a police line. Sally One-Eye almost pulled a clucker and laid an egg when she got his picture. I guess he's way high on her list of people that need to be disappeared. I know he has some very salty folks out there, and he'll be dug in like a tick on a coon hound. I'm not sure how we get him out."

They were silent a few moments when Rita abruptly grabbed her cell phone. "I just may have the answer."

Both men gave her a questioning look when she held up her phone with the display showing the 666 contact number.

"I'm going to call the devil. Jim, you wouldn't happen to have a map of the area with GPS coordinates, would you?"

Jim gave Barnes a puzzled look as he turned and opened a drawer in the cabinet. He did indeed have a map.

THIRTY

RITA EXPLAINED about Captain Hawkins landing at the National Guard Armory with her. "You know how devious Sally One-Eye is. I'm betting this is a just-in-case asset she put out here."

They had a map spread out on the counter when Rita made the call, tapped speaker, and placed the cell on the counter.

"Hawkins!" The answer was immediate and explosive. The sound of gunfire and people shouting could be heard in the background.

Rita had to resist the impulse to shout over the noise coming through the speaker. "What's your SITREP, Captain?"

"How many acronyms would you like, Sheriff? FUBARed, snafued? I don't have time to list them all. What can I do for you...say in the next fifteen minutes if I don't get fragged first?" The captain's voice was calm amongst the cacophony around her.

"How long will it take you to spin up your UAVs?" Rita locked her gaze on Jim.

"Sorry. No can do. My Gray Eagles were loaded with some GBUs, mainly anti-personnel snake and nape. We were being overrun, so I had to use them on the perimeter." Emotion was finally creeping into the Captain's voice. "I hate to kill civilians, but dammit...they started it. I don't know why or how they knew we were here, but they did. We were facing M-4s, and at least one mounted .50 cal."

"So you're out of options?" Rita was slump-shouldered, staring at Jim.

"Not exactly, Sheriff. This ain't our first rodeo. We found out Creech Air Force Base had a couple of MQ-9 Predators flying out in Nevada. That was early this morning. My controller is kind of a hacker, so he reached out and grabbed one. ETA should be in about a half hour. Once it gets here, my time on station will be under an hour. I was hoping to land it and refuel, but..."

Rita's attention perked up. "Ordinance?"

"Not good." They heard a ping on metal and could imagine the captain ducking. "It's mostly a spy plane, but it does have a couple of Hellfires on board."

"Well, it will have to do." Rita took a deep breath. "I know I'm not in your chain of command—"

"Sally One-Eye already cleared you for tactical—"

"—then my suggestion is you get your ass on the road with your Ground Control Station. Keep your Reaper in orbit."

"Roger that."

In a sharp command voice, Rita replied, "Then get yourself on the road, Captain. Once you're clear and find a secure spot, call me back for some GPS coordinates. We need to clear out a Viper's nest that's inside a cave. Is that doable?"

The captain was heard shouting orders before she responded to Rita. "Sheriff, I can thread a needle right up a mosquito's ass."

"Good, you'll need to." Sighing, Rita was shaking her head as she spoke. "I didn't realize it was that bad in Springfield, Captain. I'm sorry about your squad."

"Well, it was just harassment until today. Then we got overrun. The National Guard walking the perimeter saw the mob of people coming and hauled ass. Then the games began."

"If it's any incentive, I'm guessing the trading post and cave we're going to hit is full of people responsible for your troubles—plus their supplies and ordinance."

They could barely hear the response over road noise and a diesel engine revving. "Then it will be my pleasure. I have other intel to share when I have time. I'll re-establish comms in one hour...or I won't. Things are going to get chippy around here. Hawkins out."

RITA STARED out the window after ending the call. "Jesus Christ. What in the hell is going on, Jim?"

"Want another acronym?" He stood leaning against the kitchen counter, arms folded.

She gave him a steady gaze a moment before nodding. "Sure. Why not?"

"TEOTWAWKI. The end of the world as we know it."

Her look was skeptical. "Surely things aren't that bad?"

"Where have you been? Just in the last few days, things have started spiraling out of control. You know the whole supply chain fiasco? Now inflation is pushing forty percent, and food prices are climbing...when you can find it. The price of gas just went through the roof. The majority of our food supplies are delivered by trucks, and now they can't afford to buy diesel. We have hundreds of thousands of people flooding through our southern border every week—not all of them like us."

Rita mumbled, dragging a hand over her face. "I may start smoking and drinking again."

"Please don't." He sighed as he watched her a moment. "That ain't all. With Russia invading the Ukraine, Iran lobbing missiles at Israel, and China hitting our electronic infrastructure with malware constantly, things are a bit dicey. Even here in a fly-over country, people living paycheck to paycheck can't make ends meet, so they are stealing food for their kids. How do you blame them for that? Before the airport was attacked, there was already rioting in Springfield. These bad actors just used that for cover."

"So, what? We're screwed? No chance?" She'd gone from unbelieving to belligerent in a flash.

"We personally are in pretty good shape." He shrugged. "As for the whole picture, the rest of the common folk? The jury is out. I suspect that further intel your Captain Hawkins mentioned will confirm that."

She ran her fingers through her hair and sighed. "Well shit."

"Your vocabulary has deteriorated since we last talked." Jim smiled at her. "How are you, Rita?"

"Good question." She rolled her shoulders, trying to relieve tension, finally coming up with a tentative smile. "I'm okay. You?"

"I've been better. As you know, it looks like another relationship just face-planted in a cow pile. If I ever look at another woman romantically again, I'm just going to hand her a grenade and say get it over with."

She snorted, stifled a laugh, and gave him a sad look. "You do have a gift."

Staring at her a moment, he continued. "Stay here and coordinate with Captain Hawkins. That will make a big part of our problems go away. I got things to do."

"Negative. I'd like you to stay here." Rita's voice was firm as she stared at him. "This is still my county."

He shook his head, gazing out the window. "You see this? The raised tomato beds are being stalked again by the miniature goats, while one of the calico cats is trying to ambush a rabbit it will never catch. Do you think life will ever be this simple again? For that to happen, we need to take care of some things."

When he didn't respond, she said. "I insist, Jim."

His smile died as he looked at her. "The bikers are a danger to all of us. We're not secure until they are gone. That problem needs to be eradicated."

"Not by you. Not this time."

"If not me...who?" He quoted the old saying. When she started to reply, he held a hand up to silence her. In the distance, the rumble of motorcycles signaled an approaching storm. "That problem may be coming to our doorstep."

THIRTY-ONE

JIM PULLED his cell phone from his pocket and speed dialed Jacy.

Her answer was clipped. "Go."

"Are you close to Juana and the kids? I think we have trouble coming."

"I hear the bikes. Where do you want me?" Jacy answered in a clipped voice.

Jim thought a moment. "I want you to take the whole bunch into the maze or to the cave behind Pablo's house, whatever is fastest. Once they're hiding out and safe, you get into full battle rattle."

"Already am, boss. Most of us could see this coming a mile away. Except you, of course."

Ever since he'd known her, she was a step ahead. "Good. Your one and only job is protecting your family, along with Juanita and her brood, with one extra girl. They'll explain. Got it?"

The sound of her four-wheeler starting and spinning gravel nearly drowned out her answer. "What about Pablo? He could do this as well."

"He has his own job and knows what to do." Jim sighed and paused a moment. "Godspeed, Jacy. You're good people."

"Don't you dare take a back seat on this." Her reply was immediate. "Forget that. Get your head on straight and exterminate these vermin. We're all going to come out the other side of this alive and well. Make it happen and call me with the all clear."

Seems we were surrounded by bossy women.

He disconnected just as Rita yelled from the gun safe in the bedroom. "You've got a SCAR-H?" She came out holding Jim's new rifle, stuffing the extra proprietary twenty-round magazines in her pocket. She'd donned one of his ballistic vests, throwing an extra to Barnes. "This is sweet."

"I just got off the phone with Deputy Crewes," Rita continued. "She's a half-hour out, probably be late to the party. PJ is unaccounted for...as usual."

Barnes yelled from the front room where he was watching out the window with binoculars. "If you two will stop the love affair over a rifle, we got about twenty bikers coming up the lane. Looks like they're carrying weapons, no long guns that I can see. We're kinda outnumbered. What do you think? Parley and see what they want, or open the ball?"

"Hell with that. We already know what they want." Rita walked out to the porch and steadied the rifle on a porch post. Using the white-painted rocks placed along the drive to adjust for range, she fired a three-round burst in front of the first rider at the one-hundred-yard mark.

The riders immediately stopped and dove off their bikes, spreading out in a skirmish line. Using the scant coverage provided by the terraced pasture, they advanced up the hill.

"This doesn't make sense." Barnes watched the bikers after switching to the scope of his AR-15. "They have a couple of ARs, but mostly it's handguns and those little Kel-Tec machine pistols. They're deadly at close quarters but useless out there. We can pick them off before they get up the hill."

Jim punched a speed dial number, getting an immediate answer. "Pablo, are you in position?"

"I don't like this, boss. It's too close to home."

"No one likes this, brother. Look, I don't want you involved unless you have to. Fall back to a position between the bikers and the maze. You're the first line of defense. Juana, Jacy, and all the kids should be hidden out by now. If things go south, she can always lead them out the other side."

He could hear the distinctive sound of slapping a magazine into an M-4 before Pablo answered. "This is our home, boss. Do what you gotta do."

"I plan to. Look, we're not alone. Barnes and Rita are with me. Deputy Crewes should be plugging their escape route in a few minutes. Stay safe, brother."

Jim moved over to stand well back from the open doorway. "What are they doing, Barnes?"

Barnes snorted. "Nothing, for now. They're just laying out there waiting after they advanced, like someone needs to tell them what to do."

Jim visualized his ranch. The bikers were in front of them. Pablo was on their right flank, and Deputy Crewes would shortly be blocking their bolt hole. Although they couldn't know it, the biker's only path lay forward. What were they waiting for?

As he gazed out the front doorway, spiders were racing up and down his spine. What was he missing? There had to be something. He turned and gazed to the south, toward the recent murder scene and the observation post. Using the spotting scope he and Alina had set up, supposedly to observe the observers, he watched that line of trees a moment. There was no movement, and anyone coming from that direction would be in plain sight, but his senses were telling him something wasn't right. Before he could pin down the thought, the first bullet came through the front window. The battle for the Lazy J was on.

The deep-throated roar from Rita's SCAR-H started, sending 7.62 NATO rounds downrange. Barnes's lighter-sounding AR was firing out an open window. At first glance, Jim could see bikers falling and a couple of their bikes exploded. Their spray-and-pray tactics with the smaller machine pistols might work in the city and close confines, but here it would get them all killed. Mostly 9mm, their bullets would not penetrate the log walls of the house.

Shaking his head at the incongruity of it all, Jim waited with his lighter HK416. The M4/M16 variant was a comfortable platform for him as he waited, since Rita had commandeered his favorite, heavier rifle. As soon as either Barnes or Rita called out they were re-loading, he'd step in and keep up the fire. So far, most of the bikers had their heads down and were trying to crawl forward. It was an ill-conceived plan for men who were used to bar fights spilling out onto street corners and an occasional house to break into.

———

ALTHOUGH HARD TO HEAR THROUGH the gunfire, Rita's phone chirped. Looking at the readout, she yelled, "Gotta take it, cover for me." Placing the phone on the windowsill and pressing speaker, she said, "Go for message, Captain."

"We're finally clear of Springfield, although we have a couple of pickups on our tail. Sounds like you have problems."

"That we do. Are you ready to engage?"

"We are, although I may have to dust off those pickups first. I have a low-fuel warning light on the inbound Predator, so if we're going to do something, now's the time."

"You're a go for the coordinates I gave you. For the record, it's my call as Sheriff of Limestone County. Take out that target, Captain Hawkins."

"Roger that. For the record, it's your call to engage. Thanks for the legal cover, but I think it's a little late for that. Missiles released, and two minutes out, Predator kamikaze to follow on visual. Hawkins out."

Rita disconnected the call, looked at Jim, and shrugged. "I hope Sally One-Eye has enough pull to keep us out of prison."

Barnes barked a laugh as he turned away from his window, ejected a magazine, and slapped another one home. "We should live so long."

Jim started to reply when the reinforced back door of his cabin blew off its hinges.

THIRTY-TWO

THERE WAS no time for rational thought. Fighting down the bitter taste of stupidity, Jim turned, dropped to one knee, and started firing. The rest of the bikers' attacking force hadn't been at the tree line. They'd rappelled down the sheer bluff behind the house and were already hidden close by, awaiting a signal. He'd been too complacent, figuring the sheer bluff would protect them from an attack from the rear.

Even with surprise on their side, they were still amateurs. The first man through the opening was off balance as he followed the door into the narrow confines of the hall. He was firing his machine pistol left to right with no target in mind. Jim took two hits on his vest from the 9mm spray and pray that knocked him backward before his returning three-round burst of 5.56mm took the man down in the doorway.

Barnes yelled, "They're trying to rush the front door."

It was well-timed for the attackers. The noise level inside the cabin was deafening. Jim rose and took a step to the left as he continued firing at the men coming through the narrow confines of the back door and hall. What had he told the young man at the gun shop? Stacking bodies. The firing behind him from Barnes and Rita reached an ear-numbing crescendo. They were firing single-spaced shots and taking their time with no absence of targets.

The second man through the back door had to step over the first body and was driven to the floor by Jim's return fire. Now the third man coming in had two bodies to step over. He chose to jump and was caught mid-air by a three-round burst. The fourth man couldn't get through the door, stopping to fire through the opening before Jim's return fire took him down.

Coming around the side of a refrigerator covered in punctures and skid marks from the 9mm onslaught, Jim dropped a female biker on top of the other men. No more bikers tried to come through, and he hoped that was the last of them. He'd give them marks for bravery but nothing for smarts.

An old quote said that no battle plan survives the first shot fired, and his plan to defend his home was no different. No place is truly safe.

Loading a fresh magazine into his HK416, Jim retreated far enough to see the back door and also see Barnes and Rita. Their firing had slowed. "How's it going out front?"

"Peachy. We're running out of targets," Rita said, turning to look at Jim. "You're hit?"

"Scratches, and a couple to the vest. Hurts like hell to breathe, but I'm okay." He looked them over. Both had slight surface wounds on their backsides from ricochets that had to have come from the bikers coming in the back door spraying 9mm around. "Sorry about that. I didn't expect them to breach the back door."

"I think it's over," announced Barnes. "It looks like Pablo didn't follow your orders and hit them from the side. If there's anyone left, they're trying to do a sneaky crawl back to their bikes. I can see Crewes's Charger parked across the main gate, so that's not going to work out for them. That's a bottleneck down there, and she's the cork."

Rita pulled her phone from her back pocket and hit a speed dial. "Crewes. Pull back. If any bikers make it to your position, do not engage unless forced. Repeat. Do not engage. Let them go."

They could hear the deputy responding in a staccato voice, amped up by adrenalin. Rita disconnected.

Slinging his HK, Jim pulled his Glock pistol from its holster. "Barnes, I want you to watch my back while I clear this back door."

Barnes nodded, still breathing hard from the encounter. "Got it."

After searching all the bodies and making a pile of all the weapons and ammo on the kitchen floor, Jim cleared the outside patio area before stepping out. Grabbing the men and female biker by their heels, he dragged them out onto the cement patio. Anything else in their pockets was left until they had more time. Coming back inside, he lifted and leaned what was left of the door against the jam. At least they'd hear something if someone tried to come in that way again.

Leaving Barnes inside the building to supply cover fire, Rita and Jim filtered out the front door toward where the bikers had staged their assault. None had body armor, and the heavy incoming rounds from Rita and Barnes had decimated them. They counted twelve men and two women. Conspicuous by their absence were Mongo, Red Dog, and Boots.

Rita pulled out her cell phone and called Deputy Crewes again. "Allison? We're okay up here. For now, just hold your position and stay sharp. Any stragglers will be jumpy. Just have them drop their weapons and leave."

Her phone chirped immediately when she disconnected from Crewes. Holding up the phone's display to him, he saw 666 displayed on the screen as Rita put the phone on speaker.

"Captain Hawkins, I'm glad you made it."

"Mission accomplished, Sheriff. The video was epic until I flew the bird into their front door."

"Are you okay? You sound funny."

"Yeah, well, I lost my controller." The captain paused a moment. "He went out and engaged the two pickups to allow me more control of the Predator flight. He was a good man."

"Dammit! I'm sorry about that, Captain. Are you still in danger?"

"Negative. I'm clear. For the record, I just retired. I'm sick of this shit."

"Come and find us when you can, Hawkins. Just keep coming north, and you'll hit the city of White Rock. We'll direct you from there, and you'll be welcome. We'll have an end-of-the-world party and supply the booze."

"Damned right you will. I got a lot of adrenalin to work off. Y'all stay frosty, hear?"

"We'll try. Be advised, this ain't over on our end. Be alert when you get to our area."

"Uh oh." Hawkins's voice was sharp. "I got a line of vehicles rolling up from the south. We kind of blocked the road with our little dust-up. Looks like one has an RPG pointed at my vehicle. If that doesn't change, I'm going to launch a switchblade up his ass."

Rita gave Jim a puzzled look. "A knife against a grenade? You need to get the hell out of there."

"Negative," Hawkins said. "Switchblade 300 anti-personnel drone. I've still got a few surprises in my box of toys."

Playing a hunch, Jim responded on the speaker. "Is one of them an older man wearing a beat-up John Deere gimme cap?"

"Yeah, he's first in line. Looks like a first sergeant I had once—man could eat kittens raw."

Rita blanched and held her stomach.

"Wait one." He was glad he'd put Dunn's phone number in his contact list. The man answered at once.

"Dunn," the man shouted into the phone.

"Lawrence, this is Jim Lane. You need to disengage, and you especially need to have your man drop that RPG, M203 Grenade Launcher, or whatever the hell he's holding. Inside that ugly green mobile launching pad is Captain Hawkins, United States Army, and she is pissed. Do you know what a switchblade drone is?"

"Read about it."

"Well, she has her finger on the button." He could hear Dunn yelling for his men to stand down before he disconnected his cell call and spoke over Rita's phone.

"Okay, Hawkins. They're friendlies, just misguided. Keep your cool, let them know who you are and exactly what you did and why. The older man's name is Lawrence Dunn. Tell him Limestone County is taking care of business."

Hawkins's reply was ice cold. "No secret handshakes or anything?"

Jim laughed. "You're on your own, Captain."

"Just Hawkins. I told you the Captain part is retired. I mean it. Talk to you later."

After she disconnected, Rita asked, "Who's Lawrence Dunn? What was that about?"

"Folks weren't too pleased about what happened to the gun shop. The biker gang shot up their little town pretty good. Lawrence said he'd round up some vets to come up here and take care of business if we couldn't." Jim shrugged. "He must have got tired of waiting."

"Well..." Rita's eyes narrowed, looking at the front door. "We're not through yet."

THIRTY-THREE

"WELL, LOOKS LIKE EVERYONE IS HERE." Alina stood in the door opening, pistol pointed at Jim. "Everyone drop your weapons, or I start shooting."

Jim stood with his rifle pointed at the floor. She had them cold, and they all knew how good she was at snap-shooting headshots.

Rita and Barnes stood to one side, next to the windows. "You make the call, Jim." Rita's voice was low and husky.

"Well," Jim said. "The first thing is we don't give up our guns. You should know better, Alina. Can you talk to me about this before we all start blasting away at each other?"

Her suppressed Ruger Tactical .22 spat twice, the rounds ricocheting off Barnes and Rita's weapons. Jim started to bring his HK into play when she lined up her barrel with his forehead. "I said, drop your weapons."

Barnes was cursing and shaking a bloody hand. Rita was silent, her gaze boring into Alina as they dropped their rifles to the floor. It was a good thing their weapons had been held away from their bodies, or the ricochets would have been deadly.

"Pistols, too," Alina said, standing poised as a snake in front of them.

"Me, too?" Jim asked.

Alina gave a slight head shake. "You're fine holding your rifle against your waist. That way you can't get to your pistol. I've seen how quickly you get that out. We know each other far too well."

He turned to his friends. "Stand down...please. We'll get this sorted out." Turning back to Alina, he asked, "You still didn't tell me why. Are you back in business again?"

Her gaze seemed to canvas the room before settling on Jim. "Good guess. Actually, I never quit. Papa got bored, and Gregory did, too. They decided the Italians weren't running St. Louis properly."

He nodded. "So the times you've been gone...?"

Her smile was thin, the shrug subtle. "I had to take care of some business...thin the herd a little before our people took over." A look of resolve came to her. "This is all very entertaining, but I really need to go."

Jim was looking for anything to stall her. She was right about his pistol. He'd have to drop the HK416 to get at it. He couldn't bring the rifle up fast enough and couldn't drop it and draw before she nailed him. And nail him, she would.

"Why did you kill Bartol?"

"The shrink?" She looked startled a moment. "I really thought she could help you. I do care for you, Jim. Then I found out she was just delivering a message. That pissed me off. Of course, she took one look at me and salivated all over herself. I was going to be the star in her next book. Papa and Gregory thought she'd be a loose end, so..." She gave a slow, eloquent shrug. "Kinda like you three."

"So that's why you came back? Loose ends? Might as well clear a few things up before I die. What about Jana Hyatt? She was found near Bartol's car on the beach."

"That little blond bartender? The big gorilla took care of her. I saw it. He pulled her out of a van, picked her up, and bent her like a pretzel. And then he threw her out onto the beach. I wonder if he's Russian? We could use a guy like that." She smiled and shook her head. "I'm betting she was hoping for death by then. It looked as if he'd had her a while. I've never seen the like. But I didn't kill her. No reason to."

Rita spoke up. "How can you do this? How can you kill a man you slept with, professed love with? It makes no sense, Alina. Don't you feel anything?"

Alina gave a cold smile. "You're right, Rita. I gave him a lot more than you ever did. And in my way, I do love him. How can I not? He's a warrior." Her gaze settled on Jim. "But he's broken in ways I don't think anyone can fix. This will be a favor."

He was watching Alina closely, knowing Rita was trying to distract her. They needed an edge but wouldn't get it. He'd seen her in action. "No, Rita. Look at her. It makes perfect sense. I was just too stupid to see it. Dr. Bartol saw it at once. She watched Alina more than she talked to me. So as sociopaths go, I'm thinking Alina is a couple of wrenches short of a full toolbox, and the good doctor saw that immediately."

Jim caught Alina's gaze and held it. "Just because you perceive yourself as doing a job doesn't mean you're not a serial killer, Alina. You have a need. A hunger. You have to feed it."

"It's not like that." She centered her aim, her expression calm and serene. "This is just business."

The unsuppressed roar of the shot surprised them all. Alina most of all because the pistol was ripped from her grasp along with a couple of fingers. Screaming, she was stunned a moment looking at her hand. Seconds later, she reached for the dropped pistol, and another round took her through the chest.

Jacy moved through the door, gaze on Alina. "Sorry, y'all. I should have been here sooner. When I first saw her, I thought she was here to help."

"Oh, you were just in time," Jim said. "I owe you one."

"Yes, you do," Jacy agreed, nudging a groaning Alina with her boot and then kneeling next to her. She gazed at Alina from under the rim of her bump helmet. "Remember when we first met, Alina? I told you my .45 would trump your .22. You should have listened to me."

Alina was struggling to breathe when Jim kneeled on her other side. "I still don't understand, Alina. I guess I never will. Crazy as you were, I thought we were good together."

Alina's gaze moved from Jacy to Jim, blood bubbling from her lips. Coughing once, grimacing through bloody teeth, she replied. "It's back to the story of the...farmer... and the snake." She coughed again, convulsing once in pain before she settled back against the floor. "It's your own damned fault." Her breath rattled softly as she finished. "You knew I was a snake when you picked me up. You blame me for killing? It's what I do."

They all congregated in a circle as Alina coughed one

last time. Her hand raised like she wanted to reach toward Jim, then she settled against the floor. All that was life, that candle that had burned so hot in passion, simply extinguished, leaving a dull glaze fixed on whatever waited for her on the other side.

He felt a sense of loss, but not as great as he might have thought. Knowing Jacy was a medic, he asked. "You didn't try to help her, Jacy."

"You mean after I shot her?" She stood and nudged the body with her foot again. "Sorry. Not this one. She was evil and had way too many levels of crazy."

"Yeah." He sighed. "I guess we weren't that different, she and I. I thought she understood me."

"I'm sure she did." Jacy shrugged. "Doesn't change anything."

"You know?" Barnes had found a dish towel and was wrapping his hand. "With the exception of Jacy being the one who saved the day, did this seem like déjà vu all over again?"

"It was damned close," Rita said, turning to Jim. "Now what?"

He palmed his phone and speed dialed Pablo. "Everything good out there?"

The man snorted into the phone. "Quiet as a graveyard, boss. Which it kinda is."

"Well, better fire up the backhoe and pull a wagon. We got a shitload of bodies to bury. I'd like to get that all done before the kids start roaming around."

"On it." He paused a moment. "Remember when I said we can't be doing this here? At our home? We got lucky, boss."

"Yeah, we did. More than you know."

He turned to Jacy. "Pablo's gonna be busy. Are all the kids tucked away safe?"

"Yeah, they're having a ball in that cave behind Pablo's house. Ghost stories and the whole shebang. Juana won't let them out until she gets the word from us." She chuckled. "With the exception of Janie. That girl kept staring up this way. She actually asked me if she could borrow a pistol. When I told her no, she told me to get off my ass and go help. That's a direct quote. You're going to have your hands full with that one."

"She just lost her mother, so I doubt she's tracking too well. Don't hold it against her."

"Well," Rita said. "It sounds like she'll fit in around here just fine."

Jim walked outside, maneuvering around a couple of bikers who'd made it to the porch before dying. This wasn't his first rodeo. He'd felt it before, the disconnected out-of-body experience going through the motions— numb to the fingertips. There were too many slain, too many lives lost. Deserved or not, it didn't matter much. They'd chosen this road. He could feel the adrenalin draining away, followed by the depressive knowledge that Alina was gone. He'd been fooled because he wanted to be. There was an old saying—when your heart is hungry, you'll eat the lie. Seems he'd gorged on it.

Sitting in his chair on the porch, scuffing away expended brass with his boot, he took a deep breath, trying to relax. The distant sound of a motorcycle tweaked his nerves, but that sound was soon overwhelmed by the diesel engine of the tractor Pablo was bringing. The front-end loader and backhoe would be put to good use, maybe down the hill next to the tree line. Visions of mass graves in foreign conflicts came to mind, seen on the alphabet media, and he remembered thinking that kind of madness would never visit the Lazy J. He was supposed to be done with that. He shivered once and then stomped it down. Put it away...put it away in one of the closets in his mind...nail the door shut.

Barnes walked out on the porch with two mugs of coffee, handing one to Jim with a palsied hand as the adrenalin wore off. His voice was barely above a hollow whisper. "How do you ever get used to this, Jim?"

"Get used to it? You don't. Go home and give Wifey a squeeze or two. Bring her back to the trailer when you think it's time. You'll know when."

"Do you think we'll be safe here?"

Jim shook his head, staring across the waving field of fescue. "I'm not sure we're safe anywhere, brother."

Another lung-filling deep breath brought a small amount of determination. Rising, he moved back into the house. Rita was sitting in the kitchen, drinking her own coffee with trembling hands and staring at Alina's body. A blanket had been thrown over her, the edges dipping into the blood. Between the battle at the back door and the one in front of them, the wood-grained laminate flooring was painted a new shade of rust.

"You're gonna need a new floor." Rita's voice was hollow, lacking emotion.

"I don't know," Jim replied. "I'm thinking maybe a houseboat...way out on the water."

Jacy came in the front door with Barnes. "Pablo is here with the loader. What should we do with Alina?"

Shrugging, Jim said. "Take her out with the rest of the trash. There's more out back."

Jacy glanced at the broken back door leaning precariously against the jamb, a view of boots showing through a small space at the bottom. "Jesus."

Rita took another sip of coffee, holding her stomach against a rebellion triggered by the smell of death. "Tell me this is over, Jim. Please."

She stared at him a moment as he stood mute, gazing back at her. "Shit. It's not over."

"You heard what Alina said," Jim replied. "We know Dog and Boots are responsible for all this and that gorilla Mongo killed Janie's mother." He glanced around the cabin. All the memories generated here were not sucked away when Alina died. They'd broken in every flat surface in the house—and some that weren't. He kept trying to put those memories in a box, but they kept spilling out. "Help Jacy and Barnes take care of this mess. I'm not sure I can. Besides, I have things to do."

Rita gave him a sharp glance. "No, you stay here. I'll take care of the rest of the bikers and Mongo. That's my job."

When she started to rise, Jim's hand on her shoulder stopped her. They locked gazes for a moment. He could tell she wanted to resist, to power through the moment and take charge—felt her relax under his hand when she acquiesced. She gazed at him with tear-stained cheeks and a haunted expression.

His voice was gentle. "Not this time, Rita. Let me do what I do best."

THIRTY-FOUR

CHARLES FREDRICKSON AND MARTHA REINHOLD, a.k.a. Red Dog and Boots, stood at the tree line above the Lazy J ranch. Dog lowered his binoculars and shook his head, glancing at Boots.

"Well, that didn't go as planned," he said. "They must've had an arsenal stockpiled there in Lane's cabin."

Boots watched him with a jaundiced eye. "I think you're going to have to open another can of bikers. Your mighty horde of killers on wheels are about gone."

"About? We're done. The people I sent into the hills around this lake to commandeer homes for us never came back." He glanced at her. "None of them. And now this," he continued. "I should have killed Lane the moment we met at his house. My bluff didn't work, and now the men are all gone. I still don't see how they took out all our people down there."

"It looked pretty easy," Boots said. "Once your warriors came into the trap, the door closed behind them. They had to advance uphill against an entrenched position with greater weapons and then were flanked with automatic gunfire by someone who knew what he was doing. Game over. Lane was ready for us."

Dog gave her a quick glance. "I've only known you a few months, but that didn't sound like the Boots I know. So you're a tactical expert now?"

She stood with her pistol pointed at him. "You were given one job. Clear out this town and the area around it to make a stronghold for our people in the coming hard times. Between you and Gomez, it should have been simple."

"Well, Gomez ain't answering calls." He shrugged. "It didn't work out. There are other places..." His voice trailed off when he seemed to realize what was going on. His gaze was wary as his hand dropped toward his waist.

"No. There is no other place for you. Our people do not accept failure."

"Your people?" When he tried to draw his pistol, she broke his arm with a shot just above his elbow. Giving his shattered arm and the gun lying on the ground a stupefied look, he screamed and lunged toward her. She fired again, and his left hip was shattered. Unable to move, Dog lay on his back, grimacing in pain and wide-eyed at the approaching woman.

"Damn you! Why? I thought we were partners."

"Oh, come on, Charlie. Just because we work for the same people doesn't mean we're partners. You failed. Now I have a job to do. And if I fail, I'll get the same treatment as you." She holstered her pistol and pulled her knife. "The best part is, since I'm a woman and considering who we work for, none of this can ever be my fault."

When he tried to struggle away from her, she stepped on his wounded leg. She waited patiently for his hoarse screaming to stop. "Relax. This will be over soon. You've always wondered what I do. Now you'll know—firsthand, so to speak."

———

JIM DIDN'T KNOW where to start looking for Dog and Boots or Mongo. Somehow driving around and burning precious fuel didn't seem like the answer. Making a run through the city of White Rock, he hit pay dirt at The Gallows.

The bartender was new, a balding man in his forties with sleeve tats on one arm and a roll-your-own joint burning its life away in a brass ashtray made from the butt end of an artillery shell.

"You Lane?" The man's voice was an irritable rasp turning into a nasal whine.

When Jim nodded, the bartender continued. "Mongo said you'd be in soon."

"Where is the big man?"

The man gave a rotten-toothed grin. "He said to meet him at the old fight club spot. You're supposed to know what that means."

"I do." He gazed around the room and toward the office in the back. "Care to tell me where Dog and Boots are?"

Hacking a wet and bubbling cough, the bartender reached for his smoke. "Would if I could, it's no skin off my nose. I ain't seen them since early this morning. Looked like they was going for a ride."

It was a ten-minute drive to the clearing. He made it in twenty, wary of ambush from side roads and the brush lining the highway. An old beat-up Chevy cargo van was parked in the clearing. Between rust spots and gray Bondo filler on the fenders, he could only place the color as calico.

Mongo sat on one of the upended logs most used for chairs while watching Jim. The giant looked unconcerned as he took off his cap, tossing it on an adjoining seat. The sudden arrival of two more pickups made the big man stand nervously.

Jim stood by his truck, glancing around at the new arrivals. He'd really hoped to do this without an audience.

"A little birdie told us there was going to be a fight." Curtis climbed out of his old Ford F-150 half-ton, walking up to Jim. "You weren't going to start without us, were you?"

Glancing at Mongo standing alone in the clearing, he said. "How did you find out about this? I didn't know until a half hour ago."

"Jungle telegraph." Curtis laughed. "Actually, we're just out trolling for bikers and happened to see you— didn't want to miss it."

"This don't seem fair," Mongo called. "But I reckon I can take you two or three at a time."

Jim glanced at the pickups. Each had four men in the back with about every AR-15 platform and configuration he'd ever heard about.

"Trolling?" Jim asked.

Curtis nodded soberly. "We've intercepted six groups of three bikers each, all sent to take over cabins and homes like they tried at my place. We're looking for the rest of them. This shit has to stop."

"Hey. You forgetting about me?" Mongo stood, flexing his arms and back.

Holding his palm up toward Mongo, Jim said. "Just wait a second."

Turning to Curtis, Jim said. "You'll find the rest of the bikers at the Lazy J. They tried to pull off an assault this morning. I doubt there are many left alive for you to run to the ground. You can go help bury them if you want. All we need to find now are the two head snakes, Dog and Boots. So far, they're unaccounted for."

"We'll keep an eye out. If you need it, my neighbor still has his backhoe on the trailer." Curtis rubbed his hands together. "Now, about this fight. That's a ton of biker crap standing over there. What is he? Six-six or seven and maybe three hundred pounds?"

"I don't know." Jim gave his friend a level stare. "But this will not be a fight."

"Hey," Mongo yelled. "I got places to be. If your sheriff buddy hadn't stopped me, I'da killed your ass the last time."

"You bit me like a little girl," Jim replied. He turned and pointed his finger at Curtis. "Do not interfere."

Jim continued talking as he moved toward the giant. "Tell me something, Mongo. Why did you kill Jana Hyatt?"

Mongo snorted. "That little blond bartender that worked at The Gallows? Dog said I could have her. She was getting too bossy and then was too snooty to go upstairs with the boys."

"They could have fired her, gave her a warning." As they slowly moved toward each other, he watched the big man's feet. As the man walked, he confidently put all his weight on each leg. But then, with a brute like this, he shouldn't expect finesse or training.

"Nah. Not our way. Besides, what do you care? She

was just a good piece of meat. I broke her in." Mongo snickered. "That was before I broke her."

"A witness saw you throw her out on the beach." Jim's voice was cold as he circled the man. Since he had an audience, he wanted to nail things down in front of witnesses. He was settled in what he was going to do, knowing exactly how to do it.

Mongo grinned and then shrugged. "I did—pretty good throw, too. I just pulled her out of the van while she was kicking and screaming. At least she was until I picked her up by her neck and crotch and broke her over backward. Then I threw her away. Like I said, she was just a piece of meat."

Behind him, Jim heard several bolts pulled back on rifles. He held up his hand, not taking his gaze from Mongo. "I'll handle this."

"I don't know what you've been smoking, Lane," Mongo rumbled. "There's no way in hell you can beat me. I been chewing up men like you for years."

"Old men. Women and probably small children. You've never met a man in a straight-up fight."

The giant gave his best kung-fu bellow and rushed toward Jim with his arms spread wide. Jim waited until the man took a wide sweep with his fist. Dropping under the swing, he pivoted and kicked in Mongo's right knee. The wet-sounding pop wasn't near as loud as Mongo's scream.

Still trying to grab Jim in a bear hug, the man hobbled around on one leg. The other was bent inside at an unnatural angle.

He waited until the man made a clumsy lunge at him again. Moving under the out-flung arms, he pulled his boot knife and cut the man's hamstring on the uninjured leg, just behind the knee. Mongo went down, twisting and screaming. Jim stepped on one arm and then cut into Mongo's shoulder joint. While the man howled, he did the same for the other. In just moments, the big man was left on his back, not able to use his arms or legs.

"Jesus, man." Curtis walked to stand beside him. "That's just brutal."

Taking a deep breath, Jim tried to settle his breathing. "So is breaking an innocent hundred-pound woman in half just for fun."

"I know. I get it." Curtis was giving him a strange look. "Could you at least look out of breath or something? You just destroyed that man."

Moving back to his truck, Jim retrieved a couple of tent pegs and nylon rope. Driving the pegs into the soil with a rock, he tied Mongo's ankles to each one. Once finished, he kneeled beside the man. When the giant started to plead, Jim held the point of his knife under the man's chin.

"You'll be quiet a minute and let me talk. You can yell and scream all you want later." Getting the proper response, he continued. "That woman you killed left a little girl without a mama. I don't know what her mama's game was, why she worked at The Gallows or much of anything about her. But she didn't deserve what she got."

Jim made a show of looking into the trees. "Now you're going to be introduced to bird watching, Mongo. Here's the thing. There's a black-headed vulture that makes a home on the southern Missouri border. They're about twice the size of the turkey buzzards you'll see around here and look like they evolved from those flying dinosaurs. They are downright evil. Of particular interest to you is that they have taken a liking to the Stockton

Lake area. And of more interest? They don't really care if something is dead. The meat just has to be wounded enough so it can't get away. Everything is fair game to them. Meat is meat."

His gaze locked on Mongo's eyes, and he saw no remorse there, just a frantic search to somehow get out of his predicament. "And that's all you are. A piece of meat."

Looking at the blood pooling under Mongo's shoulders, Jim stood and looked down at the man. "I see the red ants are coming. You go ahead and yell now. It might help some."

Curtis walked with him back to his truck. "I know that peckerwood is the worst kind of killer, but damn, man. That was cold. You want me to come back later and put him out of his misery?"

Leaning on his truck, Jim sighed. "You think I'm a worse monster than he is, don't you?"

"I ain't said that." Curtis stared off across the lake. The wind was picking up, and gulls were skimming the surface, picking up bait fish. "I know you got reason. Hell, we all do. They brought it to us. It's just...I don't know. Everything is escalating—getting out of hand."

"You're probably right." He glanced back at the mound of meat pegged to the clearing. "Give him a couple of days. If he's still alive, put his lights out."

"Alright," Curtis said. "I'll have people check on him to make sure no one lets him go. If we run into Dog and Boots, you want a call?"

Jim put his hand on the man's shoulder. "Just do what the situation requires, Curtis. No quarter. They sure as hell won't give you any."

"Can I ask a question?" At Jim's nod, he continued.

"All those times you fought in this clearing—one on one, two or three on one...how did you keep from killing somebody? You damned near paralyzed me that last time. My back is still sore."

"I don't know." His voice was noncommittal, meeting the man's gaze.

"You don't...?"

Jim shrugged. "Honest answer. I shouldn't have been doing what I was doing, shouldn't have been there. Best answer I have." He gave the man a tired smile. "All my friends agree."

When his phone chirped, he accepted the call.

Barnes's voice was brusque. "You done with whatever you were doing?"

He looked around the clearing. Adrenalin from the fight with Mongo was cratering quickly, leaving him with sluggish muscles and a muddy mind. Regret would follow, but hadn't found him yet. Still, he knew the day wasn't over.

"Well?" Barnes asked again.

Watching the wind whip the surrounding trees and whitecap the lake, he sighed while returning his gaze to Mongo. He said, "I reckon so."

"Alright, brother. Get back here. All the work is done and there's a little blond hellion asking for you."

"No." He slumped into his truck, pulling the door closed with arms robbed of energy. "Tell her I'll be back in a week. She can stay with Jacy or Rita until then."

Barnes's voice was alarmed. "Hey, man. You're not going to do something stupid, are you? There are people who care about you. Where are you? I can be there in a few minutes."

"Nah, don't bother. I love the pain of mental flagellation too much to eat a bullet. Maybe I'll finish that book I'm writing."

"Your laptop is here if it doesn't have a bullet hole in it."

"I have to finish the story in my head. I'm just looking for a good ending. Once that is done, maybe I can sleep. Besides, I think the crappie are biting. We'll fry them up in a few days."

He disconnected with his friend still talking.

THIRTY-FIVE

JIM DROVE under the Lazy J arch and moved up the drive toward his house. Everything looked normal as a Norman Rockwell painting. He'd called ahead to let his friends know he was returning with a couple of coolers of iced crappie and channel cat. Barnes was supposed to have the vats ready to drop in the fish for the deep fry.

The front of the house was a beehive of activity. It seemed the youngsters and goats, kids and kids, never got tired of chasing each other. The calico cats were ignoring everything while licking their paws.

Stepping out of his truck, Barnes handed him a beer. "Welcome back, brother."

Rita was sitting on the front step next to the darkest woman he'd ever seen. "Jim, this is Captain Hawkins," she grunted as an elbow hit her side. "Retired. She's going to be my new deputy."

"Welcome." Jim shook her hand, giving her a once-over. The woman was a tall, muscular Amazon, and he was amazed at the strength she projected. There was nothing subtle about her, especially the knuckle-cracking she gave his hand. "Sudan? Ethiopia?"

"Detroit," Hawkins said. "You don't like Black people?"

He shrugged, his expression serious as he held her gaze. "Never gave it much thought. Right now, I'm hungry and thirsty. We can leg wrestle or something later for dominance. Maybe crush walnuts against our foreheads."

Hawkins turned to Rita. "I like him."

Rita snorted. "Give him time. You'll lose that feeling."

Later they lounged around the front porch, having eaten way too many fish and fritters. The children were sated and riding around in golf carts chasing goats. Each cart had a calico cat perched on the front cowling—suitably unimpressed.

"So, has the kingdom of Limestone County been squared away?" Jim asked.

"Mostly," Rita answered. "Allison is patrolling while the fuel lasts. We have the little Prius here on the charger, but she won't drive it. Says it's undignified."

"You tell her we'll probably never see another gas delivery?"

"She's still not on board with that theory. Oh, and PJ is in the wind. I'm thinking he got tired of it and drove away. His patrol car was parked at the office." Rita shrugged. "Between us and Curtis with his bunch of redneck regulators running around on ATVs, things are on an even keel. Barnes is retired—again. He and Bea are living in that trailer over there while Jacy and family have moved into the other trailer. Your little valley is filling up."

He looked at Barnes. "Where is Wifey?"

Barnes shrugged. "She caught a cold or allergy or something, didn't want to infect anyone." He grinned. "It happened right after she heard you were coming home. Sudden onset."

Looking around, Jim said. "I don't see Pablo or Juana?"

"They took the truck over to the Gomez stronghold to see if anything usable is left. Don't worry, they went cross-country, not on the road."

"I doubt they'll find anything," Hawkins said. "I blew the hell out of it."

Jim nodded. "Looks like our most wanted list is down to Dog and Boots. Any sign of our favorite bikers?"

Everyone shook their heads except Hawkins. "Hey, wait a minute. I met a biker chick. Leather vest and no shirt? More tats than sense? Mammary deprived?"

"Sounds like Boots."

"Yeah, well. She came riding up while my vehicle was still blocking the road. I'd just finished talking to Mr. Dunn when she came strolling up to me, cool as a cucumber. I'll be damned if she didn't pull a knife from her boot and try to cut me with it. Didn't say a word." She sighed. "I'd always wanted to use the line from *Crocodile Dundee* and say 'knife? That's not a knife.' Anyway, she didn't like my response much. I don't know what possessed that crazy woman. Her bike is still out there in the ditch if anyone wants it."

"You fought her with a knife?" Barnes asked.

"Oh, hell no. I shot her ass," Hawkins said. "She seemed really shocked that I didn't die of fright when she rushed me."

Turning to Jim, Rita asked. "What now? What are you going to do?"

He shrugged. It had taken a week, but he was finally starting to put all the bad memories in a box. If all the closets in his mind weren't already stuffed full, he'd be able to put it away. Still... "I can't stay here."

"Why?" Rita sounded puzzled. "I...we've worked really hard here. The house is cleaned, everything came right up off that laminate. The windows are fixed. Barnes replaced the back door with something that looks like it should be on a bank vault. It's hard to tell anything happened, except for the odd bullet hole or two."

"I don't know." Jim shook his head. "Alina made it our home. Doesn't seem right somehow."

"Dammit, Jim. Alina was a psychopath. Everyone knew that but you." Rita's voice was so plaintive everyone looked at her in surprise. "You've got to find a way to forget her. We all make mistakes."

He gazed at her a minute, wondering if that was a confession. "Then I guess the house is a monument to my stupidity."

"You can't leave." Rita gave him a serious look. "Janie needs a home. You can't drag her around the country jousting at every windmill that pops up. Face it, Jim. She's imprinted on you like a newborn calf. She'll follow you no matter where you go. After losing her parents, she can't lose you, too. It's time to step up."

"And you." Jacy walked up and joined the conversation. "She's adopted you, too, Rita."

"She'll get over it," Rita grumped.

"No I won't," a small voice interrupted them. "Have I waited long enough? Y'all said I had to wait a while before I came out."

She was putting on a brave face...a little girl trying hard to grow up. He didn't know if he liked the road stretching out in front of them. It looked crooked and full of potholes. But somehow it seemed right.

Jim stood and held out his hand. "Let's take a walk."

"I TAKE it there's some history here? I'm always up for a good story," Hawkins said softly, glancing sideways at Rita.

"Oh, yeah. Lotta history," Jacy, the resident medic, replied as she sat by Rita and Hawkins, three across on the step. They watched the two walking away—a tall man striding beside a gangling teen wannabe sporting all elbows and knees, trying to match his step. As they watched, the girl held out her hand. The man pulled his pistol and dumped the magazine into her hands, and then racked the round out of the barrel. The girl caught it in midair before taking the bullet and inserting it into the magazine. They could tell he was watching closely and speaking as the girl reversed the process and handed him the pistol.

As they watched, he gave the girl a quick hug of approval.

"My god," Rita said. "He's been cloned."

Barnes was grinning at them. "You three magpies need to give the man some slack. He'll come through without all the pushing and prodding."

"Says the man who can't get his wife to come out of her trailer when Jim is around?"

"She is stubborn, I'll give you that. But she'll come around."

Rita stood with a groan, holding her back. "Guess I better get to work."

Jacy chuckled and nudged Hawkins. "Going to go remind the boy that Alina was just a distraction and you're the main event?"

Sighing, Rita nodded. "I anticipate a lot of groveling and begging will be involved."

THIRTY-SIX

JIM LANE STOOD on a bluff overlooking the southern end of Lake Stockton. Lake levels were down due to a lack of rain, so a small beach of rock and mud rimmed the water below. Two pontoon boats were grinding and bumping into the rocks below, propelled by a slight wind and gentle waves. He was glad the wind wasn't blowing. The smell would have been horrendous.

Seagulls and vultures attended the water and beach below that was littered with bodies. The boats were covered with the bloated remains, clothing and camping accouterment were scattered about. It appeared many had tried to run down the beach and were gunned down. Other than back into the water, there was no place to run. Since it was a sheer bluff to the water below, he figured another boat had approached and then attacked.

It was simple. Someone wanted what the victims had. And killed them for it. Food, potable water, ammunition —whatever they had. More than likely any young women who weren't killed outright would have been abducted.

He sighed and turned back to the forest behind him.

Rita and Janie were standing back-to-back, watching for anyone trying to approach.

"Well?" Janie asked, impetuous as only a twelve-year-old can be.

Jim snorted. "While our world is short of food and fuel, there seems to be an abundance of bullets. Stay alert. Let's go home. We need to have a team meeting."

"I'll take point." Janie promptly walked ahead of them.

"No, you won't." Jim's voice rapped out as the girl stopped. He passed her, saying, "You still don't know what you don't know, and you're too confident in what you do know."

She stood waiting for Rita. "I don't know what that means."

Rita put her hand on the girl's shoulder. "It means you still have a lot to learn, grasshopper."

"Grasshopper? I don't know what that means, either. Y'all talk in riddles."

"What's Jim Lane's first rule of the forest, Janie?"

The girl sighed and then replied softly. "Silence rules, noise kills. I'll shut up now."

IT HAD BEEN a strange few weeks. The outside world had gone silent after a fashion. Television still worked if you liked a snowy screen or the internally saved screen saver. Phones worked—no signal, no Internet. Electricity was spotty, and he'd switched to his solar array. Vehicles worked, providing you had fuel. The much-maligned electric vehicles now ruled supreme, if you had a way to charge them.

There was still noise—the sound of an occasional engine maxed out by someone chasing, or being chased. Explosions in the distance gave them worry about the type of ordnance being used and by whom. They were thankful prevailing summer winds blew the detriment of smoking cities away from them...mostly.

The Lazy J was lucky. They had freezers full of food and enough solar power to keep them going. He knew a few neighbors were fixed up as well. But he could feel the bad times coming like spiders racing up and down his spine.

Stopping at the brush and tree-covered crest above their little valley, Rita and Janie moved to stand next to him. They were learning their lessons, and he could hardly hear their approach. Their little settlement looked peaceful. An occasional laugh from the children floated to them on the breeze. The windmill squeaked occasionally. He or Pablo needed to fix that. Their few cattle lazily swatted flies as they grazed. Jacy hadn't brought her horses; the graze wouldn't have lasted.

He was shaking his head when Rita put her hand on his shoulder. Glancing at her, he was aware that Janie had moved against him on the other side. The tension slowly trickled away.

"We'll get through this, Jim. You're still a Shepherd. Tell us what to do, and we'll do it."

A snort came from his left side. "Well, most of the time."

An electric golf cart was coming up the hill to collect them, driven by one of Pablo's kids. He was certain Captain Hawkins was looking at them through the spotting scope—or the Barrett .50 cal. optics. Once spied in his gun closet, she'd claimed that piece of equipment as hers. He sighed again, wondering how many sighs an hour constituted a habit. At least the lookout system was working.

"We'll get everyone together after supper."

His two ladies' replies were miles apart.

"As you wish."

Snort. "Yessir."

———

"ALRIGHT FOLKS, let's get this over with."

Their band of brothers and sisters were gathered on the front porch of the cabin to take advantage of the cooling breeze coming across the valley. Even the children were silent and attentive. Jim looked around at them, trying to hold the gaze of everyone, at least for a moment.

"What we've been dreading—and expecting—has happened. I think we all know that. From this point forward, we need to do everything knowing that we are in harm's way. Each of us, including children."

Juana gathered her brood around her like the mother hen she was while Jacy nodded and gave a pointed look at her boys. Janie came to sit by him on the top step like she was his second in command.

Hawkins had mounted the spotting scope at the edge of the porch, and gazed through it every minute or so, then checked her laptop screen.

Barnes and Wifey sat close by in the shade of the porch, and Rita came out with glasses of tea for the adults and juice for the little ones.

"Food. Water. Shelter. Security. That's our first concern, in no particular order. We have enough food stored and on the hoof to last all of us about a year. That's the first concern. Water is from the deep well. If solar goes out, we can use the hand pump to get it. But I need to stress this. Only drink water that's been boiled, purified, or from the well."

"Why? There's water everywhere in these hills," Wifey responded. Barnes closed his eyes, shaking his head slightly. Beatrice figured her one job was to be a thorn in Jim's side.

Janie raised her hand. "Can I take that one?"

Curious, Jim nodded.

"We just saw about thirty or forty bodies in the lake. Any stream could be contaminated with any number of things. Most springs are wet weather springs and are shallow. And it's going to get worse."

"You're a child," Wifey said.

Janie replied, "Yes, ma'am." She then muttered softly, "But I ain't stupid."

"Alright." Jim gave the girl a warning glance. "Shelter is pretty much a given. What about security?"

As soon as she arrived, he'd put Hawkins in charge of security. She'd hit it off with everyone, and the kids loved her.

"Okay for now," she said. "I'll need to talk to you later."

"No," Jim said. "If you have something to say, do it now. It involves all of us."

"You're the boss. I've been sending a little rechargeable drone up every few hours. They're small and don't have a lot of flight time, but eyes in the sky always help." She didn't look around but gazed strictly at Jim. "You sure?"

He nodded. "Give it to us."

"The roads south and east of here are clogged with thousands of people on foot, all headed toward the lake. My guess is they're traveling slow because they're stopping to eat anything they find along the way. They're like human locusts. All the cattle, horses, and smaller livestock they can catch? Gone. From what I can see, they're spreading out into the hills along the way. It's like watching those army ants on National Geographic."

"Any way of telling the attrition rate?"

"It's horrendous. There's probably a million people in the area surrounding Springfield. They're all looking for food. As I see it, the only good news is that they may run out of people before they get here."

He shrugged, speaking with more hope than he felt. "And they may not find us."

"I have an idea," Pablo interrupted. "Maybe a last resort."

"As our resident Marine who likes to break things and blow shit up, you have the floor."

Pablo nodded to Hawkins. "Captain Hawkins didn't blow up everything at the trading post. It was epic." The two grinned at each other. "That's for sure. Anyway, we found a concrete bunker where they kept explosives—I guess they were afraid to keep it in the cave."

"And...?"

"What we have is enough C4 and detonators to blow up the world."

"You're thinking of mining the perimeter for defense?"

"No, boss. What I want to do is go farther out and make such a mess that we're isolated. No way in or out. With proper use along the ridgelines, we can make our perimeter look like the maze between us and Jacy's farm."

Jim thought a moment before continuing. "A determined person could still find a way through. We'd never be completely hidden."

Pablo shrugged. "Better one person find us than a thousand. Even if they were scouts and then brought others, the mass numbers we're looking at now would never be able to get through."

"How long would it take to do this?"

"Two, maybe three days, with a little help."

"People would hear us." He looked at Hawkins. "We got that much time?"

She shrugged. "It's the best idea I've heard so far and a lot better than singing campfire songs and hoping for the best. I'm for trying it. We'll be broken arrow if we don't pull it off."

Janie interrupted. "What does that mean? Broken Arrow?"

The group, mostly of military background, looked at each other...none willing to describe the unthinkable.

Jim shrugged. "It's military slang, Janie. It started out as a code name for when a nuclear weapon was either lost or stolen. But combat troops use it for a code name for when their unit or base is overrun by the enemy."

"So, Custer's Last Stand? That sort of thing?" Her gaze was steady on his.

"We're going to try to avoid that. Look around you, Janie. We have an abundance of skills."

Glancing around at his friends, the weight of decision threatened to crumple his shoulders. "The way I see it, we treat the gathering hordes of people like a plague. And they are not the enemy. They're just hungry and desperate. We can either go out among them and take our chances, or isolate. My vote is to isolate. If we get flushed out of here, we can always figure out a plan B."

Everyone was nodding but Wifey.

"Looks like a consensus then. Let's get to it first thing tomorrow. Pablo will tell us what he needs, and we blow up the world."

———

LATER, as the evening shadows grew long and the pasture surrounding them gave up moisture in thin fingers of fog, Rita came to stand beside him.

"Janie put to bed?" he asked in a low voice.

She answered with a chuckle. "You're kidding, right? She's in her bedroom reading a book on survival tactics in the forest from your library and cleaning her pistol. I worry about her."

"We should all be reading those books." He moved to a swing and pulled her down next to him. "It's peaceful here. The things going on around us, things coming toward us...it's hard to fathom."

"Why, Jim?" Her voice barely carried to him. "Why is this happening?"

"Doesn't matter, now. High gas prices leading to curtailed delivery? Doesn't matter. Food shortage? Doesn't matter. A fuel shortage already, then the politicians ship most of our ready reserve overseas? Doesn't matter. Pandemic? Doesn't matter. The law of unintended consequences has struck, the tipping point reached. One day it just all fell apart."

Shaking her head, she settled against him. "Nothing matters, then?"

"That girl in there reading the survival book. Jacy's kids being taught everything a combat medic can teach; Pablo's kids being taught everything that old Marine might know—those things matter. Everything we do from now on needs to ensure the children's survival."

"Do you think we can make it? Can we teach them enough, quick enough?"

He pulled her close against the chill of the evening and tried to put conviction in his voice. "Yeah. We'll make it."

The night was still, the slight breeze carrying smoke from a distant fire. Sporadic gunfire winked on distant hills as a calico cat, worn out from shepherding giggling children, came to rest on the top step of the porch—its world at peace.

It was full dark, so Rita couldn't see the lie on his face, couldn't read his mind as she did with regularity. He took a deep, shaky breath and slowly exhaled.

Until we don't. Until we don't.

A LOOK AT BOOK FOUR:
SHEPHERD'S SWORD

FULL OF DESPAIR, THIS APOCALYPTIC THRILLER STARTS FAST AND HURDLES TOWARD THE END IN AN ACTION-PACKED FIGHT FOR YOUR LIFE.

Mason Law works for the Army, specializing in rescuing people from far-away places. When he walks out of the jungle with his latest charges in tow, he is greeted with the news that his wife has died of a strange illness.

Immediately transported back to Springfield, Missouri, he finds the world as he knew it unraveling. With no fuel for transport, no electricity, and—most importantly—very little food, he witnesses society coming apart at the seams.

Despondent and looking for a will to live, Mason barely has time to get his wits about him when General Slade requests he extract his daughter and take her to Sanctuary—a safe house built on Lake Stockton. And since Mason owes the General big time, he accepts the mission.

Pitting himself against rogue military units and hordes of starving people out of their minds with fear in a trek through the collapse of society, Mason resolves to complete his task...or die trying.

AVAILABLE JUNE 2023

ABOUT THE AUTHOR

Darrel Sparkman is an award-winning author of novels, novellas, and short stories. He's been included in three western anthologies, worked as a feature writer for *Saddlebag Dispatches* and blogged a short time for *Sundown Press*. His ideas come from a diverse past of serving as a combat search and rescue helicopter crewman in Vietnam and volunteer Emergency Medical Technician First Responder. He has worked as a professional photographer, computer repair tech, and was once part-owner of a commercial greenhouse operation and flower shop.

Darrel is enjoying semi-retirement and finally has that job that wakes him up every day—with a smile on his face.